THE MAJOR AND THE MINER

In an era when same-sex love is a crime, what is an ex- army major to do when he falls for a sexy young coalminer?

Run out of the country town because of his illicit relationship, former army major Dr. Damien Bouton flees to the relative anonymity of a poor, inner-city suburb where he deals with the loss of his lover, Josh, ministering to the needs of a startlingly eccentric mix of supportive characters. Josh, his eyes and his heart newly opened to love, chases after his lover but, in his innocence, falls prey to con men and the razor gangs that abound in Depression-era Sydney. When Damien and Josh's paths finally cross again, they are almost strangers and their social circumstances make any sort of relationship impossible. Until fate steps in. But is it too late for them to rekindle their love?

The Major and the Miner
ISBN 978-1-911478-41-6
Copyright©2011 – 2019 Barry Lowe
Cover art and design by Dawné Dominique

This is a revised and expanded version of *The Major and the Miners* first published by loveyoudivine Alterotica.

Published by
Lydian Press 2019
Find us on the World Wide Web at
www.lydianpress.com

THE MAJOR AND THE MINER

BARRY LOWE

Lydian Press

CHAPTER ONE

~

WELCOME TO SEASPRAY BAY

T here is no doubt it is good to be back in the city with the scandal behind me. Ironically, it was the scandal and the accusations it involved, since withdrawn, that have been responsible for my success, although I was not to know this at the time. As a result, I spent many sleepless nights and, on more than one occasion, contemplated ending it all the only way I knew how.

I'm a doctor you see, a very good one, but had the Medical Association struck me off the register I don't know what I could have taken up to earn a living. The Great Depression raged, people went hungry, anarchy threatened. Now in the year 1935, I can look back on it and almost be grateful to the upheaval for the comfort and love it has brought me. There is still the very real fear of blackmail. Mud was flung once, it did not stick but a second such accusation attached to my name would be terminal.

Forgive me; I'm wandering – a habit of mine. My name is Dr. Damien Bouton. About three years ago I allowed it to be spelled and pronounced Button as a favor, perhaps patronizing, to the people of the idyllic coastal village of Seaspray Bay, named for a ship that foundered on rocks in the area in the early eighteenth century. The hamlet was settled some time later and initially thrived as a north coast hub of the fishing industry. Later a rich seam of high quality coal was found to run under the area and an ugly mechanical behemoth of a mine was constructed on the headland overlooking the quiet sandy bay as if to scare off any competition.

It was here I found myself in God's year 1932 at the behest of the company, which employed me to care for the workers and their families. It was a laborious job. I was on a very generous monthly salary that meant my life was at the mercy of the villagers who, unlike the majority of the country, were getting their health care for free. While most were grateful for the company's consideration, a few, usually gossipmongers and malingerers thought nothing of interrupting me at all hours of the day or night merely for a chat or for psychosomatic illnesses. A few even saw my bachelorhood as a means of marrying off unwed daughters.

I was thirty-six years old, of appealing appearance, of athletic build, an inch shy of six feet in height. I had served on the battlefields of France during the Great War after enlisting against my parents' wishes. They did not live to see, by war's end, my rapid promotion to the rank of Major. I also found myself much decorated. Someone must have believed me brave, although I felt I did no more than my fellow soldiers. The trinkets meant little to me. It was not something I spoke about unless with other veterans of the war. I was not one of those chaps much taken to jingoism. I did my duty; I survived.

The story really begins in my third month on the job. I was looking down the coal-dust throat of a woman made old beyond her years by washing her husband's or her son's clothing and breathing in the choking soot that will ultimately kill her. I would know if it was a husband, a son, an uncle or a 'friend' if I had been in the town longer. I was learning fast, faster than I ever would have imagined when I became the recipient of the coal company's largesse.

The local doctor had retired suddenly on medical grounds – death, they called it – and I became the General Practitioner to the sorts of people my mother would have called the salt of the earth. They didn't complain; they just got on with it. Disease and dying were part of the cycle of life along with eating, sleeping and reproducing. I did what I could to alleviate the suffering and gave a silent sigh of resignation when I knew it was in God's hands.

My patient, who merely wanted her pain alleviated, did not expect a cure. It was no use telling her to rest, as there was no such thing here. She gathered her shopping basket of groceries from the one and only general store, which also served as the local post office and petrol station, as well as tourist tea rooms during the summer, and I let her out the side entrance. She had been the final patient for the day when I'd last looked in the Waiting Room. I went to lock the surgery door to discover a young man reading an outdated magazine. What I noticed immediately was not that his lips mouthed the words he was reading, but his beauty surpassed even that of the surrounding coastal landscape: his hair was the color of the fine sand on the beach, and his eyes bluer than the waters in the bay. My breath caught in my throat. I must have given an audible gasp because the young man smiled.

"Hello, doc. You got a moment?" he asked.

I ushered him into my office too dazzled to speak. He stood in front of my desk rather than taking the comfortable leather chair meant for patients. A few inches shorter than I, he was fit, tanned and wore the cap and rough clothes of the villagers. But I'd never seen him before. I would certainly have to remedy that even though one of the reasons for taking on this job was to avoid the temptations that the city offered. Here I expected the temptations to be much less.

"I won't take up too much of your time," he said. "My mum told me I should ask you to supper this evening." He blushed.

"What?"

"Mum said as you being a bachelor gentleman and having no one to look after you then you probably need a proper feed every now and then 'cause gentlemen don't know how to cook good, wholesome grub."

I did have a woman in three times a week to clean and cook for me, but the days she didn't attend I lived on cold meats and leftovers.

"Don't expect nothing fancy," he said. "I said to mum that Dr. Button is no snob even though he's from the big city and has probably et at all the fancy cafés, but he knows you can't beat good home cooking." He paused and smiled expectantly. "Please, sir, say you'll come. It's to show our appreciation for all what you done for us. Me."

He stumbled over the word appreciation as if he'd rehearsed his little speech, but it just made him all the more endearing. However, I was at a loss. I didn't recall him. "What exactly is it you think I've done for you?"

Disappointment clouded his face. I looked again at those eyes.

Suddenly, it struck me. "Joshua?"

"Yes, sir. Did you not recognise Joshua, sir?"

"I should have known you. Why, those eyes, lad. They must drive the local girls crazy."

He blushed again and fidgeted with his cap.

"Take a seat while I lock up."

I quickly set about closing the surgery for the day hoping that no one would disturb us. As I did so I remembered the awful circumstances under which we had met. The caterwauling siren as I attended a sick woman in her bed at home. I say sick, but Mrs. Clohesy was a slacker who needled her poor husband and her two daughters and visited my surgery with more regularity than the locals to their water closets. And she was about as welcome. She had set her sights on winning me for one of her daughters. She was meeting with strong resistance and her feigned illnesses were increasing.

Even the unfeeling Mrs. Clohesy winced as she heard the wail from the mine shaft, winced as all the people above ground in Seaspray Bay would be doing at that moment. I grabbed my medical bag and ran outside. I tore up the dirt road surrounded by womenfolk in dread for their sons and husbands, but they gave me space and did not jostle me because a few seconds delay on my part could mean the difference between life and death.

By the time I reached the pit, men were being winched to safety while word was reaching the union representatives that the accident had been minor. A few of the men laughed, not so much at the feeble pun as with relief. One man had been hurt. They carried him on a stretcher, blackened from the coal except for a red slash across his leg where his trousers had been cut open as had the leg itself. He was conscious, barely, the pain excruciating. I kneeled down in the dust to examine the injury. It was severe, more than my little surgery could handle. His tibia was shattered and protruded in an ugly break through the skin on his lower leg. All I could do was clean the wound, patch him up, and ease the pain for what was going to be a long and painful journey to the nearest major hospital.

I leaned over and whispered words of comfort to the poor man, but his face was so covered with soot and coal he scarcely looked human. Apart from his eyes. They were astonishingly blue. Like the sky. I just stared into them until his groan of pain interrupted my preoccupation. I had a group of the miners carry him down to the surgery, where I did my best with limited resources. It would take too long for an ambulance to reach the town so a group of the men organised one of the colliery lorries into a makeshift hospital transport that would do its best to meet the ambulance coming down the Pacific Highway. I would go with him until we met.

The poor man groaned as I prepped him for the journey, trying to speak through the morphine I had given him. "Danny. What about Danny? Did he get out all right?" Because of the injured man's sudden agitation, it was imperative he remain as still as possible, I had one of the miners go to fetch Danny to join our little expedition.

Slowly the truck crawled its way along the dirt road to the highway, every bump and pothole agony for the prone man who, nonetheless, kept up a steady chatter with his mate. "I thought you was a gorner," Danny said with a stoicism which belied the catch in his voice.

"Nah, takes more than that to get rid of me," the victim said. I looked away as he sought his mate's hand and squeezed it. I had no wish to intrude on their mateship. "You and me has too many plans. Why, here I am at age twenty-four and I ain't ever seen the city." He fell in and out of consciousness, but every time he woke, Danny was there to feed the dreams and keep his mind off the pain and the even more painfully slow journey. Danny never let go of his mate's hand until the injured miner was transferred to an ambulance just under an hour later.

On our return journey I let Danny sleep. His exhaustion and concern were palpable, even though I was curious about their background. Now Joshua had returned to his family with a cane and a pronounced limp.

We walked toward the cottage he and his parents and his sister shared, a small weatherboard dwelling that was brightly painted and made homey by the small garden of flowers near the front door, a garden of more practical vegetables at the back, plus a wire coop for hens. Joshua was prolific in his thanks for all I'd done – damn little, I thought – but he was convinced that he would have lost his leg but for my timely intervention. He was so enthusiastic in his thanks and so damn cute, I couldn't help but cast sidelong glances in his direction as people called out their best wishes to him as we passed.

We entered the cottage by the back door. His mum, with a stray hair covering her forehead, wiped her hands on her apron, which she was attempting to remove as a sign of respectability.

"Josh, you shouldn't of brought the gentlemen through the back door. That's common. I thought we brought you up better," she said and clipped him playfully across the back of the head. "You'll have to excuse Joshua, sir. His manners has slipped since he's been away. I think city life corrupted him."

"I saw damn little of city life from my hospital bed, mum."

"Language!" his dad shouted from the sitting room where he was smoking a foul-smelling pipe as he read the newspaper.

"Tea will be early, Dr. Button, I do hope you don't mind but dad has a night shift and must get away shortly, and Joshua gets tired easily though he's not likely to admit to it."

She was a tiny woman, not much over five feet, with her son's blond good looks. The years had bent her, but she retained a lively sense of humour and was obviously devoted to her children. Joshua's sister, Eileen, was a pretty little thing of eighteen, upon whom Joshua obviously doted.

The dad was gruff but friendly and delegated the rule of his weatherboard kingdom to his wife. He was content to read his newspaper and smoke his pipe, and drink beer from his ice chest as long as he had a clean vest when he needed it and food on the table as required. He was not much for socialising, so our conversation was short lived after his perfunctory but heartfelt thanks for saving his only boy. After again attempting to put my part in his son's recovery in perspective there was little else to say, so grunting he went back to his paper, and I wandered into the kitchen to talk with the rest of the family as they set the table. I attempted to help, but was shooed away.

Shortly, there was a knock at the back door and a young man's head poked inside. Eileen shrieked with delight and swooped on the visitor, showering him with eager hugs and kisses. Like Joshua, I barely recognized this attractive young man as Danny, Joshua's mate. Scrubbed clean of the coal, he was almost as prepossessing as his friend. Where Joshua was blond, Danny was dark although it would have been difficult to tell who was the taller, so neatly did they coincide.

Danny, who had ostensibly come to visit Eileen, was promptly invited to stay for tea, an invitation he accepted with alacrity, but it was apparent to me that the real reason he had turned up was his and Joshua's mateship, now under strain as Danny was expected to be affianced to Eileen as she had recently celebrated her eighteenth birthday.

Their easy rapport was born of a lifelong friendship. I learned later they had grown up, attended school, come of age, and more or less did everything together. They were, or had been, inseparable.

During the plain but delicious meal of lamb chops and basic vegetables, Joshua was restless, sometimes awkward. Danny's attempts to draw him out went unrewarded. Joshua's mum put it down to the pain he still suffered. Wanting to change the subject, she asked about my war experiences. Reluctant as I usually am to speak of such matters, I endeavored to sparkle as a guest, entertaining them with a few of my more publicly acceptable anecdotes even though they brought back painful memories of my friendship with a young soldier whose death still haunted my dreams. Our close friendship had been a revelation to me as to my true nature, something I left unexplained to my hosts. I noticed, however, Joshua look at me with quizzical interest.

At meal's end, Joshua's father headed off to the pit and Danny conceded defeat in his task of livening up his best friend, finally turning his attentions to the more grateful Eileen. I helped Joshua's mum with the washing up even though she complained vociferously that she was capable of doing it on her own. I was cunning. I knew that by helping with such a simple task it would endear me in her esteem, perhaps leading to further invitations, for I had become quite smitten with Joshua. It had not gone unnoticed by Danny, who growled quietly at me across the table.

When the dishes had been washed and dried and stacked back in their cupboards, Joshua's mum excused herself and went to listen to the radio in the sitting room and generously issued a general invitation to drop in any time. Joshua and I were left alone and the awkwardness was increased by a certain tension on my part and also, I sensed, on his. We kept breaking into silly smiles whenever we looked at each other. But we had no privacy with his mum in the next room and Danny and Eileen on the swing seat in the back yard.

"Why don't we take a stroll down by the beach?" I suggested. "The night is warm and I could do with some fresh air, having been cooped up in the surgery all day."

"Mum?" Joshua called.

"Go ahead love. Just be careful of that leg of yours," she shouted from the next room.

So she had been listening.

"I'll be in good hands." He laughed. "I'll be with a doctor."

"Perhaps we can call into the surgery on the way back so I can have a look at the job they did at the hospital," I said, more loudly than necessary.

"It couldn't hurt," Joshua agreed. "They said I should get it checked regular like by the local doctor. No use delaying, I suppose."

I mumbled good night to the lovebirds as we left and I felt Danny's hatred burning into my back as we reached the main road.

We walked on in silence until I said, "Your mate Danny doesn't like me."

"Danny's always been the jealous type. Anyway, it's not like it's me breaking up the partnership, is it? He's the one getting married..." There was more bitterness in Joshua's speech than I would have expected.

"You can still be friends after he's married, can't you?"

"It won't be the same," Joshua said, closing the subject.

We walked down to the water's edge across the little ribbon of sand, romantic beyond expectation. I wanted to take him in my arms, but there were others on the beach engaged in their own romantic trysts and they would see us. A sudden wave crashed against his bad leg, threatening to knock him down. As I held him to prevent his falling, I knew. As did Joshua. He gazed into my eyes, and I fancied I saw desire. At that moment, we didn't care that the legs of our trousers were wet through, as were our shoes.

I was getting good at laying false trails, so in a voice loud enough to carry to those already on the beach, I invited Joshua back to dry his clothes, and at the same time I could take a look at the injuries to his leg. We walked in silence, hopeful that our reading of each other had not been a misinterpretation. Back at the surgery, Joshua removed his trousers without speaking. I hung them up to dry.

Standing in his loose underpants, ragged but house-proudly clean, he looked incredibly handsome and expectant. I asked him to remove his shirt. He shivered in his vest with his hands across his groin in an act of unnecessary modesty. I helped him up onto the surgery table, getting him to lie on his back.

He looked away as I examined the scar than ran the length of his calf. It was a vicious thing, but injury was a given when you were a miner. Impulsively, I leaned over, kissing the disfigurement, brushing my lips along its entire length. To feel Joshua's flesh had an electric effect on my groin. My cock was hard in an instant. Obviously, Joshua was also in a state of arousal because he made an adjustment to his crotch through his underpants.

"Look at me," he said in despair at his shattered leg.

"I am and I'm having a hard time from keeping my hands off you."

"Don't then."

"You've done this sort of thing—"

"With Danny," he said bitterly. "But then you've already guessed that. Best friend stuff. Experimenting. And once properly. The day I came out of hospital. I spent a night in a hotel room with a stranger I met in the pub." He paused. "It was better than I ever could have imagined. I couldn't wait to get back here to tell Danny." He stopped, thinking he had revealed too much.

I leaned over, placing my lips against his. He opened his mouth to welcome me. I had worried that he would find kissing another man like this offensive, unnatural. I went in gently, but he threw his arms around me, sucking my tongue into his mouth like a thirsty man discovering an oasis. We tussled for supremacy. I ran my hand across his vest, feeling the hard muscles beneath, but my ultimate destination lay farther south. Slowly, I slid my hand beneath the band of his underwear. I felt him tense. Perhaps I was going too fast.

"Please," he said. He sat up to enable me to remove his vest. He squirmed out of his underpants as I ran my hands over his magnificent body, pinching his nipples, making him moan softly, teasing my fingers down his sandy trail of hair until I brushed the head of his cock. He gasped, his prick slit oozing pre-cum. I knew it would not take much to bring him off, though I was hoping he would be good for more.

It was uncomfortable here in the surgery. I wanted him in my bed, but I dared not break the spell lest he panic. I lowered my head to lick the head of his cock. "Sweet Jesus," he gasped. I ran my tongue along the shaft down to his balls, lathering them with my spit before licking my way back to the head again. His choked moaning increased when I placed my warm mouth over his cock, sucking it inside. A few slow strokes to get my rhythm and my face was impaled on half its length, licking the underside with my tongue as I pushed my head down. I gulped in air and sank my lips down the entire shaft so that my nose was in his patch. He sat bolt upright on the table as if he'd been struck by lightning. He held my head attempting to pull me off his cock and at the same time attempting to slam it in deeper. "Oh my God," he gasped.

I opened my throat, gagging slightly, knowing he was a matter of strokes away. "I can't hold off, I'm going to shoot. Take your mouth away." I had no intention of doing so just to tell him I had no intention of doing so. I wanted to taste him, to swallow his beauty. I felt his cock contract then shoot his spunk, filling the back of my throat. He shot three or four good loads, finally falling back against the pillows exhausted even though I had done all the work.

Now came the difficult part. Having achieved orgasm, there were numerous ways he could play it: accuse me of sexual assault, get up and walk away not mentioning it again, or...

"You swallowed it?" he said in awe.

"Uh huh."

"Doesn't it make you sick?"

I smiled, assuring him I enjoyed the taste.

"What would you like to do now?" I hadn't wanted to ask, but we had to make a decision one way or the other.

He blushed and asked, "Can we do it again?"

I couldn't keep the smile off my face. "We can do it as often as you like. But not here. We'd be more comfortable in my bed."

So it was we found ourselves lying on the covers naked and in each other's arms. He had lost his reticence. He kissed more gently now. He had learned restraint. Gazing at my body, in muscularity inferior to his own, but still tight enough with little flab, he flicked at my nipples absentmindedly. I stilled his hand, putting my lips to his chest and biting down gently. His sharp intake of breath revealed how sensitive, and erogenous, his nipples were.

I caressed him, making him sleepy. "I didn't know it could be that good," he murmured.

"What experience did you have then?"

"With Danny, we would just watch each other bring ourselves off. There was no touching, though I wanted to. I think he did as well. We just didn't dare. We would wrestle, especially when we went swimming. I would feel him get hard when he touched me. I only had to look at him and I would get hard. We didn't do it so much as we got older, but every now and then, it was like a drug you have to go back to."

"Did Danny feel the same way?"

"I don't know for sure," he said. "But it was always Danny who started it. I never had the nerve."

"What about the man you met after your hospitalisation?" I ran my fingers through his hair. He almost purred with satisfaction.

"He kissed me. I was shocked. I didn't know two men could kiss each other. Not like that. I imagined I was kissing Danny." He added quickly, "Not that he was ugly, this new bloke, but I guess it's what I always wanted to do with Danny but didn't know it. Then he put his hand on my… "

"Cock?"

"Is it all right to say that?" His face registered surprise.

"As I've just had your cock in my mouth, I think it's permissible."

He laughed. "You're funny. Anyway, he put his hand around my cock and pulled me off. And then he wanted me to do the same for him. I put my hand around him. It was like..." He struggled for a moment. "I can't describe it. Like I'd come home. I never wanted to take my hand away. But I gave him a pull and he squirted. We'd taken the room for the night, but he got dressed and told me to stay if I wanted to as it was paid for, but he had to get home to his wife and kids. I had so much to think about, but all I wanted to do was rush back here and tell Danny."

I pulled him to me and kissed him, but he pushed my head gently toward his groin in expectation of a repeat performance.

Joshua left around midnight. I only know because he leaned over my sleeping face, kissed me chastely, and whispered "Thank you" before he let himself out the back door for the short walk back to his own home. That kiss showed, at least, there were no hard feelings – if you discounted the very hard organ between my legs – still I remained worried about repercussions. I was not foolish enough to expect reciprocation, as there had been none, or a repetition of the night's eager couplings, so I took myself in hand and within moments had done the job Joshua was too embarrassed or too...well, I didn't really want to spoil the moment by inferring too much.

I fell asleep wondering if it were possible to ever find someone as sweet and beautiful as Joshua to share my life. I ran my fingers across my lips remembering his sweet kisses.

CHAPTER TWO

~

A SERPENT IN PARADISE

I did not see Joshua for another week, unusual in a village so small, so I assumed he was avoiding me because of guilt. I was concerned that our basic lovemaking had somehow unhinged him, that he might cause harm to himself or others. Yes, the others I had in mind were me. I meant not physical harm, but harm of a rather more sinister nature – exposure.

As the older man I would, naturally enough, be seen as the predator. Joshua would be the innocent prey, although our consummation had been entirely mutual. I had seen this sort of incident frequently enough in the past.

I was unable to sleep with any calm; I have never been comfortable with suspense. It was not busy at the surgery, so I left a note pinned to the door that in case of emergency I could be reached at the Carter residence. If the matter was not urgent, I merely asked that the patient take a seat in the surgery until such time as I returned.

As usual, Joshua's mum was in the kitchen when I knocked at the back door, although it was wide open. Few people in the village bothered with locks. She was surprised at my visit, but greeted me warmly.

"Come in, Dr. Button. Would you like a nice cuppa tea? I'll put the kettle on."

"Thank you, Mrs. Carter, but I don't want you to go to any trouble."

"No trouble for you, doctor. After all you've done for our Joshua."

I refrained from repeating that my part in Joshua's recovery was minimal. Perhaps it was for the best if she believed otherwise.

We exchanged pleasantries about the weather, Mr. Carter's health, matters that scarcely touched on the personal, before we moved into the sitting room. It was cosy. No other thought had been put into its furnishings than the comfort of the occupants; therefore, it was welcoming in a way that more fashionable salons were not.

Mrs. Carter allowed me the comfortable armchair her husband normally reserved for himself, while she perched on the settee that looked somewhat faded, a little like Mrs. Carter's own beauty although she radiated good humour and hospitality.

"I'm afraid my husband is at the mine, Dr. Button." She assumed I was there to see the man of the house.

"I'm actually here to enquire after Joshua," I said, trying to keep my voice level.

"He's up at the mine as well."

I was almost apoplectic with concern. "But he can't possibly..."

"No, no, no," she soothed. "He was getting restless with nothing to do. If I may be frank, he was getting under me feet. So he's taken himself off to see if he can get a job in their office. Filing papers, you know, anything at all like that. Just until his leg heals proper." She leaned forward conspiratorially. "We're not rich folk, Dr. Button, and without Joshua's wage coming in his dad has had to take on a few extra shifts. And the pittance Eileen gets helping out at the school doesn't go far when a young girl wants to look her best for her sweetheart. If you know what I mean."

I smiled that I did. I relaxed, as her attitude toward me had not changed in the past week; in fact, she was more confidential than ever, so my fear of the worst was misplaced.

"I was just concerned that Joshua had not been back for his check-up. He still needs regular observation, I didn't want him to neglect it," I lied.

"Heaven forbid, Dr. Button," she said. "I have told him the very same thing myself. Just between you and me and the fence post, I think Joshua wants a job at the front office as much to be able to repay your kindness as to put extra bread on the table."

"I don't expect payment, Mrs. Carter. The company reimburses me very well."

She looked startled that I might expect financial compensation. "Oh, it weren't a payment. It was more along the lines of something personal he had in mind. He was ever so cheerful when he came home the other night from your surgery. The next day it was Dr. Button this and Dr. Button that. You would have thought the sun shone out your arse." She blushed and looked at me fearfully. "I do apologize, Dr. Button, I don't know what I'm saying. It's just I haven't seen Joshua so happy since the accident."

"Absolutely no apology necessary," I said sincerely. "And young Joshua will find my arse shines no brighter, I hope, than anyone else's."

Mrs. Carter whooped with laughter that I would use the same vulgarity in front of her, and her humor was so infectious that we were both still smiling broadly when Joshua walked through the door. His face had telltale signs of disappointment, but he disguised it when he saw me with his mother.

"Mum? What's the matter? Are you ill?"

Mrs. Carter wiped the corner of her eyes with her apron. "Me? Ill? Never been sick a day in me life," she said. "Would you like a cuppa, love? You look plumb tuckered."

"Wouldn't mind," he said despondently.

"I'll make us a fresh. The other's well stewed by now." She stood to go to the kitchen. "You'll have another, doctor? You keep him entertained, Joshua, while I make it."

I had been on the verge of leaving, but now that Joshua was here I hesitated. My heart banged in my chest and my stomach felt empty on seeing him again. I knew the signs.

"I told Dr. Button you were up at the mine looking for work," Mrs. Carter called from the kitchen as she stoked the fuel stove.

"Mu–um," Joshua complained.

"Any luck?" I asked.

"None." He cast his eyes down. "They aren't hiring at present, and they might even be laying off some of the girls. Things are tough."

"Come and work for me then." No sooner had the thought entered my mind than I found it on my lips. It had bypassed my common sense.

He looked at me suspiciously. "What would I have to do?"

I chose my words carefully. "Only what you're comfortable doing, no more." He understood my drift, but in case his mother was listening, I added. "Obviously your leg is my prime concern, but a little help in the surgery would not go astray. You could run it on those occasions I'm out. And the building itself could stand a little handiwork. There are leaks and drafts which don't help the patients' well-being."

"What do you think, mum?" he called.

"I think you should get down on your knees and thank God for a man like Dr. Button," she said as she brought in the refreshed pot of tea.

Joshua and I both laughed, but whether it was at the image I had of Joshua on his knees ministering to my sexual needs I don't know. The deal, details to be worked out later, was sealed with a hot cuppa.

Later that same afternoon, Joshua visited the surgery after the final patient had been treated. He was hesitant and unsure. I sensed his discomfort. I would have to lay it on the line.

"Look Joshua," I said. "What we did last week…"

"I don't want to be bought," he said, mustering as much dignity as he could.

I noticed, what was it? Fear? Expectation? Desire?

I took a deep breath. "What we did last week…that is not part of your duties if you come to work for me. Is that understood?"

He smiled. "I thought you might want me like a common whore," he admitted meekly.

"Oh, I do want you Joshua. Like no man I have ever wanted before. But as an equal. I would like nothing more than to repeat and keep repeating what we did, but I respect whatever it is you decide with regards to that. You have a job here regardless."

"You want me?"

"More than I can say."

He was in my arms so quickly he almost knocked the breath out of me. He roughly sought my mouth, cutting off my protestations. I had never known a man so eager. After returning his kisses with equal ardour, I made him sit down on the other side of the desk, so I would not be tempted to strip him and have my way on the spot.

"I couldn't get you out of my head, Dr. Button. After that night, I kept touching myself, thinking of you while I did it. I nearly came back here so many times, but I thought a sophisticated gentleman like you was just having a bit of fun with a lad like me. I didn't know two men could feel like that. It did my head in. So I kept away."

I looked at him, wondering what I had done to deserve even a few months with this remarkable man. "I missed you more than I can say, Joshua. That week was the longest any man has had to endure. I do feel that way about you. I have tried to fight it because I thought perhaps you may have used it against me."

He was vehement in his denial. "No! I would never do that!

I believed him.

He pushed his hand across the desk shyly. I held it. "Will you teach me?" he said quietly.

Joshua blossomed in his new employment. It helped his ego to have work, so I ensured there was enough that he did not feel it was charity. It helped his parents financially, and he was popular with patients. He helped with lifting the more infirm onto the surgery table, he would walk them home, he would explain to the men in words they understood when I used medical obfuscation. I even began to teach him nursing skills, which some patients felt unsuitable for a man although young women would often feign a bruise in the hopes Joshua would tape their leg or their arm.

We kept honing Joshua's skills in another department as well. Our afternoon sessions continued with as much passion as they began. Josh, as I now called him, was a quick study, thriving under my tutelage. He was becoming as adept at pleasuring me with his mouth as I was with him, although his early attempts had been painful until he learned to retract his teeth. He was an eager student, wanting me to set as much extra curricula practice homework as I could endure. Our relationship bloomed. Tentatively, we began to make plans for a future together, which would mean wrenching him from the village when I returned to the city.

I also became a regular fixture at the Carter table, sharing food with them. The only person displeased with the arrangement was Danny, who became morose as his relationship with Josh cooled and mine heated up. It began to affect tea, as they called their evening meal, to the extent I felt it better for all that I not be there. I began having my meals at home. The Carters were embarrassed, accepting my explanation that I had medical business that kept me busy, but the truth was I felt it only fair as Danny was to be part of the family and I would always remain an outsider. With time, it was not uncommon for Josh to spend the night at the surgery, ostensibly in the spare room, which we had set up for such an eventuality, always ensuring the bed appeared slept in, although it never was, before the cleaning woman turned up three times a week.

Danny's temper only increased with Josh's voluntary banishment from the family hearth, leading him to white ant my reputation with the Carters.

* * * *

"There's a gentleman at the door, sir," Eric, my manservant, announced discretely.

"Who is it, Eric?"

"He said his name is Daniel Page, sir. Shall I tell him to make an appointment?"

My blood froze. I thought Josh and I were safe here in the city, away from the gossip and accusations of Seaspray Bay. It had been three years or more, yet still I was haunted by it.

"Did he ask for me or Josh, Eric?"

"He was hoping to have a word with you, sir."

I sighed. "Show him in here, and, Eric."

"Yes, sir?"

"If you have a mind, be at hand."

"I understand, sir. You're expecting trouble?"

"Perhaps."

Josh and I had no secrets from Eric. We had deliberately set about building a life and a practice where we could be comfortable and be ourselves. We had only two servants, but we had vetted them carefully. Eric was a fine gentleman's gentleman who turned his hand to all manner of tasks above stairs, as they say. His partner, John, was our cook. We liked them, they adored us. They were a generation above, but thrived in our house among our close friends.

Eyebrows had been raised about having a male cook, but his sumptuous dinners had won over all but the most intransigent of opinions. Some people had even tried to lure him away, without success, for where John went, Eric followed. They were a pair and could not be split up. I met them when I shared their favours, individually and as a couple, when I first arrived in Sydney. They became stalwart friends. At that time, they served different masters, making it difficult to sustain their relationship.

Once my medical practice began to establish itself, courtesy of the grapevine of like-minded men, and I had moved to larger premises in the city, which became my home and my surgery, I had no hesitation in asking them both to come with me. They jumped at the opportunity and had been with us since. They were as loyal and as discrete as we could possibly hope for.

"Daniel Page, sir."

I stood, but kept my back to the man who had just been announced. I could scarcely contain my anger.

Eric read my mood and advised, "Take a seat, Mr. Page."

What did he think he could achieve by coming here now?

* * * *

I lay on my back because I wanted to watch Josh's face. We had been leading up to this moment, but I did not want to hurt him. He had fucked me weeks earlier, and while admittedly his first attempt was lacking in finesse, what it lacked in experience it more than made up for in stamina and perseverance. Josh insisted on practicing until he made perfect. I was more than happy to oblige because his blond cock felt right at home embedded in my arse.

That night he wanted to try to take it. He had seen my enjoyment and was disturbed he may have been missing out on something. I tried to explain that the pleasure was different to what he experienced when he fucked me. Still he insisted. I was glad. I had long harboured a desire to insert my cock inside his warm and inviting arsehole. I had fingered him on occasions, inserting two fingers until his grimace forced me to stop.

I again had two fingers inside his well-lubricated arse as I attempted to reach his prostate, but he was having difficulty accepting the penetration. I had relaxed him by biting his firm arse cheeks, almost driving him mad with desire when I inserted my tongue in his vulnerable hole. Squirming in pleasure, he begged me to fuck him, but my cock was much bigger and thicker than my tongue, and he was having such problems I thought the night would end disastrously. I told him we could try again at another time.

"No," he said with determination. "I want it now. Lie still."

He squatted in position over my cock while I held it, greased and ready, pointing at his beautiful arse. He parted his cheeks with his hands, tentatively lowering himself over my cock until I felt the head push against his sphincter. I had chosen this position because Josh could control the depth and regularity of our lovemaking. Beads of sweat broke out on his forehead as I pushed gently. I told him to relax, but he was fighting it.

I was about to give up on the enterprise when, in frustration, Josh said with finality, "Oh, fuck it!" forcing his arsehole down over my cock. The look of surprise and pain on his face was followed by an understandably vocal, "Holy fuck!" His immediate reaction was to unimpale himself, but I spoke to him softly. I held him firm and soothed him. "Relax, Josh. The pain will go away. It was a brave thing you did. I guarantee it will start to feel good in a few moments." I was trying to convince myself as much as Josh.

His breathing became more relaxed as he raised himself off my cock then slowly reinserted it. If he didn't actually look as if he were enjoying himself, he also didn't look as if he were in too much discomfort. I let him regulate his movement, pushing himself down further and further on my aching cock until he was right down to my balls. He looked at me and beamed.

"It's reaching places I didn't know existed," he said.

I could have explained that my cock was rubbing against his prostate, but that was just too academic for what we were both feeling. "Hold still, Josh," I said, slipping out from under him while at the same time turning him on his side. We fumbled a bit until he was on his back and I had his legs on my shoulders. I pushed my cock against his arsehole again, sliding in easily. Leaning forward, I planted wet kisses on his face and mouth. "I love you, Josh Carter,' I whispered.

"I never want this to end," he whispered back.

I increased my thrusts as he pushed back against me, holding his cheeks apart for better access. I closed my hand around his cock. It was hard as coal. I would not last long even though I was attempting to prolong my pleasure as well as Josh's. "I'm gonna cum," he moaned. "Fuck me, fuck me good."

Never one to turn down a request like that, especially from a handsome man like Josh, I sped up. Soon my cock was so sensitive I could feel my balls churning. I gasped while Josh, whose cock was pulsating in my hand, kept repeating 'yes' under his breath. We both must have howled to wake the dead when I shot my spunk into his warm, wet arsehole. He spewed a load on my fingers and his own chest.

"G-o-d," he panted. "That was so good. I want to do it again."

"Give me a chance to catch my breath and we can." I pulled out and lay on Josh's sticky body, kissing him deeply.

That was how they found us when Danny burst through the door. He wasn't alone. He had brought Josh's mother with him.

"I told you," Danny said in triumph.

Mrs. Carter just looked at us, but her face gave nothing away. I grabbed for the sheet and pulled it over our naked bodies and over Josh's embarrassment. Mrs. Carter pushed Danny out the door and closed it quietly behind her. About twenty minutes later, Josh confronted his old friend in the village's one and only pub and beat him so badly the hamlet's lone policeman was called out. Danny was hauled to my surgery where he screamed he didn't need a doctor, while Josh ran back to his parents' house. I had difficulty patching up Danny's wounds without wanting to inflict maximum damage.

The cop, to his credit much embarrassed by the enquiry, asked if I knew what had precipitated the argument. I volunteered that I had heard Danny was spreading rumors about discovering Josh and myself in a compromising situation. He admitted he had heard the same and that, with my permission, he would like to examine my bed. I complied and we both went into the room that had been the scene of our discovery shortly before. The bed was made, but the cop pulled back the sheets and ran his fingers across them. "Clean, but slept in," he said to himself. Unbeknown to him we had swapped them with the bedclothes in the spare room. He turned to me and said, "You've not had time to wash them and they are not stained as you would expect from what Daniel Page described. I would normally have Joshua Carter examined, but as you're the town's resident medical practitioner it would be a conflict of interest."

I agreed.

"So, I guess that leaves it up to Mrs. Carter to confirm or deny whether you will be arrested or not, Dr. Button. Good-day to you."

CHAPTER THREE

~

THE DOCTOR'S DILEMMA

*N*ews of the contretemps and its cause had spread around the town like a virus. Sides were taken in expectation of a right juicy scandal, most of the villagers coming down heavily on Josh's side as the injured party against me. Danny had ensured that. I expected little sympathy, so I used the time to pack in expectation of imminent arrest. I had almost completed putting away my medical instruments when there was a knock at the back door. I had taken the precaution of locking myself in lest I be subjected to vigilante justice.

Peeking through the window, I saw that it was Josh. I opened the door quickly. He entered carrying a battered old suitcase. He smiled and embraced me warmly, if somewhat cautiously.

He almost danced with glee. "She was magnificent."

"Who was?" I asked, almost too stunned to enquire.

"Mum. Not only did she swear that nothing like what Danny saw had occurred, she said she and Danny had entered the surgery, not the bedroom, and had come in on you examining my leg, which was no more than she expected of you as part of your job as a doctor. She swore she had seen nothing untoward and got so angry at Danny's charges she threatened to have the courts on him unless he took back the allegation immediately. And, and, wait for it, she topped it orf by telling him he would never be welcome in the Carter household ever again, and that went for Eileen as well.

"Danny mumbled something about being drunk or something stupid, and the copper said he'd have to have a good think about all this. When he left, mum turned to me in front of Danny and asked how long it had been going on.

"I admitted ever since I came back from hospital. 'And do you intend keeping it up?'

"I told her I couldn't stop and got all teary. 'I love him,' I told her. She said, 'I know, love,' then she turned on Danny. 'If I so much as hear another word about this, Daniel Page, I'll cut your balls off and serve them to you on a plate, you hear?' He nodded, then she dismissed him just like that. When we was alone she asked me what I was gonna do now. I told her 'I dunno.' She said, 'If you want an old woman's advice, if he'll have you, go with him. There's nothing in this place for the likes of you. Your future will be much brighter, for all the pain that might be involved, away from here'.

"She helped me pack and tried not to cry, but we both had a right old weep, I can tell you. She gave me some money from her rainy day jar and..."

He finally broke down.

"Take me with you. Please."

"You don't have to beg, Josh. I wouldn't leave without you. I'd rather die."

He kissed me harder than he ever had before, holding me like a man scared to let go. "Don't leave without me," he said. "I'll go and organise us a lift to the station. It's too far to walk." He flushed with the sense of adventure as he ducked out the back door.

"You won't change your mind, will you?" I called after him.

"Never," he said, but he noticed my concern. Noticed enough that he came back and held me tightly. "I will never leave you." To reinforce his words he crossed his heart in that naïve gesture of which children are so fond. He made me joyful. I mussed his hair. "Ten minutes. Fifteen at the most."

* * * *

I was shivering. "Ten minutes. Fifteen at the most."

The command would come along the trench, followed by foot soldiers clambering up the wooden ladders and over the sandbags to confront hell. There would already be a few lads ready to soil their pants at the thought. We were green; we'd been in France but a few days. The sound of war was so foreign to our antipodean ears, and so foreign to our easygoing concerns, it seemed less the great big adventure to us colonials who had enlisted to fight for Old Mother England, and more a major blunder into which we'd stumbled, eyes closed, to the wider implications of our stupidity.

I had never been one to shirk my duty, and I found strength in the easy mateship of my fellow Australian squaddies. We made up the AIF 5th Division and, with the British 2nd South Midland, we were dug in near the French village of Fromelles some ten miles from the picturesque town of Lille on the Western Front.

Ted was shaking so hard I handed him my last cigarette to calm his nerves. We weren't supposed to be smoking now, but the officers turned a blind eye to any sort of action on our part that calmed the nerves. They weren't like the martinets that whipped the Poms into shape and who were more concerned with the niceties of ceremony that they saw as the epitome, as well as the saviour, of the British Empire.

Most of us knew this could to be a fatal exercise, although none of us was keen to speak it aloud. It would be just another stupid waste of life in a whole series of futile vainglorious exercises that resulted in mass slaughter. What made it more difficult to bear was that our heroic exploit was merely a diversionary tactic for the more important offensive about fifty miles to the south at the Somme River. We'd gleaned the information from the little we'd overheard among the officers, who were as disquieted as we enlisted men. That was of little concern to our commander, General Richard Cyril Byrne Haking, commonly referred to as, out of earshot admittedly, The Butcher.

He was equally loathed by his officer class as he was by the common soldier, including those that ever got to hear of him before they were sent out as fodder for the German artillery. He was a man of the old school, walrusmoustached, a believer in that outdated maxim that the person on the attack had the advantage, and that, even in war, every soldier, no matter his rank, should be a gentleman. It would have been the gentlemanly thing to do to excuse The Butcher's military beliefs on the grounds he'd taken a bullet to the head in the early part of the war, but he'd previously penned a book espousing his beliefs, so there was no getting away from the indisputable fact, The Butcher was an ass.

* * * *

I finished packing my medical equipment and my clothes, and only enough that I could carry with me. Anything else could be replaced. I sat at the old wooden desk that had been my comfort since I first arrived. It had witnessed a myriad of illnesses and injuries and would now witness my ultimate humiliation as I wrote out my resignation to a company that would shortly demand it if I didn't fall on my own scalpel. It was one of the most difficult epistles I had ever attempted, the wastepaper basket testimony to my feeble attempts to explain myself. Eventually, I realized there was no point prevaricating or explaining. I wrote a simple, bland letter of termination explaining that circumstances made it impossible for me to continue as the village doctor. I didn't bother to explain the particular circumstances; they would know them. Better not to put anything in writing. With economic conditions as they were, I knew the company would have no problem in replacing me quickly although I dreaded a mine emergency in the interim.

By the time I had sealed the envelope with my resignation and tidied away any evidence of my occupation in the cottage, it was getting dark. I noticed a gang of men had gathered out the front of the surgery, muttering belligerently, a triumphant Danny amongst them. When he saw me peer out the window, he sauntered toward the surgery door. As he was alone, I opened it without inviting him in. I glanced at my watch. Josh had been gone for close to two hours.

Nodding my head in the direction of the assembled men, I said, "The tar-and-feather brigade?"

Danny was enjoying my discomfort. "If you're lucky."

"He loved you, you know," I said quietly.

Danny froze, then spluttered angrily. "You're a sick bastard. You've corrupted him."

I sighed. There was nothing I could say to this man.

"And where is he, eh? Your little Joshua."

My look of concern must have encouraged him. "He's not coming, that's where. He thought better of it. He knows now you were just using him."

"Does he, indeed?" But my confidence was rattled.

"Why don't you just piss orf back to the big city where poofters like you belong. We don't want your sort here."

"That's precisely what I intend."

"What are you waitin' for?" He smirked. "Aw, you're not waitin' for your little bum boy, are ya? Didn't I tell ya? He won't be coming."

"If I leave, will you do me one favour? For Josh's sake?"

"I might."

"Give me a moment."

I closed the door and went to the desk. I scribbled a note telling Josh how he could contact me in the city and sealed it in an envelope, writing his name on the front. I had to trust that Danny would deliver it. I would not insult him with money; I was relying on his sense of justice.

"Please give that to Josh," I said as I handed the note to Danny at the door. He examined it carefully and saw that it was sealed.

"So, you're goin' without him?"

"You said he wasn't coming."

"I did, didn't I?" He looked pleased with himself as he turned, swaggering back to his mates. I closed and locked the door. I was gathering my bags together as the first stone shattered the surgery window. Loud, menacing threats were hurled at me. I determined to wait a while longer for Josh. I didn't believe Danny that he had changed his mind. Something unexpected had detained him. I was relying on Josh to organise transport as I did not fancy my chances with the crowd in the street. Tar-and-feathering was the least of the problems I faced. These were brutal men whose fists did their talking for them.

As dusk spattered shadows across Seaspray Bay, I made a heart-sickening decision, taking the opportunity to slip out the back door carrying my possessions in two suitcases and a pack I had strapped to my back. In the shadow of the hill, keeping low behind the grassy hillocks, I managed to crawl and squat my way to emerge a few hundred yards down the dirt road from my tormentors. I heard their impatience and knew it would not be long before they either wearied and went home, or Danny geed them up enough to attack the surgery.

I felt gutted that Josh had forsaken me. What else could I think? He had obviously changed his mind, otherwise he would be with me now. No longer caring particularly for my own safety, I picked up my suitcases and marched down the dirt road toward the highway. There, surely, I would snare a lift to the nearest railway station and make my way to Sydney. I would leave this small-minded village behind. I would immerse myself in the city and forget the past few months. Seaspray Bay no longer existed.

It took a good hour to reach the new Pacific Highway and a further half before a kind Samaritan took pity on my dusty form to offer a lift. I was miserable company for the journey to Gosford railway station, a considerable distance to the south through rolling hills of farms and bushland peppered with its grey gums that stood sentry like an army of pale ghosts against the dying light. By the time I reached my destination it was dark. Fortunately, the station had a cosy refreshment room where I bought a cheese sandwich, which tasted of cardboard and despair, and a cup of weak milk tea while I sat at a small wooden table that appeared as miserable as I felt. I waited for the train, which would steam me the fifty-five or so miles to Sydney.

Never in my life had I felt so forlorn as I did now, wallowing in my unhappiness, afraid to give in to my teary-eyed depression which I covered by frequently blowing my nose in my soggy linen handkerchief in an attempt to convince other waiting passengers that I had a cold.

As the mighty steel locomotive steamed into the platform, a uniformed guard struck the metal plate inserted in the brick wall of the ladies waiting room with a metal rod, the resultant clamor a warning to travellers to climb on board. I took the precaution of wrapping the leftover sandwich in a clean handkerchief in case my hunger returned during the long trip. I was going to change trains at Hornsby, the city's most northerly suburb to catch one of those on the electric line. Since my time as doctor at Seaspray Bay, the mighty marvel that joined the city of Sydney with the northern shore of Port Jackson had been completed and a new underground section of the railway built from the southern end of the bridge to the main terminus at Central.

The Sydney Harbour Bridge was a potent symbol of a city flexing its muscles in a modern world. The Iron Coat Hanger, as it had been affectionately dubbed, dominated the city and the harbour, its sandstone pylons and its great grey skeletal metal beams a beacon of modernity. There seemed no better symbol of my new life than that welcoming crossing. I was determined to experience it firsthand. It would, in part, make up for my ignominious return.

I found an almost empty compartment, struggled to stow my bulky suitcases above the seat, yet hesitant to sit. I heard the station porter blow his whistle, so I lowered the window to glance out at the platform. I looked toward the overheard bridge where a few late passengers were running to jump on board, clenching my hands in hope that I would see my Joshua running for his life to be with me. But as the carriage jolted forward, I knew it was not to be. I pulled up the window against the billowing smoke from the engine, sinking into the leather seat and into my despair.

If I did not overcome my funk, I would be no good to anyone, least of all myself. The dearth of conversation in my carriage was as a result of an elderly matron in widow's blacks whose severity matched my own. And the only other solitary gentleman, rude as all young men are today, merely grunted acknowledgement of our existence before burying his head in a lurid penny dreadful novel which seemed to engross him for the remainder of the journey. I was to be denied even civilised conversation, which would have, at least, occupied my mind for the two-hour journey.

I pulled down the blind and leaned into the corner of the carriage in an attempt to establish a course of action. In my haste I had left everything to chance, a rather haphazard circumstance for someone usually as well organised as I. I had already begun telling myself that it was in Joshua's best interests to stay with his family, for I had nothing to offer him but a life of uncertainty; that it was my selfishness that sought to wrench him from family and friends to a life of who knew what in a city he had never seen and which he had probably never imagined. No, I had done the right thing by leaving without him.

When the train pulled into Woy Woy station, a young man and young woman got into the compartment. They were all giggles and excitement. I judged them newly married, for they had eyes for no one but each other, speaking in whispers huddling their heads close together as if exchanging the most delicious of secrets. I smiled at their obvious joy, keeping the bitterness of my own situation at bay. I chastised myself it was the second time my heart had led me astray, and the second time I had put another man's life at risk.

In that frame of mind, I dozed as we steamed toward the big city.

A loud knocking startled me awake. A hubbub of voices shouted. For a moment, my surroundings confused me, and I panicked. As my eyes focused, I noticed the other passengers in the carriage glancing my way. I was aware I had gasped or made some such sound as I woke, but they shrugged their indifference, going back to whatever they had been engaged in previously.

The knocking seemed to be coming from my head or thereabouts. I had been leaning against the thick blind that covered the window to my side of the compartment. The knocking was coming from outside. The train had come to a standstill, and the sounds of activity were obviously from the station. I pulled the blind up and weary faces peered in. At first I thought they were passengers who would clamber aboard until I noticed they held aloft cane baskets with the scrag end of long, thin bottles with which they were attempting to entice us.

I glanced at the station name in large painted letters attached to the side of the waiting room. Hawkesbury River. This was about the half-way point to the city. We would spend just enough time here for a second engine to be shunted behind the carriages for the arduous climb up the steep incline to the tiny hamlet of Cowan. The chattering classes on the platform were selling the local produce from the small village of Brooklyn, which hugged the bend in the river and which, in turn, produced the local delicacy: oysters. Those that weren't consumed by the inhabitants or shipped off to market were sold in glass bottles to the passing railway trade.

Lowering the window for a little fresh air, I was inundated by the hawkers who descended on me like a horde of annoying mosquitoes, buzzing about me insistently until I had an overwhelming desire to swat them away. They jostled and screeched at me, each attempting to sell an identical product, each undercutting the other's price in an attempt to flog off the last of their stock so they could go home. I commiserated silently, but had no intention of purchasing their wares.

"For heaven's sake, man, close the window. The noise is deafening," the young reader in the carriage called above the din.

I turned and mumbled an apology, pulling up the window and drawing down the blind as the porter's whistle signalled the train's departure.

* * * *

The whistle sounded very close now. I was running for my life, and I could hear them getting closer. The back alleyways were dark and forbidding and, at any moment, could lead me to a dead end. It would be a tragedy for it to end like this. I glanced back. Ted was right behind me. He had that mischievous smirk on his face like this was a great big adventure rather than what it was…a matter of life or…well, it wasn't really life or death, more like life or disgrace.

We'd fallen asleep on the cramped single bed only to be awoken by loud banging on the door and shouts from the other side. We'd taken the precaution of locking the door against intrusion and discovery, but from the sound of an increasingly hysterical landlady we'd been discovered. We'd been told that this modest terrace in Pyrmont, a depressed, grimy suburb within walking distance across the swing bridge from the city itself, was 'sympathetic'.

Old Mum Doreen would never rat on us, but she could ill afford to spend time in front of the magistrate. She was a good, old sort. Nonetheless, because we knew her loud hammering, hollering and her fumbling with the keys at the lock were a signal for us to 'do a bunk', as she put it so colloquially, I put my hand over Ted's mouth and shook him awake. In a few seconds he was alert to the situation, already hurriedly getting dressed. I did the same as we heard Mum Doreen, God bless her, telling her rowdy companions …the police…MPs…that she had brought the wrong keys and that she would have to go back down to the parlour to get the correct set. There were curses from the men who were with her and a severe rebuke from Mum that she would have no profanity in her house, she was a God-fearing woman and kept a clean establishment. There was a communal mumbled apology as we heard Mum descend to the floor below.

The room's one window looked out onto the back and side walls of a matching set of terraces. I slid it open quietly. It was intentionally well oiled for just such an emergency. I heard a secret "psst" from below. The top of a makeshift ladder was suddenly propped against the sill so Ted and I could scramble down to the backyard below. "Bloody coppers! They'll be the death of me," Mum hissed, her aversion to profanity gone. It was for public consumption only. "Good luck, boys. Look me up when you're back in town."

She hugged us both in turn to her ample bosom, pecked us on the cheek before revealing the easy escape route she had prepared, and used frequently it seemed, before patting us on the arse, whispering, "Go, go!" We scrambled under corrugated iron and over back fences to the consternation of the local dogs, hearing shouts and a whistle from the terrace as we scrambled away.

The zigzag of alleyways and dunny lanes were confusing at first, but we knew to head back toward the city where we could blend into our surrounds and become just two more anonymous people in a grey landscape. Our one fear was that they may have blocked the bridge, but luck was with us. We stopped running and walked briskly so as not to attract any undue attention. A paddy wagon sped by, but it was not on the lookout for us. Yet. We managed to camouflage ourselves amongst the dock workers who were pouring across the bridge to the Pyrmont wharves, although we were walking against the tide.

There were a few calls of "Good on ya, mate," and a few slaps on the back as they passed. I knew they would not have been as supportive of us as soldiers had they known we'd spent the night in bed together sharing our illegal love with our bodies caked with each other's semen.

* * * *

The train steamed through the suburbs, which made up Sydney's outer perimeter. The tiny villages cut into the threatening bushland, which periodically burst into savage summer flame, threatening their very livelihood. They were unhappy places to live. Tents had sprung up along the railway line between Cowan and Asquith, families eking out an existence, not a life, in these dark, early years of Depression among the ubiquitous metal signs counting down "18 Miles to Griffith Bros Teas", promising that civilisation was waiting at the end of the journey.

I had pulled up the curtain as the train wheezed to a stop at the top of the incline. Now, as we approached Hornsby, there was activity in the compartment. People would alight there for a change of trains, as I would myself. After the small village stations we had passed most of our journey, Hornsby was a blaze of activity. Steam trains puffed like angry animals on the country train platforms while the new electrical carriages, more sleek and modern than their black metal behemoth brethren, hummed as they prepared for the journey back to the city through the burgeoning North Shore suburbs whose patina of leafy laissez-faire only marginally disguised wealth and consumption from prying eyes.

Farther south, we passed solid middle class suburbs of brick Federation houses until the train pulled out of North Sydney station on to the new tracks to the bridge. There was a palpable sense of excitement in the carriage. Many of us had obviously never seen this new metallic monument to man's modernity, the city's architectural claim to world prominence, or else, the sight was so new and dazzling that it still had the power to awe.

The railway had originally terminated at Lavender Bay for the ferry across the short open expanse of the beautiful harbour but now, as we pulled out from the station sandwiched between the sandstone rock face that had been excavated to make way for modern transport needs, I could see the illuminated majestic slate grey curve of the bridge's vast expanse against the night sky. It was, indeed, a sight to inspire not only awe, but confidence in progress, in modernity.

I stood in the carriage, as did other passengers, to the bemusement of the regulars, to marvel at the lights on the ferries and small craft going about their business like so many fireflies scattered on the water. As we closed in on the city itself, the foreshore cast a welcoming glow. My heart quickened. I had expected to share this with Joshua. Now, the seething mass of humanity could only promise a tired man the embrace of other lonely men like myself until I could forget the pain.

I had opened my heart twice, and twice it had brought tragedy. I would not make that mistake again.

CHAPTER FOUR

~

GOOD SAMARITANS

 $\mathcal{M}$y luck was in. I rapped on the front door of the double-storey Victorian brick terrace which, while there was a valiant attempt to keep it trim and neat, had seen better days. Its owner was obviously house-proud but not so much so that she wanted to draw attention to her abode or get the neighbors' noses out of joint. The hand of working class gentility was apparent everywhere from the tidily swept cement entrance to the polished tiles on the tiny verandah, however there was no gentility about the big bosomed harridan who answered the door with a scowl that would have done proud to a gargoyle atop the General Post Office in Martin Place.

The appearance of a friendly face was too much and I burst into tears, something I am not prone to doing. Mum Doreen looked along the street to see if there were any stickybeaks about before clasping me tightly, helping me into the warm embrace of her home. Both she and the house smelled of dark chocolate, the one luxury she afforded herself. I learned later she kept blocks of it in her wardrobe among her dresses and her stockings and that is what gave her the particular scent.

Before my interruption, she had been listening to the wireless, a scratched black Bakelite box that sat on her old wooden kitchen table, as sturdy and weathered as she was, a teapot with a chipped spout wrapped in an embroidered cosy in front of it. A cup of cooling milky tea was quickly removed before she got me to sit down, and then fussed about filling the kettle with water before putting it on her kerosene stove, the ritual cuppa being the one tenet of faith shared by all women of her ilk. She found her 'good' teapot in the china cabinet, as well as a new multi-colored cosy which looked for all the world like a layered hat with a bobble attached. She also got out two of her best china cups and saucers.

This pretension of elegance was rather spoiled when she spat on her one teaspoon and wiped it brusquely on the edge of her dress before depositing it in the saucer of the cup she placed nearest to me. By this stage my sobbing had run its course and I wiped my eyes on my linen handkerchief and blew my nose.

"Better now, love?" she asked, swirling the hot water to warm the pot before emptying it out the side window. She spooned the black leaves from a tin tea caddy branded with the name of a popular importer, poured over the boiling water, then added a goodly portion of brandy which she kept in a cupboard under the sink. She scooped a small jug through the billycan of milk on her window sill, placing it alongside the sugar bowl. As the tea was drawing she found a paper bag of broken biscuits and scattered them on a plate which she pushed in front of me.

"There you go. A nice cuppa tea and a biscuit'll cheer you up."

I remembered I had the remnants of my sandwich in my coat pocket and took it out, offering her the half.

She shook her head. "Ta anyway. You eat it; you look like you could do with a good meal."

So far, apart from the sobs, I had remained mute. The tea did me an immense amount of good and I began to compose myself as Mum Doreen watched me reclaim my equilibrium. She had switched the wireless from a serial which I had obviously interrupted to popular music of a particularly mawkish nature until even she could not stomach the platitudes and clichés being expressed and switched it off. I was grateful for the silence. As I struggled to formulate a story palatable enough to placate her inquiries, she said forthrightly, but with concern, "Man trouble, love?"

I nodded, fearful that if I spoke it would open the flood gates again. I'd held myself in check, with great difficulty, since I had left wretched Seaspray Bay, left the man I had loved for too short a period, the man who had abandoned me after his faithful promise of a new life together. The whole story came flooding out of me as if in repeating it the pain would drain away but, even as I related my misery, it merely reinforced my despair.

I had a little money put aside, after all there was scant enough to spend it on in the coastal hamlet I'd called home. Having to start again, find a suitable area that was not already over-serviced by general practitioners, build up a practice in one of the worst depressions the world had ever seen, seemed so overwhelming I could not see a place to start. I was tired, not surprising considering how much had taken place in less than twenty-four hours.

Tomorrow would seem, if not brighter, at least a little less daunting. The empty feeling would heal eventually, that much I knew because I had been through it before, just once, although I wondered how many times I would suffer so miserably at the hands of fate throughout my lifetime.

When I'd exhausted my tale of woe, I slumped against the kitchen table, my head in my hands, my face dirt smeared from my earlier binge of crying, my hair dishevelled, and my collar and tie askew. What did I expect Mum Doreen to say? I was not her problem.

Throughout my tale which I told in much too elaborate detail as if mapping it indelibly into my mind so I never made that mistake again, we were interrupted by a steady stream of men of all ages and positions in society through the front door. Mum Doreen moved my luggage into her parlour so that it was out of the way of the newly arrived guests. To a novice it looked as if she ran a men's boarding house.

She met the men at the door with a cheerful good word, sometimes a hug, sometimes a quick peck on the cheek, but always with a quick wit and an even quicker sleight of hand as she collected her 'rent.' I had, in fact taken advantage of Mum Doreen's rooms on a few occasions myself. The modest establishment was clean and non-judgmental, like its proprietress.

"What you need is a good night's sleep, love."

I stood and adjusted my collar. "I needed someone to listen."

"I know," she said simply. "It's what I do best."

I went to retrieve my bags wondering aloud where I could find suitable gentlemen's accommodation at that time of the night. I was sure there would be Spartan overnight rooms near the main railway terminus at Central although I was much too fagged to walk back there.

"You'll stay here tonight," Mum Doreen instructed. "You're much too buggered to go walking anywhere in your condition. I'll make up the lounge in the front room; you won't be disturbed there with the comings and goings through the night. If I'd known earlier that you was coming I could have put a room aside for you but, well, a woman has to take a penny where she can get it and what with everyone out of work and men reduced to begging on the streets I have to take it when I get it and I'm full up tonight."

I saw her glance at the unwieldy grandfather clock whose constant ticking was at once restful and an irritating reminder of life's transience. She pulled bank notes from between her breasts, stacked them neatly on the table, flattening any that had become creased or crumpled, emptied the last crumbs from the paper bag of broken biscuits, then counted the cash and placed it carefully inside. A few moments later there was a knock at the front door.

Regardless of the effusive welcome she had given each and every one of her visitors, I noticed that Mum Doreen tensed every time there was a knock. I listened as she greeted whoever was at the door. Her tone was less congenial and her guest did not seem inclined to enter. I gathered from what I overheard that he was with the local constabulary and prone to call on a weekly basis to pick up said brown paper bag to distribute among his confreres at the sandstone police station down the street a ways.

When Mum Doreen returned she shrugged. "It keeps them orf me back. And they try to give me notice when Vice is in the area." It had been the Vice Squad pounding on the door when Ted and I had been rudely interrupted during one of our overnight furloughs here during the Great War.

It was none of my business.

The brandy had relaxed me and although I knew from experience my emotions would refuse to shut down, my body certainly would. After she'd completed her transaction, Mum Doreen helped me to the front parlor whose decoration was rampant floral. It was in the curtains, it was in the carpet, and it was in the cushions that were scattered among the comfortable old furnishings. I didn't care whether my head rested against roses or magnolias as long as my head rested.

The lounge was not as comfortable as a bed but I was in no condition to complain. Grateful for shelter, I undressed to my undergarments, folding my coat, shirt and trousers neatly over the back of an old armchair, before lying down and covering myself with a patterned rug – tartan rather than florid blooms. I wondered what Josh was doing at that moment. I didn't wonder long as the combination of the warmth of Mum Doreen's hospitality as well as the warmth of her front parlor plus an ample helping of brandy-laced tea, propelled me to sleep.

Mercifully, my night was not broken by dreams, at least not any that I recalled. A small mercy, for once I awoke and looked about me it brought back the desperateness of my situation. I groaned self-indulgently at my predicament.

"Here, you'll need this." Startled to full awakening by a voice in the room with me, I sat bolt upright and immediately regretted it. I moaned before allowing my head to fall back on the pillow. I was lifted gently as I heard a familiar effervescence in a glass that was pressed to my lips. The carb soda slid down easily smothering the nausea; the throb in my temple would require something stronger.

"Mum said you might need a little something to straighten you out." The kind Samaritan allowed me to sink back into the cushion while I focused my eyes, glued with the thick crud of my dried tears. I picked it off, rubbing my eyes until I could see clearly. He was an older man but in remarkably good shape, I could tell because he was clad only in the bottom half of pajamas.

He saw me looking. No, I was doing more than looking – I was admiring. He smiled at my presumption. "Like what you see?" I looked away, embarrassed at my forwardness, and that I could so readily forget Josh. My sigh was deep and heartfelt.

Seating himself hard against my body he threaded his fingers through my hair before running them down my spiky unshaven cheek. "Poor Damien." I was about to remonstrate with him that it was none of his damn business when a loud sob shook my frame. He put his arms about me and just as I had last night with Mum Doreen, I let myself go – totally. I held nothing back and cried like I never had before.

Well, perhaps, once before.

* * * *

The bombardment had kept up for over ten hours. You get used to the noise, but you don't.

Contradictory, I know. Your ears remain alert for the shell that may take you out, but by the time you hear it all you can do is flatten yourself against the earth and hope, or pray to your God. Anything else is just noise.

There's no understanding if you aren't there. It's beyond description, particularly my feeble efforts. The poets captured it best but even Siegfried Sassoon and Wilfred Owen, great as they are, become poor wordsmiths, no more than workmanlike, when it comes to the sheer bloody horror of what our country expected of us.

As six o'clock approached, I felt sick to my stomach. My nerves were taut, my fear keeping me on edge. I had seen men snap at this stage and shoot themselves in the foot, or worse, rather than face almost certain slaughter at the hands of the machine guns terminally trained on their position. We were expected to 'act like men', as The Butcher put it, and clamber out over the top to run like rabbits toward the barbed-wire embrace of death or disfigurement across the battlefields of France and Belgium.

And for what? Because some poppycocked inbred potentate of some quagmire in Europe with a name we'd never heard of before had copped an assassin's bullet. For that we were expected to play clay pigeon to an artillery barrage. It didn't seem like an equal exchange to me. Had the Archduke Ferdy ever heard of Australia, ever once asked about me?

Too late to think about that now. Perhaps not. What better time to get angry than when you confront a pointless death? That's when you began to question the stupidity of what you had volunteered for. The hollow sloganeering that had seduced you into replacing your usual scepticism, your usual common sense. We were told it was our 'duty'. But why were those who so freely bandied about that hideous word, with all its trappings of class privilege, tucked up at home in their beds or in their cosy living rooms reading tenth-hand reports of our deprivations, dipping their heads in token acknowledgment of our sacrifice, while we shivered in rat infested hell holes. It was all bullshit. I knew that now.

"All rights, lads."

Ted panicked. I squeezed his hand. No one was likely to begrudge him that. The youngest among us, he was terrified. Rooted to the spot. He smiled weakly at me, hopeful I would keep him safe.

It was time. We outnumbered the Germans. That was a good sign, wasn't it?

The signal was given and we clambered up and over, the element of surprise a slight advantage. But not for long. Anyone with an ounce of sense knew an incessant bombardment would be followed by an attack. My chest hurt as I ducked and weaved across the battleground, our target less than 450 yards away. We were to take the Sugarloaf, as we'd nicknamed the German salient because of its particular shape, which dominated our position from its height above us.

It was still daylight when we attacked so the element of surprise was short lived. We were to strike from the north. It was madness. The only instinct was for survival as we rushed forward. As much as I could I ran ahead of the frightened Ted who, with grim determination etched across his face, seemed to really believe I could somehow keep him alive. We learned later that the enemy, with the advantage of cover, had mown down so many as we valiantly attempted the impossible. I couldn't blame the German soldiers, had the situation been reversed we would have done the same.

We over-ran the German trenches with loss of life on both sides. It had been easier than we'd expected except that now we were isolated and up to our armpits in mud and slimy water. But at least Ted had come through his baptism of fire, now by my side, and flushed with excitement. That was worrying because men tended to do extraordinarily foolish things when they thought they were invincible.

CHAPTER FIVE

~

AN APPEALING OFFER

$\mathcal{M}$en don't cry, I reminded myself but it did no good. The two great losses of my life crowded in and left me defenceless. In the end the emotional breakdown would be cathartic and enable me to continue with my life, relegating the continuing pain over Josh to a compartment in my heart that I would acknowledge, and then only reluctantly, in moments of self-indulgence. Pain has a way of making itself heard.

But pain and tears eventually subside, except in madmen, and I began to feel foolish in the arms of a man I had never met, making myself vulnerable to all kinds of mischief. It was also distressing that his close proximity had, unbidden, excited me. My rigid cock was pressing against his side and he could not have failed to notice it. I reddened, shifted uncomfortably until he released me, and begged his forgiveness for my behaviour.

Rather, I attempted to beg his forgiveness but his mouth covered mine as I spoke. I was surprised he did not immediately recoil from the bitter early morning foulness of last night's cheese sandwich and the large helping of brandy. When he did not I gave in to his embrace, allowing myself to be cared for. It was what I needed most now. Some men I know have almost driven themselves to exhaustion by always being in control, whereas I have learned through my medical practice that sometimes men need to relinquish that stubborn masculine authority. The time was ripe for me.

As he kissed me gently, he ran his hands beneath my undershirt. They were smooth as butter, not those of a man engaged in manual labor, and felt good against my skin. In return I trailed my fingers along his spine, feeling the strength in his powerful back.

He disengaged from me gently, the absence of his touch distressing for a moment until he stood and untied the drawstring of his pyjamas, allowing them to drop to the floor. His prick was already at full mast and I had but little time to admire his strong physique, well-proportioned for a man of his age which I estimated to be around fifty, before he was guiding his shaft toward my mouth. My lips opened hungrily as he pushed slowly, savouring the sensation when he reached my tongue. Lapping around the head of his cock until he moaned his appreciation, I felt him slide toward the back of my throat. I relaxed and took him all, holding firmly to his arse cheeks, squeezing them like yeasty dough, not daring yet to finger his hole.

He pulled my undershirt up to my chest and must have liked what he saw as he increased the pace of his thrusts into my mouth. The heat of our activity was putting pressure on my own weapon and I wriggled out of my underpants, finally kicking them off. My cock stood proud.

My unknown lover retrieved his prick and lifted me up, pulling my vest up over my head so that my nakedness now matched his. He stood back to admire me, licking his lips like some old-style music hall villain. I laughed, as he'd obviously intended.

I looked him in the eye. "You have the advantage of me, sir." I hoped I hadn't sounded too formal.

"Eric," he said and put his hand out. I was about to shake it when he made his real target obvious. He wrapped his fingers around my prick. I laughed again at his feint. The sides of his eyes crinkled in amusement.

There was not much else to say. We were two adult men, totally naked in each other's company, both sporting cocks that were eager to be satisfied. As the lounge was inadequate for two adult men he sat on the floor and pulled me to him. We sat facing, fondling each other's cock until we felt to continue in this activity would lead to an unsightly mess on Mum Doreen's ruddy floral carpet. Pushing me backwards, Eric soon engulfed my prick in his mouth. The niceties of our earlier coupling gave way to the more immediate activity of releasing our pent up loads.

I motioned for him to reposition his body above mine so that his cock could gain entrance to my mouth. He did so with alacrity and I guided him into my warm opening. He was a tight fit but I concentrated on my labour of love, the position not the most comfortable for sucking cock, while he concentrated on my own ache. We were both men of experience and it was not long before I felt myself ready to explode into his mouth. I guessed from the rapidity of his own strokes into my gaping mouth and the sound of his nostrils flaring that he was on the brink himself. As he seemed disinclined to take his mouth from my prick, and there was little chance of my removing mine from his, I prepared for the shudder that would accompany my release.

Eric shot first, filling my throat to overflowing with his pungent spunk so that it oozed back on to my tongue. Moments later my ejaculation flooded his gullet and he swallowed greedily. Some men are averse to this practice, although I love swallowing a man's seed, and Eric seemed to be of a similar inclination. The sexual tension in our bodies relieved, we relaxed, Eric crawling up to envelope me in his strong arms. He kissed me, the taste of sperm comingling on our tongues. I wished that I could stay like this until Josh was a faint memory. I must have fallen asleep for I awoke to find myself back on the lounge, a fully dressed Eric standing over me.

I stretched leisurely. "Breakfast?" he asked. My stomach rumbled my answer. He tossed me a dressing gown that was clean but had seen better days. "No need to dress for meals here." He closed the door after himself and I heard him whistling as he passed down the passageway. Slipping into the gown which smelled of mothballs, and rolling up the sleeves because it was obviously meant for a man much larger than myself, I ran my hands through my hair in an attempt to appear less unkempt but I need not have worried.

The kitchen was a confusion of activity. The remnants of various breakfasts lay scattered across the table: jam pots with lids ajar, a sauce bottle with its cap sadly missing in action, a container of lard, the poor man's butter, greasy and uninviting. Chipped plates and saucerless cups were stacked alongside smeared plates in the sink. A sailor was just polishing off the last of a slice of toast and dripping as he kissed Mum Doreen, resplendent in her floral nightie covered by a threadbare pink chenille dressing gown, her feet adorned with faded slippers to keep her off the cold linoleum floor. He nodded to me as he hurried down the hallway, calling his goodbyes as the front door slammed shut. Two other men, who looked as if they were heading out to work in the factories or on the docks nearby, stole glances at me as if measuring me up as a partner for some fun. They tipped their caps and I nodded back, smiling broadly at their approval.

Eric pulled out a chair and I sat; only half awake as yet. Mum Doreen sluiced out one of the less chipped cups and poured me a strong brew, minus the brandy this time. She was a kind-hearted soul but a bit heavy handed on the spirits for my liking. I sipped the tea, listening to the general chatter that went on about me. It was immensely good natured and I learned the two lads, Jack and George, shared an affection for each other that they could only consummate occasionally at Mum Doreen's premises. Once they were comfortable in my presence they were confident enough to hold hands. It was at once sweet in its innocence and bittersweet for me in that it brought back visions of Josh.

I excused myself and got up to look for the privy, which was in the backyard, a forlorn patch of grass clumps hemmed in on two sides by the walls of adjoining terraces so that the sun cast a watery warmth on to a simple garden bed where a few scrappy vegetables, carrots and cabbage mainly, were attempting to make their presence felt. At the back of the property was a paling fence which I remembered from my experiences clambering over it with Ted, one step ahead of the Vice Squad many years before. Then came a dunny lane with the grand name of Paternoster Row before more backyards and carbon copy terraces, only discernible from one another by the jerry-built extensions at their rear.

The privy, a brick outhouse, with a full wooden door according more privacy than usual for these conveniences, was comfortable and clean, with a stack of torn newspaper convenient as arse wipes. But I had no need for that at present and soon slipped out of the small room only to bump into, I wasn't sure, George or Jack? I mumbled an apology for keeping him waiting as I thought he was there to use the toilet, but he merely cupped his hand over my balls and squeezed, planted a wet kiss on my lips cheekily before scaling the back fence and was gone.

Perhaps being back in the city did have its advantages. That simple grope lightened my spirit so that I returned to the kitchen with a smile a mile wide on my lips. I saw a look pass between Mum Doreen and Eric over my change of mood. It was only later that I discovered Jack, for it was he I met in the backyard, always welcomed the new patrons in such a familiar manner. Certainly, his heart belonged to George, but his body belonged to any man who cared to take advantage of its easy availability.

A plate of warm crisp toast awaited me and there was real butter and strawberry conserve. Mum Doreen excused herself to get dressed leaving me alone with Eric. He was at the stove and the smell was tantalizing. "This will be ready in a moment," he said over his shoulder as he whisked the mixture in the frying pan. While I waited my hunger got the better of me and I buttered and ate a little toast. A few minutes later he spooned the fluffiest scrambled eggs I had seen outside a quality restaurant on to two plates and slid one in front of me.

We ate in silence, apart from my constant congratulations on his culinary skills, which he brushed off with disarming modesty. When I'd finished, I pushed the plate aside with satisfaction, buttered my second piece of thick toast and spread it liberally with jam. Lest, dear reader, you think me greedy, I had every intention of compensating Mum Doreen generously for her hospitality. If she had not taken me in, I would have been obliged to seek alternative accommodation elsewhere for the night and I am not one to take advantage of a person's kindness.

I was also effusive in my thanks to Eric, who had finished his meal before me and was boiling the kettle, I thought for more tea. He cleared the dishes from the sink; they'd already been scraped of their excess earlier, emptied the hot water into an enamel bowl adding soap flakes, and then cooled the water sufficiently from the tap until he could comfortably submerge his hands.

I was not to be allowed to shirk my duty. Rummaging through a drawer he found a tea towel and threw it to me, a pile of clean dishes, already draining, awaited my attention. I finished wiping them then stacked everything on the table for I was not familiar with the house and where they belonged. I unwound into the ritual of drying up; exchanging pleasantries with Eric as he attempted to draw me out. Under normal circumstances I would have been more reticent at discussing my personal life but he freely traded information of a personal kind so I reciprocated.

I had already decided I would spend the day seeking temporary accommodation before looking for an area to set up a new medical practice, not an easy task at the best of times let alone in the worst of times as they were now. I had been through the process before and knew the problems ahead. The reason I took the job in Seaspray Bay was because my previous surgery in Bondi Junction, which I had chosen because I thought it would be recession proof, revealed that I was no pundit. I was woefully out of touch.

Eric would be of little help as it was beyond his expertise. He worked as a manservant for old money, money that was not reliant on the vagaries of the stock market, in rather palatial quarters, at least by the way he described them, in Darling Point, a snobbish suburb tucked along the harbor foreshore with magnificent views of the new bridge.

He was in the process of telling me about his employer when there was a loud knocking at the door. I tensed but Eric assured me it was unlikely to be the Vice Squad at this early hour of the morning, besides which the transient population had long since departed. There was loud shouting and more heavy knocking. I heard Mum Doreen emerge from her room cursing and caught a glimpse of her adjusting her corset as she waddled down the hallway.

It was the scream that had us dropping the plates we were holding, pushing and shoving as we ran to the front door, believing something dire had happened to Mum Doreen. Instead, she was kneeling on the front step slapping the face of a young woman the front of whose dress was soaked with blood. A young man stood watching the scene wailing his distress.

"Kitty. Kitty! Can you hear me?" Mum Doreen was pleading.

I took control. To Eric I said. "Go and clear the kitchen table. Go on, man." I turned to Mum Doreen. "Go and put the kettle on. I need water and clean rags. Now!" I'm afraid I spoke more rudely than is my wont but time was of the utmost importance. "You," I said turning to the young man. "Carry her inside and lay her on the kitchen table. Carefully." He was dazed enough to follow my instructions without hesitation for I did not have time to argue. I went to retrieve my medical bag from the front parlour, and then hurried to the kitchen where Mum Doreen commanded, "Let the doctor through lads so he can go about his business."

The young man, whom I guessed to be the patient's boyfriend, baulked at my cutting Kitty's dress. "It's her best frock. She won't half be mad when she finds out." Mum was sympathetic, but firm. "It doesn't matter, love. It's ruined anyway. Blood like that won't come out no matter how many times you boil it."

She had poured hot water into a clean bowl by the time I'd finished cutting away the young woman's garments, exposing her groin. The young man turned pale, gulping air. Mum Doreen steered him quickly to the kitchen door. Shortly, I heard him throwing up in the backyard. Eric remained calm, attuned to my demands while Mum went to the front step to wash off the blood before it congealed into a sticky mess.

By the time I had completed my job, a cup of tea and sweet biscuits were awaiting us. The lounge suite that I had used last night was made up as a hospital bed with a heavy blanket as an undersheet – just in case. The young woman, Kitty, needed rest. She had lost blood, great clots of it, but she would be all right. She had drunk some weak tea with sugar and nibbled at a biscuit, all she could stomach at that time, while her boyfriend who looked almost as bad as she did, held her hand.

The three of us adjourned to the kitchen to leave them in privacy. Mum Doreen cleared up the rags I had bloodied taking them immediately to the large copper she had in the back yard. She got the fire going quickly and poured a few buckets of water to soak the cloths in a handful of soap flakes. "They'll be a bugger to get clean," she muttered. Then she examined Kitty's torn clothing to see if it was worth salvaging but shook her head sadly. "Nice piece of linen gorn to waste."

I collected my instruments to sterilise, sluicing them in boiling water in an enamel bowl. I was shown the bathroom to wash up and given a jug of hot water which I mixed with cold until it was the right temperature before climbing into the bath, lying back against the cool tub. It was shallow but enough for me to bathe and was lukewarm by the time Eric brought more hot water, pouring it carefully at the foot so as not to scald me. He sat on the edge of the bath and took the flannel from me to rub my back. It was a liberty, a familiarity I would have allowed few men.

"Mum and I have been talking," he said, choosing his words carefully. "You can tell me to mind my own business if this is none of my concern but the way you handled yourself this morning..."

He paused to allow me long enough to tell him if it were none of his concern. I said merely, "Any fool of a doctor could do what I did."

"What of Kitty?" he asked.

"She'll be fine in a day or two. I'll explain to her what she has to do to look after herself. Something the backyard butcher should have taken the trouble to do then we wouldn't get into situations such as this."

"But." He hesitated. "What of the police?"

"What have the police to do with it?"

"Isn't it your duty to report it?"

I laughed. "It's my duty to do a lot of things. When I don't believe them to be in the best interest of my patient, or myself for that matter, I turn a blind eye. I trained as a man of medicine, not a snitch."

Eric looked downright pleased with my response. He rinsed the soap from my back and handed me a towel. "I'd like to buy you a drink, doc. If you would allow me."

"Perhaps a small one because I have things to get done today."

He was gone before I'd even finished my sentence. I got out of the bath to dry myself, luxuriating in the clean feeling all over my body. Eric brought my clothes, withdrawing to allow me time to dress. He had also brought me shaving equipment. I thought it senseless to imitate a modesty I did not feel as he had not only seen my cock he had had it in his mouth, swallowing my spunk. By the time I was back in the kitchen, I was clean shaven and looked my usual respectable self. The young man was seated at the table and stood to shake my hand profusely as I entered the room.

"I can never thank you enough, doc, for what you done for me Kitty an' she'll thank you herself as soon as she wakes up. You saved her life. You're a regular miracle man."

I let him exhaust his gabbling because it was relief for him. "Kitty's mum and dad won't let Kitty marry a young bloke like me. No prospects. Not in times like these. We love each other, but. I want to do the right thing but with no steady job." He shrugged his resignation. "A man has needs, you know what I mean?"

"Then next time you should use a condom." I handed him two from my satchel. "But I would leave it a while before you even attempt it no matter what your needs. Kitty's needs are more important just for the moment."

He looked sufficiently chastened so I curtailed the lecture.

"I would make an honest woman of her in an instant if only her parents would let me." He was downcast. "We don't want to elope." He left the option hanging.

He shook my hand again. "If you're ever in trouble, doc, just leave a message here for Bert an' I'll come running. I owe ya." He thrust a few silver coins into my hand and disappeared before I could say I didn't require payment.

I handed the money to Mum. "Give this to Kitty; she will need it more than I do. Besides, if Bert is not working he can ill afford to lose this much money."

"Oh, he's working all right," Mum snorted, "Though not work as you and me would think of it."

I encouraged her to go on. "He's a local lad, born and raised in Pyrmont. A good lad. His mum and dad live a couple of streets away. Same with Kitty. Sweethearts from birth, we like to say. They've always been thick as thieves, the two of them. Always expected them to get hitched. But, come the crash. Bert can't get work. Oh, he tried. Tried really hard. When there was nothing, well, it's easy for a young lad strong as Bert is to fall in with easy money."

"He's a thief?" I asked.

"Worse'n that," Mum said. "He's one of the Loo mob. One of Tilly's boys."

I was familiar with the razor gangs of Woolloomooloo and Surry Hills through newspaper reports. At war with each other over territory and the control of, so it was said, prostitution and sly grog. With hotels closing at 6pm men were always on the lookout for bootleg booze and Tilly Devine and her nemesis Kate Leigh were only too willing to oblige. A few years before, new gun laws had been introduced with severe penalties for those caught with concealed weapons, so razors became the new choice of the criminal classes. Severe damage could be accomplished with cut-throat razors and some men wore their savage scars as badges of honor.

There had been a notorious battle for supremacy in Kings Cross in 1929. It had raged for an hour or more, both sides suffering major wounds. I wondered whether Kitty would still love her Bert with a deep razor slash across his face – that being the likely outcome of his flirtation with a life of gang crime. But I was hardly in a position to pass judgment on the lad.

"Come on," Eric cajoled. "Let's get started. This is my one day off and much as I love Mum I don't want to spend it all here."

"Is it all right to leave my bags and come back for them later?" I asked.

Mum and Eric exchanged looks.

"Kitty is fine. She needs rest and some light broth when she wakes up and she should be fit to return home this afternoon. If she has any more problems, I'll give her my contact details," I said.

Mum assured me she could take care of the nursing duties so Eric and I took off along Harris Street turning toward the Pyrmont Bridge and into the heart of the city. It was a fine day to walk rather than attempt to climb aboard the clattering trams that passed by. As we strode toward the tall sandstone buildings in the city proper, I marvelled that the Americans had built a tower that stood 102 storeys above the streets of New York City. I could not imagine a tower of such magnitude on the streets of my Sydney no matter how fast it was embracing the modern world.

At Pfahlert's Hotel, just down from Scots Church on the corner of Margaret and York streets, opposite the quaint and lush Wynyard Park, I realised almost immediately that the men in the bar, all middle class respectable had much in common with Eric and myself. It was not apparent unless you were a member of the fraternity, then it was bleedingly obvious. I made a mental note that it was a place to visit to be among like-minded men and perhaps find a companion for the night or, if compatible, longer.

There was no use pining for Josh. Once I got myself settled, I would write him a letter, I held hope that he would reply if only to explain his change of heart, but I had a living to earn. My meagre savings were needed to set up a new surgery and I could not afford to fritter them away on trivialities.

Eric seemed eager to talk so we shared stories about our lives until I got a real liking for the man and, in turn, I believe he got a liking for me, although, I did sense he was hedging. I thought he would reveal what concerned him in his own time. One drink turned into a second, and as we had strolled at a leisurely pace it was near the lunch hour and we decided to eat together before I spent the afternoon searching for digs.

"That's what I wanted to speak to you about," Eric said after the waiter had taken our order.

I smiled. "I thought you had something on your mind. Well, come along, spit it out man."

He was hesitant, as if afraid he would insult me. "I know you have little enough ready money."

"True," I agreed.

"And at present you have no preference for an area in which to set up."

"Equally true."

He took a deep breath. "What about Pyrmont?"

"It's a possibility," I admitted, although I wondered at scraping by tending to people at the lowest end of the social scale who barely eked out a living themselves. I suspected they would be impatient with illness, reluctant to seek medical help.

"Mum would like to make a deal and she's asked me to negotiate with you."

"I'm listening."

"She's willing to turn over the front parlor as a living space for you, and the room adjoining to set up as your surgery. You have the run of the house, except the private bedrooms of course, and Mum would be glad of the company at meal time." He'd blurted it out in one quick breath.

The offer was most unexpected, but I was not naïve enough to think the arrangement was without advantage to the old woman as well. It certainly deserved consideration. I proffered a few token negatives but Eric quickly swatted them down. Everything, it seemed, was negotiable. I told him I would give it my serious consideration and we let the subject slide.

Eric spoke warmly about his lover, John, a decade his junior, with whom he'd shared his life for the past fifteen years. John also worked in one of the city's grand mansions albeit as a cook. Because of their conflicting schedules it was common for them to go weeks at a time without their one day off a week coinciding so they sneaked pleasure in each other's company whenever they could, usually reserving a room at Mum's when they were able to share an overnight together. They both lived for the day that they might find employment in the same household. That would make their lives less unbearable.

It was a sad world that separated lovers so.

I took my leave, promising to keep in touch, agreeing that as soon as was practicable I would meet John. I was assured I would like him as much as I had already liked Eric. It seemed the lovers were not unduly jealous. I had enjoyed my short foray with Eric and would certainly take the opportunity to repeat it if the occasion arose.

The city was pulsing with activity as I walked along the busy main thoroughfare of George Street, gazing at the shop window displays although they did not really register as my mind was weighing up the pros and cons of the offer. As I turned down Market Street to Pyrmont Bridge the positives far outstripped the negatives. The major obstacle to my acceptance was that the people of this area were not likely to be a stepping stone to my desire for wealth and fame as a society doctor. In my snobbishness, that is where I saw my future.

By the time I was back at Mum's I had all but made up my mind. She met me eagerly at the door when I knocked, so over the ubiquitous hot cuppa we ironed out our differences. She made few demands, the rent was modest and the cancellation of our agreement was at my discretion. If I failed, Mum was adamant she was not one to flog a dead horse and I could move on in my own time. Our sticking point was the floral carpet in what would become my living space. The smaller room next door would serve as my surgery, while Mum's kitchen would just have to do as the waiting room until we could sort out something better. I wasn't likely to be inundated with patients in the beginning at any rate.

I could work without a receptionist. But still, there was that carpet. Mum could not understand why anyone would dislike it so vehemently, especially a man of such discernment and taste as myself. In the end our compromise was reached through the simple expedient of money. Or lack thereof. I simply could not afford to have the carpet replaced even if Mum had been agreeable. She wasn't and I didn't. What I could afford was a large rug.

Within two weeks, with a lot of help from the denizens of Mum's 'boarding' house and a few sympathetic locals who warmed to the idea of a doctor in their midst, we'd painted the surgery and I had installed a neglected second-hand desk which looked chic and professional in its new home. I had also managed to find an examination table going begging and had it hauled back to Pyrmont. The most expensive item of all was the rug, a deep burgundy Persian rug that Mum declared was 'much too busy' for her liking and 'give me flowers any day.' But even she had to admit that I had transformed her front parlour into a warm semblance of a home. She had been forced to move her second-hand sewing machine into her bedroom where the light was not as good but she was still able to make dresses and trousers and manage repairs to supplement her income, most of which came from renting out rooms to what the law described as men and women of ill repute.

The women were mainly working girls and their paying customers, or young lovers who weren't prepared to consummate their love on the grass in the park at night, lovers such as Kitty and Bert. There were a few working men who were paid for their services, mainly sailors who brought 'clients' up from the Montgomery Hotel, a notoriously rough pub frequented by wharfies, sailors and their admirers, at the western end of the bridge.

The majority of the clientele for Mum's rooms were men. Men who preferred the company of other men. She liked them. They were less trouble than the working girls, less belligerent than the sailors, and were fun to talk to. She became a de facto mother to many of the regulars, thus her nickname, Mum Doreen, which eventually became just plain Mum. She never spoke of a husband or children, but she was not a daughter of Sappho either. And I never saw her with a man in her room. Not that I was looking particularly.

The official opening of my surgery in Harris Street, Pyrmont, coincided with the unveiling of the brass plate proclaiming my status as a general practitioner and the universities at which I had gained my credentials. Mum was so proud to have it on her front door she would polish it daily. Unless, it was raining.

Business was slow at first, the locals were wary, and Kitty and Bert could hardly advertise their satisfaction of my skills without bringing down opprobrium as well as the law on their heads. Many a day I would sit at the kitchen table chatting with Mum waiting expectantly but vainly for a patient. Occasionally a local would call in to enquire as to the cost of consultation. I pitched it in the local currency, what the market would bear, although as often as not in the beginning that was the promise of payment when things got better. Or else a dozen eggs from their chook pen, or produce from their garden, and less often a rabbit which Mum would serve up in a hearty stew that night.

If I wasn't becoming wealthy overnight I was at least comparatively happy. I had written to Josh, careful to give him my address, but as the weeks passed, I gave up all hope of receiving a reply. Although the pain faded into the background it never went away entirely and I would sometimes find myself sighing for what I had lost.

That loss was made bearable by the friendship of Eric and later, John. They continued to frequent Mum's rooms when they could arrange time together and would often stop into my living area to chat before or after their coupling. Eric would sometimes call on his day off just to keep me company and we would take turns in servicing each other's needs.

CHAPTER SIX

~

PRACTICE MAKES PERFECT

Mum had a habit of knocking on my door at night for a bit of a chin wag. If I felt like it, I would answer, invite her in, leaving the door ajar so she could keep an ear out for any late customers looking for 'privacy' or the ominous knock of the Vice Squad. Their visits had tapered off once I opened my surgery, although initially they burst in to give me the third degree only backing off after they looked into my background and verified my bona fides and my war record. I neglected to tell them about my time in Seaspray Bay and their records would not have picked it up because I had anglicised my name to Button while a resident of the country town.

I had been settled here for about six months, slowly building up my practice, when there was a sharp tap at the door. Not Mum's usual knock. Someone was striking the door with a cane. Occasionally, one or two of the regulars would drop in for a bit of pleasure if they'd had no luck elsewhere. I did not mind in the least as it kept me satisfied and I didn't have to go out searching. On the few occasions I had tried, my thoughts kept turning to Josh and ruined the evening and the pleasure of any partner I may have managed to pick up.

The knock was insistent so I went to the door in my shirt sleeves. A well-dressed, and obviously wealthy gentleman, his face showing impatience, was about to knock again.

"If you're looking for Mum Doreen, she's usually in the kitchen at this time of the night," I said politely although I was nonplussed by the arrogant disdain with which he regarded me. When I had first taken up residence here I did get men knocking on my door because it had always been Mum's room, until they got used to the idea of my being there. I hadn't had one of those for months.

"I'm looking for a Dr. Bouton," he pronounced it Bowton and I corrected him gently. "I don't care how he pronounces his goddamn name, I want to see him."

I was taken aback by his belligerent attitude and wondered if he were the father or husband of any of the women I'd treated.

I remained calm. "If you care to glance at the plate on the surgery door," and I pointed to the room next to mine, "You'll find the office hours are prominently listed."

"This can't wait," he bellowed.

"I'm sure it can," I said quietly, and began to close the door in his face. A rule of mine is that I will never be spoken to in such a manner no matter the position of the person.

"Dr. Bouton," a gentle female voice interrupted me. She had taken the time to pronounce my name correctly. I had not seen her standing in the shadows farther down the hallway. She was wearing a hat with a dark veil that covered her face. "Do forgive Cecil, he has only two tones of voice: bellowing or asleep."

I laughed. Cecil rubbed his finger along his collar in embarrassment.

She continued. "You are quite right, it can wait. But waiting until tomorrow would be, shall we say, inconvenient."

There was something familiar about her voice and I tucked it away in my mind for future reference.

"Do come in to my sitting room and I'll see what I can do." I stood aside as she entered and the man known as Cecil followed behind somewhat more sheepishly now.

I pride myself on keeping my abode tidy and uncluttered. I offered the mysterious lady, for she was indeed a lady of some breeding, the arm chair, while apologising for my coatless appearance to which she tushed endearingly while Cecil coughed his disapproval.

"Which of you is it who wishes to consult me?"

Cecil harrumphed; the veiled lady spoke over him. "If you would be so kind as to give me some advice." I nodded. "It is of a personal nature. Women's business," she emphasized.

I grabbed my coat, shucking it on as I opened the door. "My surgery is next door. If you would be so kind."

She followed me out and I bade Cecil take a seat. I left him examining my room with obvious distaste.

I sat behind my desk as she sat upright in my patient's chair. I opened my notebook, took up my pen. "Now, Miss…" I waited.

"Smith," she said firmly.

"Miss Smith. Is there an initial?"

My index of patients was top heavy with Smiths. I cared little what name they used but I did need an initial in case of subsequent visits and these were precisely the clients who did return again and again. They usually appreciated my discretion at not pushing them for details they were not willing to divulge. However, the woman before me was the most secretive I had ever had consult me. She made no effort to remove her veil and in deference for her need for anonymity I did not ask her to do so.

"V. For Valerie," she said. Most of them gave their real Christian names and I knew at once she had also. She was Valerie Sweet, the Music Hall star. No wonder she was incognito. I could guess now that she was here for one of a small number of procedures.

"How can I help you, Miss Smith?"

"You may just as well call me Valerie, Dr. Bouton. You have obviously guessed who I am so I can take off this bloody veil. It's suffocating me."

She did so and she was even more beautiful in person than her posters outside the Tivoli or her photograph which appeared regularly in the society pages.

"That's better. Now I feel I can speak frankly," she said turning her smile upon me.

"Please do," I encouraged. I could see why so many men fell under her sway, and had I been at all that way inclined I, too, would have been her abject slave.

She watched me quizzically. I was obviously not reacting the way she expected. Then her face lit up. "Oh my goodness, Dr. Bouton. You're queer. Please tell me you're queer." Without awaiting my confirmation which I would have freely given, she clapped her hands and gushed. "How simply marvellous. We shall be great chums then." She visibly relaxed and her mood became much freer and chattier.

I let her go on for a while before bringing her back to the reason for her visit. She patted her stomach. "It's this. You understand?"

I nodded.

"For my career's sake I cannot afford it. I am unmarried and intend to stay that way for some time yet. I enjoy my life and there is no place in it for a child. I know I sound vain and selfish. Well, perhaps I am."

"Is it?" I nodded toward the room next door.

"Cecil's? Good heavens, no!" she shrieked. "Cecil is a dear, dear friend. Spoils me dreadfully, but nothing like that." She leaned toward me conspiratorially. "You've seen him, darling. Would you suck his dick?"

I confessed I wouldn't, not even for good money and we both shrieked with laughter. Then she became serious.

"Can you do it?" she asked.

"Of course. It's a comparatively easy process."

"*Will* you do it?"

I had patched up a few of the local girls after backyard butchers had taken to them with a wire coat hanger. I understood although not necessarily condoning the act. The Depression raged and an extra mouth to feed was a backbreaking imposition. And, too, many of the girls were unmarried.

Never having been asked to perform the illegal operation I had not previously examined my conscience as to its morality. I had long since booted God from my vocabulary and killing was less terrible now that I had been through the war.

"Have you—"

"For various reasons which I won't bore you with, it is unwise for me to go to Macquarie Street. And the idea of a backyard," she shuddered theatrically. "That is simply too gruesome to contemplate."

"The father?"

"Some stagehand or Stage Door Johnny. Or someone from the cast. I have no idea. I have a large appetite for life, Dr. Bouton. I do hope you are not one of those old fashioned types who believe only bulls should have all the fun."

I confessed I was not but then she began pushing me to be the solution to her problem. I said I would think it over and let her know tomorrow by post at the theatre. I guaranteed I would treat her request with the utmost confidence. She showered me with the prospect of an extraordinary fee although I told her it was not necessary. Her requirements also included the procedure be performed on a certain date because she would be between revues at the Tivoli leaving sufficient recuperative time. I reiterated my answer would be with her the following day.

"I confess I don't like to be kept in suspense, Dr. Bouton. But I like you and I do hope you will see your way clear to help." She placed the hat and veil back on her head and we went to get Cecil, who was keen to leave. I think the area and the house insulted his sense of propriety.

At the door, Valerie hesitated before lifting the veil and kissing me sweetly on the cheek. "I do hope we shall be friends, Dr. Bouton," she whispered before Cecil helped her into a hansom cab he had asked to wait.

I performed the surgery three weeks later, at her home in Vaucluse, where she remained to recuperate while feeding the press the misinformation that she was going to Brisbane for a short holiday before beginning rehearsals on her next show. She hoped the press would respect her privacy and if they were 'good boys' she promised them lots of photo opportunities upon her return. They seemed to buy it.

I attended her daily and it was a pleasure to wait on her. Cecil got used to me, becoming almost friendly when he learned I was a "goddamn queer" and therefore no threat to him. Valerie later began sending me tickets to her shows at the Tivoli to which I invited Mum Doreen who wore her Sunday best and was thrilled to be introduced to the star herself at the opening night party of *We're in the Money*, at a mansion in Potts Point, although she pleaded age and left early.

Valerie took my arm to introduce me to swells and hangers-on. She made a point of recommending my services, medical not sexual, to both men and women and with the rise of an eyebrow or the quirk of her mouth managed to impart my discretion as well as my willingness to take on cases that others might find, well, uncomfortable. Cecil, who seemed ill at ease in the party atmosphere, stood apart from the young crowd but I made sure I went to speak to him for which he seemed grateful, again thanking me effusively for looking after 'his' Valerie.

After a couple of hours of theatre talk, which I found vacuous, and with which I could never hope to compete, I decided to call it a night. I went in search of Valerie to wish her good night. When I finally found her, she was wide eyed and flagrant, the tell-tale residue of white powder visible about her nose. She rubbed it away when she saw my expression. The drug had been criminalized a few years earlier, its distribution now in the hands of the razor gangs.

She would not hear of my leaving so early although I declined her invitation to 'party hard' with her friends. She did not seem slighted by my refusal. "Come on, there's someone I want you to meet. I think you'll like him." I followed her along hallways of gilded opulence that could so easily have been ostentatious but which were, in fact, the result of a keen eye.

Finally we turned down a wide corridor at the end of which were two large wood panelled doors muffling a hubbub of voices. There was also the distinct odour of expensive cigar smoke which became more pronounced the closer we came. Valerie rapped and then pulled the doors apart. The conversation ceased and all eyes turned toward us. The air was thick with smoke and a number of gentlemen in dinner suits lounged on divans and in padded chairs, smoking and quaffing from large brandy balloons.

The reason I couldn't tell you the exact number of men present in the room was that my attention was immediately taken by a young man, I estimated his age at about 26 or 27, with slicked hair the color of deep-seamed coal, eyes of the most piercing olive green, and skin like caramel. He eyed me suspiciously then nodded to Valerie, his face breaking out into a smile that revealed his strong white teeth. If I sound like I'm taking inventory, well, I was smitten badly and I intended soaking up every morsel of this magnificent animal for my dreams. I use the word animal deliberately, because when he rose from his seat to greet us he moved with the grace of an African cat. He swept her into his arms and kissed her passionately, as much for show, I thought, as for affection. Then he turned his attention to me.

He meant to dazzle, and he did. Here was a man of such elegance, such style, he could seduce with a smile, enslave you with a handshake. Until, that is, I was introduced and the blood froze in my veins. This was Enzo Fabrini, the man considered the biggest criminal mastermind in the city, the man who supposedly had the police, as well as a number of prominent politicians, in his pocket. It was rumoured that he controlled most of the rackets, from prostitution, and sly grog through to cocaine trafficking. He was a man to be feared.

When Valerie mentioned his name, my hand was already in his strong masculine grip so he must have felt me flinch. His temper was legendary as was almost certain injury if you stood in his way. I hoped he was not easily offended. He did not release my hand. In fact he placed his second over it and I was held in a vise-like grip. He wanted me to know who was boss, as if I had been in any doubt of it.

"That's all for tonight, gentlemen," he said. "Please feel free to join the party and enjoy yourselves." The room emptied to a chorus of 'ciao' and much backslapping until only the three of us remained. Enzo had his arm wrapped casually around Valerie and gave her a smooch which revealed more about possession than passion. She in her turn was using all her acting skills to disguise her true feelings for this man: fear. After swapping a few whispered pleasantries he slapped her playfully on the arse and dismissed her. He turned away and I was about to follow Valerie when he said without turning around, "Close the door on your way out, Val. No, you stay Dr. Bouton. We have business to discuss." It was a command, not an invitation.

Only when the door closed behind the retreating Valerie did Enzo turn to address me. There was nothing intrinsically hostile in his manner; it was more like he was dissecting me to see what made me tick. He held out a brandy and had one of his own. "Sit. Sit and we will talk." He went back to his chair which dominated the room like a throne, removing his coat and draping it over the back. I sat on a divan facing him.

"Valerie tells me you're a doctor?"

I nodded.

"A good doctor."

"I like to think so." I was playing modest because I had no idea where this conversation was headed. I waited for him to go on.

"My organisation needs a good doctor, if you get my drift."

I didn't.

"Let me get to the point. I need a doctor who is good at his job but knows how to keep his mouth shut. Valerie assures me you're that doctor."

I didn't want him to get the wrong idea. "I don't mind, uh, bending the rules when I believe they're stupid. However..." I let it hang.

"Okay, doc. I get it. There are some things even too far for you. Fine. I can respect that."

If this was a job interview it was one of the strangest I'd even come across.

He stood abruptly. "Valerie tells me you're queer?"

Before I could answer he had unbuckled his belt, his trousers and his underpants soon down around his ankles, his shirt pulled up and his cock at half-mast. Sure the guy was handsome, and from the brief moments of observing his cock, well endowed, but I do expect a semblance of seduction before I succumb.

"What do you think?" he asked.

I stuttered. I had no idea how I was supposed to react.

"It would help if you came over and examined it more closely."

That was it. I didn't need any more foreplay than that simple request. I was across the floor, kneeling close to his prick in a matter of seconds.

"You know who I am, I felt you tense when Val mentioned my name. No need for that, doc. Only people who do the wrong thing by me need fear me. And I think we're gonna get along just fine."

I looked up. The view was magnificent. His stomach was flat and muscular. I could spend years rubbing my hands all over that from my position of subservience. I suspect he liked to see people kneeling before him.

"If you know who I am you know I got girls. Lotsa girls. I pride myself on how clean those girls are but, eh, you know how things are, human nature being what it is, there's a little slip-up here a little infection there. And I'm a man with big appetites. I'm Italian. What more do I need to say, eh?"

I was staring at his thick Italian sausage, the foreskin hooding most of the head, the slit peeking through. "Hey, queer boy, I'm speaking to you. You hear what I'm saying?"

"You want me to make sure one of your girls hasn't given you an infection?"

"Right. What the fuck, we're men here. Just tell me if I got the clap. I got a wife. She's a good woman, you know what I mean? Church on Sunday, prayers every night, grace before meals. But she don't know shit about how to treat a man. I don't want to give her no disease but."

While he was speaking I was trying to work out a method of examining him without actually touching that magnificent cock. He must have read my mind.

"You can touch it. I know how it's done. Just don't go getting any ideas, eh, queer boy."

The man was an arrogant ass and I wanted nothing better than to squeeze his balls until they burst. I'm lying. Yes, he was an ass, but what I really wanted to do was wrap my lips around that beautiful uncircumcised prick and have him fuck me like he did his girls. Instead I put out my hand and peeled back the skin and squeezed the back of his glistening knob. A small blob of pre-cum emerged.

I looked up still holding his cock; he towered over me, and asked, "Does it feel like you're pissing razor blades? Is there puss in your urine?"

"No."

"Have you had the clap before?"

"A coupla times."

"Does it feel like those times now?"

"No, doc."

I told him I could do a more thorough examination when I had my medical satchel with me and if he wanted me to attend him the following day then we could arrange that. He agreed, and I was about to stand up, when he said brusquely. "You're not gonna leave it dripping like that, are you? That's unhygienic."

I looked around for something with which to wipe away the drool of pre-cum and short of using his shirt tail, or my own, there was only one solution. The most he could do was kill me. I leaned over, licked the pre-cum from his knob then engulfed his prick in my warm mouth. He was taken totally by surprise and with his legs caught in his lowered trousers, he staggered backwards to get away from me, bumping against the armchair behind him. He fell backwards, sitting down hard, while my mouth stayed suctioned to the prize. I had seconds. My tongue went into action, slathering around his shaft as I took it all the way down my throat, appealing to whoever the gods of cocksucking are that I would not choke and have to relinquish this beautiful weapon. They must have heard and were on my side because I took his cock right down to the base, bobbed back up to the top, and rammed my mouth back down again.

Enzo's hands gripped both sides of my head to make me stop. I plunged a third time and stayed there. He gasped and I felt his hold relax. I almost had him hooked. I slowed the action minutely to give me time to swirl my tongue beneath his foreskin, to chew it gently, then to slide down his pole dragging my tongue and my lips the length, in an effort to suction the juice from his balls.

"Ah, shit, queer boy. You're better than any girl. They don't like it. But you do, don't you queer boy?"

I wasn't about to take my mouth off his cock to answer him so I nodded as best I could.

"You know I'm not queer, don't you queer boy?

I thought that question required an answer so I took my mouth off his prick long enough to mutter "uh huh."

"I just like to be sucked good. That's all it is."

Now that he was assured on his non-queerness he leaned back into the armchair to concentrate on my oral manoeuverings. After a little hesitation he put his hand on the back of my head to guide me, pushing me down to his balls, my nose buried in his jet black pubic hair, holding me there until I thought I might pass out from lack of air.

Mostly, however, he allowed me to set the pace, and I fluctuated between fast, bringing him to the edge of ejaculation, then slow, backing off to give me longer to enjoy this unexpected pleasure. He had long since given up resistance and was openly moaning his appreciation. That's when I heard the panelled doors slide open and a voice say, "Hey, boss. Oh, shit!" I froze. Enzo put his hand on the back of my head keeping me in position but made no attempt to hide what was going on.

"Close the fucking door on your way out and don't let anyone in until I tell you. Okay?"

There was mumbled assent and the doors closed once again.

Enzo sank his cock down my throat. "Suck it, queer boy. Suck it good."

I let him fuck my mouth because he was used to being in control but once he realised he was better leaving the job to me, he let me get on with the work. I lifted my mouth off and ran my tongue down his shaft until I reached his balls. I sucked them gently, lathering the hairy sack with my spit. I made my way back up to the slimy head to lick off the drooling string of cum, and swallowed. He was smiling so I took a chance. I lifted his shirt to his neck and took one of his nipples in my mouth and sucked it for a while before I nipped it with my teeth.

"Holy shit!" he muttered.

I squeezed his other nipple between my fingers, returning my mouth to his cock. His breath became laboured as I began slurping down his cock. I knew it was time to bring him off. Reluctantly I relinquished his nipple and his carved brown chest and put my hand around his balls. I wanked him with my other hand until he bucked, and then I slammed my face down, bobbing like a mad man until I felt that tell-tale clutch in his balls. He pushed his cock as far into my throat as he could and arched his back.

I felt the blasts of his spunk and didn't stop swallowing until he slumped in the chair. I licked him clean, noticing that I had shot my own load in my trousers. I had been so occupied giving him pleasure I hadn't noticed my own. I pushed his deflating cock back into his underwear and cautiously did up the buttons on his fly. I was sorry to see him pull down his shirt to cover his muscular chest and stomach. He stood to tuck it into his trousers before going to the door to issue instructions to the guard. Then he turned back to me.

"Say five o'clock tomorrow, if that is convenient for you to inspect the girls."

That hour was agreeable to me.

He let his guard down just a little. He shook my hand and held it in his. "And if the girls don't like it but you do, who knows?"

He opened the door for me. As I was about to pass he thrust his arm out in front of me preventing my exit. "Don't get the idea I'm queer."

"I don't."

He let me pass. "Hey," he shouted after me as I walked down the corridor, back to the party. "Queer boy. Another thing my girls don't like. They don't like it when I drill them in the arse. Maybe you do."

He couldn't see me smile

* * * *

So the months settled into a routine. Every week I would go to Enzo's mansion to inspect his girls and, unless he was busy, I would inspect his cock in great detail as well. He even got comfortable enough that he would invite me to stay and share a drink with him, but never dinner at his family table. I noticed a remarkable lack of gang members on the occasions I visited. He could not afford this little secret to become widely known. Every now and then it led to self-indulgent soul searching on his part and he would become brutal and rough. On those occasions I went home bruised and battered although he was never violent.

True to his word, he fucked me in the arse on my third visit. It was more by way of an experiment and I knew he enjoyed it, though impossible that he enjoyed it as much as I did, but it seemed as if it was a step too far for his teetering masculine self-worth. It was never repeated.

My practice flourished thanks, in part, to Enzo and Valerie. I attended to the locals, many of them floor hands at the CSR factory, set up at the end of Pyrmont peninsula, who worked in appalling conditions, terrific heat one moment and bitterly cold drafts at the next, hot water and cold water sloshing around them all day so their feet were never dry and their toes became pulpy and nasty: toe rot. There were more mundane illnesses such as measles and coughs and colds, the occasional birth, sadly the more than occasional death, and the steady stream of terminations. The only difference with my more respectable patients was they did not suffer from foot rot, but rather diseases more common to the affluent.

I suppose things would have continued in the same manner until I'd built up a bank account enough to allow me to leave my Pyrmont home for something more salubrious. My emotional life was on hold. My love for Joshua had not faded but I had managed to keep it in check so that I was not incapacitated in my day-to-day existence. I had sufficient contact with sympathetic partners that I did not want for sexual relief but it did little to relieve the emotional gap in my heart.

I was content if not happy although at the time I could not really tell the difference. Things would have continued this way except that Fate has a habit of intervening to bring you down a peg or two. It was my weekly turn at Enzo's mansion. He was tense, pacing the floor when I arrived. It had taken me a while to understand why he wanted me to examine the girls at his home but now I understood. It ensured they turned up and it was safer than at the brothels he ran, which were subjected to periodic raids. It was much more difficult for the Vice Squad to get a warrant to raid his home.

He had left me to get on with my task. The girls had become friendly once they knew I was queer and not likely to expect certain favors, like their last physician. I would have much preferred to be examining the veins on Enzo's luscious dick but I didn't get paid for that. At least not in cash.

I was examining Hazel, one of the newer girls, who was still not comfortable with the weekly parade, when the door burst open. Hazel screamed and attempted to cover her privates. I turned to remonstrate with the intruder. It was Enzo. He grabbed Hazel and her clothes and pushed her out the door. She ran for it.

My complaint died in my throat as I saw men, bloodied beyond recognition, being walked or carried along the corridor. I turned to Enzo.

"Razor fight?" He nodded. "Right, I need as much hot water as you can muster." Enzo screamed to one of his men who scampered off to the kitchen. I moved armchairs and the divan to allow space to lay the men down. "What about the carpet?" I asked, as there would be blood.

"Fuck the carpet! These are my men."

There were five in all, and I had them positioned so I could examine them quickly. The cook arrived shortly with water and I asked that she clean the men as gently as possible with clean rags, careful not to open the wounds.

A quick examination showed that four would be all right with my immediate help. The fifth, his face covered in blood, looked hopeless. I wiped the blood from his eyes to force them open with my thumb to search for signs of life. They fluttered open. A cry caught in my throat. They were as blue as… I would know those eyes anywhere.

It was Josh.

CHAPTER SEVEN

~

AT DEATH'S DOOR

He was dying. I'd forced his eyes open after wiping the blood from his face with a warm, damp flannel. I'd been about to give up on this man because he'd been injured so severely until I'd gazed into the bluest blue that even the sky could not match.

"Josh."

His eyes fluttered, life draining out of him. I cried out in despair.

I saw him attempt to focus. I thought he knew me.

I was more frantic now. "Josh. Hang on. Don't give up. Fight it. Bloody fight for your life."

Enzo kneeled down beside me. "Is he..?"

"As good as," I whispered.

"You know him?"

"Knew him," I said.

Enzo stood and ordered the other four men helped from the room and made comfortable elsewhere in the large mansion. "Will they be all right?"

I nodded. "Bed rest. As little movement as possible. Their wounds need time to heal. They'll have some nasty scars but they'll wear them with pride, I expect." I didn't bother looking up at Enzo; I was concentrating on the man who'd broken my heart.

I could have let him die for what he'd done to me but I'm not a vengeful man. Apart from my Hippocratic oath necessitating I do everything in my power to save lives, even though the triage nurse at Sydney Hospital would have long since given up on this poor bruised body on the carpet, I needed to hear Josh's story and why he had deserted me.

A superhuman effort was required but Enzo, who seemed inordinately fond of his henchman, had a bed set up in the living room and offered me access to any medical and pharmaceutical help that it was within his powers to provide, and his powers were incredibly far ranging.

I patched Josh up with what was to hand and sent a list of necessities to Enzo who, in turn, sent his men to beg, borrow or steal everything on the list. If I had never appreciated the particular skills of pickpockets and thieves before, I certainly did now, faced with their ability to supply material comfort to Josh.

He was obviously well-liked among his underworld confreres and they would tiptoe into the sick room and doff their caps asking after their mate. I had done all I could in a makeshift manner while I awaited the more modern and more difficult to procure medical equipment, especially for a general practitioner. Once he was sleeping soundly, albeit uncomfortably, I called upon one of those mates to watch over him, with explicit instructions he was to raise the alarm if Josh's condition changed in any way, while I went in search of Enzo.

I found him chatting amiably to one of his injured foot soldiers. I took the opportunity to examine the injured man and assured him that relief from his pain would be forthcoming. A quick nod from Enzo confirmed that. After a few more pleasantries, a perfunctory but genuine clap on the shoulder, Enzo drew me aside and ushered me to his office.

Exhausted, I sank into a chair opposite him and he handed me a brandy. I was in no state to refuse, quaffing the liquid so quickly it burned my throat and made me light-headed.

"When was the last time you ate?" Enzo asked.

Having no concept of time passing since the array of bloodied bodies had arrived I muttered some barely coherent hour to Enzo's consternation.

"Good lord, man. No wonder you look ill." He stood up abruptly and pressed on a gold bell in the corner. A few minutes later the cook came scurrying into the room. She gave a curt nod to Enzo and turned to me, "How is he, doctor? Will he be all right?"

My doctor's opinion was that, no, he would be dead by morning, until I looked at the window in Enzo's office and noticed for the first time sunshine streaming outside. "What time is it?" I mumbled blearily.

"It's ten o'clock in the morning," Enzo replied. "Have you stayed with Joshua all night?"

"I must have," I mumbled, incredibly weary.

"And, is he…"

"I left him alive. Barely."

I heard the relief from both people in the room. Enzo, I now realised, believed I had sought him out to give him bad news.

"You need rest if you are to save him," Enzo said.

"And something for that stomach of yours, I wouldn't wonder," the cook added and with a look from Enzo hurried away to prepare something for me.

"You'll need help," he said once we were alone. "You can't do it all on your own."

I desperately wanted to, but I knew I couldn't, and without rest I was likely to make a mistake that could prove fatal. "If a carriage could be sent to my premises with a request to…" I stumbled over her name and realised I knew her only as "Mum Doreen. She's a woman with a stomach of cast iron and adept at learning quickly. I could do with her help as a nurse. If I could beg your indulgence to transport her to and fro when I need her. She runs a business and will need to return home each evening."

"The cat house in Pyrmont?" Enzo said matter-of-factly. I was acutely aware of tone when people spoke of Mum but I could not detect even the remotest censoriousness in his voice. It would have been unthinkable that Enzo would not have checked on my background and discovered where my practice was located.

Josh's mate, whom I'd left at his bedside rushed through the door and Enzo was about to berate him when I was up out of my chair and out the door before he could even open his mouth. The young man ran to keep pace with me, panting. "He woke up, doc. He seemed to be okay. He looked at me and groaned and said something like 'I thought you were…' then he went right back to sleep."

Once back in the makeshift hospital room I noticed Josh was sleeping less peacefully, tossing with pain. In my eagerness to talk to him, I had thought less of his comfort and more of myself. I prepared the syringe and sent the morphine coursing through his tired body to bring him blessed pain-free relief. My questions could wait for later.

The cook sent up a tray of cold meats and boiled eggs, with bread and cheese and a pot of tea. She was a good old stick and knew a hot meal might sit uneaten whereas this one could serve at any time during the day. I nibbled a little just to settle my stomach. About an hour later, as I wiped Josh's brow of perspiration, proof that his body was fighting the infection, Mum Doreen burst into the room like a tank battering down a farmhouse door. In her wake came Eric.

Mum was removing her coat and hat and threw them over a chair with scant regard for whether they got crumpled or not. I noticed Eric pick them up and fold them neatly, a true professional.

"What do you need?" Mum said rolling up her sleeves. She looked down at Josh and then saw my bleary eyes. "Is this him, love?" She knew it had to be something important for me to bring her here like this. "Looks like they carved him up like a chook dinner at Christmas." She was brutal in her assessment, no sentimentality clouded her vision. She placed her hand on his brow and shrugged. "Too early to tell if he'll pull through, eh?" She set about taking over. "Right, you look like shit and you're no use to anyone," she said to me. "Introduce me to the boss and I'll sit a while. By the time I gotta get back to my boys, you'll be rested."

I wasn't about to argue and, after giving her directions to Enzo's inner sanctum, I lay down on the lounge for a quick kip. Eric sat beside Josh and held his hand. "So, this is the lad who caused you all that pain? I can see why. A real beauty. He'll break many a heart as he goes through life." I fell asleep while he was still babbling.

When I awoke I looked at the clock believing I had napped for a matter of moments, startled that it had been six hours since I had put my head down. I sat up groggily, someone had placed a blanket over me while I slept. My mouth tasted of cotton wool and I needed to empty my bladder urgently. Eric had obviously long since departed for his employment but Mum Doreen was seated beside Joshua's bed, her knitting needles clacking, as she chattered inanities at the sick man. For a moment I thought Joshua was conscious.

Mum interrupted her one-sided conversation. "Have a good sleep, love?" Before I could answer she continued. "I took the liberty of bringing you a change of clothes. Casual like, I didn't think you'd be needing your good suit at the moment. I'll take it back with me and press it and bring it back tomorrow. His temperature has come down a little but it's still too high but he's resting easy so you hurry off and have your bath. I'll still be here then Mum's gotta get back. There's a Depression on and a woman's gotta eat."

I stumbled over to take a closer look at the sleeping figure and, indeed, he did look more rested, so I knew he was in good hands. Mum was already regaling him with another of her funny anecdotes regardless or not of whether he could actually hear her.

Enzo was at his desk going over papers when I knocked. He beckoned me in. "Is the old battleship still here?" He smiled as he said it. "If I had a few more like her on the books I could control most of this city. She's not scared of anything. Ordered the staff around like she owned the place." His tone was one of admiration rather than irritability.

"She's a formidable woman is Mum Doreen," I agreed.

Enzo got serious. "Any news?"

"His condition hasn't worsened," I said.

"I've been thinking," he said. "If Joshua would be better off in a hospital, I'm prepared to face the consequences."

He must have seen the distress on my face, for he added quickly. "No, it's not what you're thinking. I trust you implicitly, but I want what is best for him."

"So do I," I said with a choke to my voice. "I did think about it and whether my motives in keeping him here were self-interested. And, yes, they are. But I can give him my undivided attention and, with the, um, goods your men have managed to supply me with, I believe his chances are better here than in a hospital ward where his obvious criminal status would have the police intervening in his medical treatment and his survival would be very low priority indeed."

"I was just checking," he said. "I assume you would like a bath?"

"That would be good, if it's not too much trouble."

"Use Victoria's. I've sent her away with my daughter. I don't want them involved."

He called one of the maids who took me along to a plush bathroom, all ostentatious gold taps and gilded mirrors. She drew the bath for me and once she had left, I stripped off my crumpled clothes and sank into the hot water and immediately felt the tension leaching from my body. The maid had swirled an ample handful of salts in the steaming water and it was that which lulled me into a stupor from which I could scarcely rouse myself. When the water turned lukewarm I knew it was time to relieve Mum at Josh's bedside.

I felt clean and reinvigorated as I changed into the casual clothes she had brought with her. I was glad to be free of the collar and tie, the suit coat, and I went back to the sick room with a new determination. "You look almost human again," Mum greeted me as she folded away her knitting.

I did not know how to express my thanks. I burbled like an embarrassed child and she patted me on the back. "No thanks necessary. After all you've done for me; this is little enough repayment from my side. If you send the carriage tomorrow I'll be back again." She paused. "If you want."

"Of course I want," I said quickly.

I escorted her to the waiting car and she sat in the back waving like an East End Duchess as she disappeared down the driveway. As I went back inside I hoped I would one day learn to enjoy life like she did.

It was days of constant care, ensuring infection did not take hold and carry him off, and keeping up his salts to avoid dehydration. His temperature was coming down slowly, and within three days there was a marked improvement. I was seated beside the bed bathing his body, careful to avoid his wounds as best I could so as not to cause pain. Using a flannel cloth, I bathed his armpits before rubbing down over his beautiful tanned bicep to his tough working man's fingers.

"Damien?" he groaned.

I sat stock still. I dared not even breathe.

He said it again. I looked up at him. I'm afraid I had tears in my eyes. He tried to raise his hand but was too weak. "Am I dead?"

I laughed. Laughed out of all proportion to what he said. It was contagious and he began to smile before a low guttural sound emanated from his chest, but it soon gave way to a sharp intake of breath, signifying pain. He grimaced and my relief was short-lived.

"I'm bloody starving," he said.

I stood up to ring the bell for the cook. "I'll get you something. Don't try to move just yet." He took no notice of me and attempted to sit up but cried out in pain. I rushed back to prop pillows behind his back. He grunted, squeezing my hand fit to crush my fingers. But I would not complain about a small inconvenience like that. Josh was back. Not completely whole as yet but on his way to recovery.

"It is you, Damien?"

"Have I changed so much?"

"You match the picture I carry in my head exactly, as if it was yesterday."

I ran my fingers through the hair that fell over his forehead. "And you are even more handsome."

His cheeks flushed and, to cover his embarrassment – and delight – he held my fingers to his mouth and kissed them. We were interrupted by the cook who had anticipated my request and brought up a small repast for myself and a bowl of rich watery broth for Josh. She beamed when she saw him propped up in bed and watched as I fed him slowly, every swallow an agony even though the meal was necessarily lukewarm to my instructions.

"This is dish water," he said, then looked sheepishly at the cook in case he had offended her. "What I need is a good steak, with potatoes and carrots and…"

I spooned another mouthful of broth to keep him quiet.

"All in good time," I said. "For now, it's the cook's delicious dish water that will have to suffice."

He thrived on it, complaining bitterly every time it was spooned into his mouth. He was up to liquids but it would be only a matter of time before he moved on to solids. I was in danger of infantilising him and needed to step back. Reluctantly, I turned over his care to a trained nurse and went back to my home and my surgery in Pyrmont, which I had sadly neglected over the previous week. My heart wasn't in it and even though Mum and Eric attempted to jolly me along, I lived only for the hour or two I spent at Josh's side when I went to check up on him.

Our initial talks were awkward as we both blamed the other for our separation. When Josh was tired and in pain I would lull him to sleep with tales of my life over the past year, careful to censor some of the more salacious moments. He, in turn, had no such qualms when he related what had happened to him in the intervening months.

He was obviously still raw from what he saw as my betrayal and punished me with rather lurid accounts of his pleasures as well as his pains. And he had experienced both, revealing a prodigious appetite for life that I never would have believed possible of the shy and inexperienced young man I'd left in Seaspray Bay.

CHAPTER EIGHT

~

GETTING SHAFTED

*A*nd so, dear reader, this is Josh's story as best I can remember. It's unpolished, like its storyteller. He told it while he lay in pain, heartsick with worry. It was fragmented and repetitious but I have removed the repetitions from the narrative. Please forgive its crudity, its forthrightness but that is how Josh relayed it to me, sometimes, I think, to give me greater distress. It's a tale of today and its morals are timely.

* * * *

I was so excited when I left you because we were going off to the city and make a life together. I never even dreamed that sorta thing was possible. It was all so new to me. Sure, I was sad to leave mum, especially when she got all teary, but she knew I would leave the nest some time.

She looked me in the eye when she asked what my feelings were for you. "Mu-um," I said, trying to look away. It's not something a grown man wants to talk to his mum about, is it? But she wouldn't give up. "I never felt like this about a girl, if that's what you're asking," I said. She could tell I was speaking true.

"What about Danny?"

"What about him?" I said 'cause I was playing for time.

"Does he like girls? Or is he like you?"

"He likes girls. He likes Eileen."

"You and Danny ever done anything like you were doing to Dr. Button?"

"No." It was only partly fibbing. Mum knows I can't lie to her.

"Anything at all, like that?"

"Like what?" I thought she would be too embarrassed to say what she meant.

"When you was growing up you two was inseparable. I often wondered what you got up to. Sometimes you looked like you was up to no good."

"Just kid stuff, mum," I told her truthfully.

"Not grown man stuff like with the doctor?"

I looked her in the eye and told her I hadn't. But I think she was still worried. I was about to go and get a mate to do us a favour and drop us off at the highway but dad stormed in. He was ropable, said he heard rumours at the mine about some 'unnatural acts' as he called it being perpetrated on his son. I knew it would get round quick enough because Danny was spreading it like a grass fire and the copper wasn't too discrete neither.

Dad just stood there bellowing; like that would have any effect on the situation. Mum kept trying to calm him down and that just made him madder.

She told him Danny's story was all a pack of lies, that she'd been with him and nothing had been going on. He calmed down a bit after that.

"Anyway, Josh, they want to see you up at the mine office. That's one of the reasons they sent me down here."

"I'll go and see them tomorrow. I'm not in the mood right now," I told him. I was eager to get back to you.

"You'll go and see them now, young man. Don't give me any of your lip or I'll take my strap to you. You're not too old, you know."

Mum looked worried because she knew you were waiting for me.

"Leave the lad alone. He's been through hell today." Mum was always sticking up for me and dad didn't like it.

"You bloody well get yourself up there now son. You want a job? Well, if you don't snap to it when the owners tell you to you could be out on your ear. And then where will we be? What with Eileen's wedding coming up, we need every spare penny we can get. There's a Depression on, you know." That was his favourite saying. *There's a Depression on, you know.*

Before mum could get involved, I said, "Okay, I'll go now." It would give me the opportunity to organise our lift. I was way behind schedule in getting back to you but I knew you'd still be there.

I raced up to the mine office but they kept me waiting. People came out to stare at me so I knew the rumours had travelled right through the village. It made it easier to leave. One of the girls was kind and made me a cup of tea while I waited, all the others giggled behind their hands.

It seemed like ages before I was called into this big wood panelled office. I'd been there once before when the boss had sat me down for a talk about my future after the accident and told me they'd look after me and that there was no point going to the union about the accident because that would only affect my dad's position at the mine.

The boss asked me how I was and I just said "Fine, thanks," and left it at that. He couldn't look me in the eye. There was a long silence then he just blurted it out. "We've heard rumours here at the top of the hill…" He sorta paused to give me a chance to jump in and deny them but I just sat quiet like. "Whether they're true or not, we, uh the company, can't afford to have those sorts of stories circulating. It's bad for business. And anything that's bad for the mine is bad for the village. You understand that?"

I said that I did.

"We'd like you to take some time to think about where your future lies. Obviously, there's no job for you at the mine any more. Not since your, ah, accident. It would be foolish to think you could ever be sent back to work." I knew he was lying because men with worse injuries than me were back down the shaft. "And there's no work here on the hill in the office."

He went into this long speech about the mining community being like a big family and how we all had to look out for each other. He went on and on and it was all bullshit to make himself feel better, not me. In the end he handed me a cheque for pays outstanding and a little bit extra to tide me over. He even had to look at my name inked in on the cheque because he couldn't remember it. What a bastard!

Then he handed it to me. I held out my hand to shake his but he turned his back on me and mumbled, "Good luck in the future. Close the door on your way out."

I was so angry I almost threw the cheque in his face but I remembered mum could use it. I tried not to cry on the way back and made a quick detour to the hauler to tee up with him to pick us up in about twenty minutes. I guess I didn't realise how long I'd been gone. I rushed back to the house, but my eyes were all bloodshot and my dad looked like thunder when I went in the back door.

It wasn't hard to see why. Danny was standing there, smug as a cat that's swallowed the cream from the top of the milk. He was two sheets to the wind and had my suitcase with him.

"He's gone," Danny grinned. "Left you behind."

I saw dad look at the case.

He kept his temper. "What did the office want, Joshua?" I knew it was bad. He only ever used my full name when he was angry.

"What do you think dad? They pissed me off. Gave me the sorry speech and showed me the door. Told me to think about my future. Preferably as far away from here as possible."

"You mollycoddle the boy," he shouted at mum. "No wonder he's turned out the way he has."

Mum flew at him. "Exactly how has he turned out, eh? He's a fine young man. Any dad would be proud to call him son. But you wouldn't let him get a real job. No, you had to have a son who followed you down the mine, like your dad did before you and his father before him. Well, look what it's got him. He's a bloody cripple. He'll never work in the mine again, he'll never get a good job anywhere with that leg, and you're too bloody gutless to tell him. Go on, look your son in the face and tell him what his future is."

Dad struck her across the face with the back of his hand. She stood there and glared at him, neither of them was going to back down. She walked quietly into the bedroom and closed the door. I turned on dad and told him what had gone on up at the office. I didn't spare him anything. Danny slunk away like a coward. When I'd finished I went and knocked on mum's door.

"Mum, it's Josh. Let me in, please."

She opened the door. She'd been crying and was dabbing her nose with a hankie. I gave her a hug and pushed the cheque in her hand. I told her to use it for herself. She made a fuss but I wouldn't take it back. I told her I was still going to the city and that I'd write and send her money whenever I could. I'd send her my address when I had a place to stay meanwhile she could write care of the General Post Office. And if you ever wrote she was to tell you where I was and pass on your details to me. I was gonna blubber real bad so I gave her a quick cuddle and a kiss and left. I grabbed my suitcase from the kitchen table; my dad was sitting very quietly in the dark in the lounge room.

I ran down to your place but you was gone. No note, no nothing. I couldn't believe you had just up and left. I knew you musta had your reasons but it still hurt. Me mate dropped me at the station and I ran across the overhead bridge, the train was just pulling out. I scrambled down the steps three at a time; I thought I saw you standing at the window watching out. I hoped it was for me. I ran along the platform screaming but the steam musta covered me and you didn't see me. The train picked up speed and I couldn't get hold of the door to hoist myself on board.

The guard on the station told me there would be another one in a coupla hours, the last one for the night. I bought a one-way ticket. I was burning my bridges. I was never going home again. When I set myself up I would shout mum a trip to the big city and she could go shopping at all the big stores like Mark Foy's and Marcus Clarke's and Buckingham's. She could shop for herself and buy clothes that fit not stuff outa a catalogue that she had to take up with her old Singer. And I'd take her to a proper restaurant like Repin's Coffee Inn in Market Street what she's read about in the *Women's Weekly* where she could have an American-style fried egg sandwich for three shillings and sixpence with tea or coffee thrown in. For a bob extra she could have savoury mince on toast. She'd always wanted to try coffee. She'd heard so much about it.

On the train down I was sorta scared but happy. Maybe if I'd known what was in store I mighta turned round and gorn home. I stared outa the window until it got so dark I couldn't see no more except the occasional light in a window or a car headlight on the highway as we got closer to the city.

I couldn't believe the bridge when I saw it. For a moment I thought the train was gonna go over the arch and said 'Sugar' out loud. A coupla people looked at me and I apologised for the bad language. When we got into Central – the noise. People everywhere even at that time of night. I had a pie and a cuppa tea but it didn't taste like anything, I was so excited.

Two lads a bit older than me came and sat at my table. They were a friendly pair and we got chatting. They saw my suitcase and asked where I was from and I told them about Seaspray and I'd come to the city to get work. They introduced themselves. One was Maurice and the other one was called Tony, he looked a bit woggy to me. They asked what sort of work I was after cause they said there wasn't much going being a depression an' all. I told them I was a hard worker and was prepared to turn my hand to anything.

They looked at me funny and Maurice said "Anything?"

I told them, "Anything that I can handle. Like I don't think I'm cut out to be an opera singer or anything like that."

They thought that was real funny and asked if I knew anyone in the city. I told them about you but they didn't know any Dr. Button. I wasn't such a country bumpkin that I thought they would but if you don't ask...

"Where are you staying tonight?" Tony was curious. He was older than Maurice I woulda said and much tougher looking.

I told them I was gonna look for a cheap hotel and then look for a room in a boarding house starting tomorrow.

Maurice looked at Tony and I saw him wink. "No need to waste your money on a hotel, mate." He said. "We got enough room for you to doss down tonight, eh Tony?"

"Sure, mate. Save your money for when you really need it."

"That's real kind," I said. "We hear such awful stories about city folk back home."

"Nah, we're just nice guys," Maurice said and gave a sorta funny laugh.

They paid for my pie and cuppa tea before we took orf back to their place. We walked up a coupla the back streets of what they called Surry Hills but there was no way I coulda found my way back. When we reached this terrace house they said they shared with some friends they knocked on the door, they said they left their keys at home, this big fat sheila in a floral nightie, opened the door. She had so much powder on her face it was cracking. She started to abuse the two guys until she saw me and then smiled and told us to come in. We went through to this parlour out the back. There were a few lads my age sitting around smoking and they didn't half stare when they saw me.

One of them, he told me his name was Johnny, came over and sat on my lap. He nibbled at my ear and whispered, "Watch your money with those two. Hide it before you fall asleep." I'd heard about this sort of thing and had already taken the precaution of hiding my money in my sock.

We sat around drinking until I was feeling a bit woozy and Maurice and Tony suggested we say goodnight and adjourn upstairs to their room. I thought it strange that they had to ask which room it was of the woman in the floral nightie but thought they musta been as pissed as I was. The three of us laughed loudly as we bumped our way up the steep narrow stairs to the first floor where they pushed open a door to the first room they came to. This sailor, totally naked, had his cock inside what looked like a young lad, told us to 'Fuck off!'

I shook my head to get a better view but by that time Maurice had closed the door. A little way down the hallway we came across an empty room which must have been theirs although it was very sparsely furnished and had only a bed and a wash basin. I had no idea where they kept their clothes for there was not a wardrobe or a chest of drawers to be seen, although neither would have fitted in the room without cramping it severely.

Maurice took off his clothes and lay on the bed in just his underpants and a singlet. Tony encouraged me to do the same and suggested I hang my good clothes over the door knob to keep them off the dirty floor. He had brought my suitcase up with him for which I was grateful, not that it contained anything of value, except a change of clothes. He placed it on the bed and then produced a small bag of a white powdery substance. I asked if it was drugs.

"No, lad," he assured me. "This is Bex powder. Maurice and I take it to ward off a hangover in the morning because we must be up at sparrow's fart for work. Right, Maurice."

"Mmmm," he said. But he was almost drooling over the powder Tony was tapping onto his thumbnail which I noticed he kept peculiarly long. He built a little snow mound then offered it to Maurice who snorted it into his nose. My mother occasionally took Bex or Vincent's APC but I had never seen her sniff it. She usually took it with a cup of tea or a glass of water as the taste was so awful. Tony saw me watching with a quizzical look on my face. "The body absorbs it much faster through the nose rather than the stomach where it has to contend with all that nasty stomach acid."

That makes sense, I thought. *I must tell mum.*

Tony tapped another small mound onto his thumb nail and offered it to me. I hesitated. "You don't want to spend tomorrow with a terrible headache spewing your guts out do you?"

I didn't, but I still wasn't sure. Tony held it to his own nose and sniffed. "You want some or not?" He sounded impatient with me. He'd been so kind to take me in I thought I'd better say yes to make myself agreeable. The mound he made for me, I thought, was bigger but it was probably just a trick of the light.

I held Tony's hand as I sniffed the end of his thumb and the powder flew up my nostril, feeling fizzy and a little painful. It also made me cough and I wanted to sneeze but Maurice held my nose until it subsided. "You wouldn't want to blow it straight out again would you?" he said.

We lay talking for a while although there was barely enough room on the bed and one of us would soon have to move to the bottom so we could sleep. About fifteen minutes later I felt Tony press his body against my back. He was hard in his underpants, pushing his erection against my arse. Maurice turned in to face me and moved his hands down to my cock and began to play with me.

Before you, Damien, I had had practically no experience at all and to find myself between two men who obviously had sex on their minds was a real eye opener to me. I'm sorry, Damien, but I got excited. Maurice began to kiss my face starting at my forehead and then my eyes, the tip of my nose, my cheeks until he reached my lips. I couldn't help myself. I felt so lonely and abandoned. I started kissing Maurice and pushed my hand under the band of his underpants and began to wank his cock. It was a nice size and hard as mine. He slid down the bed and pulled my undies down until my cock was free and standing hard as a soldier. He put his mouth around it and began to suck. I was naked from the waist down and I could feel Tony pushing his prick between my arse cheeks. I didn't try to stop him, in fact, I wanted him to.

I told him there was Brylcreem in my suitcase. He rubbed it into my arsehole and then pushed his knob against me. He hurt like hell. I told him to stop for a minute until I got used to it because he was bigger than I was used to. That pleased him, but then he said, "You'll be able to take an elephant without any trouble soon." He and Maurice laughed but I didn't know what he meant.

He started thrusting and it felt good especially as Maurice was sucking my cock. He was good at it. He wriggled around and asked me to suck his at the same time. I couldn't believe I'd only been in the city a few hours and here I was with two good looking men around my own age indulging in the sins of Sodom, as the local minister would have said. I wasn't just indulging, I was having a whale of a time.

I wasn't as good at sucking as Maurice but he seemed pleased enough that I was doing it at all. He held off, whether because he was intent of pleasuring me or I wasn't good enough at it, I was soon flooding his mouth with my spunk. He spat it on the floor then he and Tony pushed me over on to my stomach and raised my arse so they could put pillows under me. Tony began to fuck me harder and it hurt a little even though he'd used the hair cream. He grunted and swore in some foreign language, then rolled off me and wiped his cock on the sheet. Maurice took his place and began fucking my arse as hard as Tony had. He came quicker and with less words. He patted me on the arse and said, "Thanks, mate. You could make a fortune with that arse."

I was feeling dizzy and must have fallen asleep although I woke up later and the woman from the door was showing another gentleman to the room. They must have been very crowded. But he got undressed quickly and he pushed his stubby cock inside me. It hurt and I asked him to use the Brylcreem but he took no notice. He grunted and then was gone.

All night men seemed to be making their way to the bedroom and I noticed the door woman collecting money once the men had felt my arse. I guess in the fog of my brain I knew what was going on but I didn't care. The powder I'd sniffed took care of that. A couple of the boys I'd seen downstairs sneaked into the room between visitors and had their way with me. All except Johnny. He cradled my head for a while to make sure I was doing okay and got me a drink of water to slake my thirst as a couple of the men had spunked in my mouth.

"They do this to all the new boys," he said sadly. "If you don't fight it, you won't get hurt."

He began fondling my prick and it got hard again. He crawled beneath me, guiding my cock into his arsehole. It was sweet and juicy and I loved the feel of it around my cock. I didn't even mind when the door opened and the woman of the house began screaming at Johnny. But he didn't budge.

She stood and watched a while then I heard her say, "What the fuck, it's late, there'll be no more tonight." I'd never heard a woman swear like that before. But then she lifted her nightie and I saw a big hairy belly like a wharfie and a huge hard cock. She was a bloke.

"Come to mama," he said as he kneeled between my legs. His aim was good because he pushed straight into my arsehole. I screamed but he pinned me down and began to bang my arse like a pile driver. That pushed me further into Johnny and soon enough the feeling front and back felt good enough that I didn't care anymore. I must have fallen asleep because when I awoke I was alone and my arse was very sore.

I dressed quickly, knowing that I wouldn't find the money that I had hidden in my socks, or my suitcase. They had left the Brylcreem though. I hurried downstairs but no one was stirring. Everything I'd been warned about in the city was true. I'd fallen for it. I felt such an idiot. I went to the privy in the backyard and evacuated the spunk that I had taken during the night. I just prayed that I had not picked up a disease because I did not know how I would explain that it was in my arse. I didn't even know for certain if you could get it there.

I crept back into the house and searched until I found the man-woman's room. She was snoring loudly with one of the boys I'd seen last night wrapped in a hairy embrace. Her room was done up like a cheap bordello, not that I've ever seen one, but it's as I imagine one to be. She was obviously trusting because the top drawer of her bureau was open and she had just stuffed pound and ten shilling notes in there for counting later. I knew some of it was earnings made from my arse and throat and I felt no guilt relieving her of it.

I took it all, and then returned a few crumpled ten shillings' for the use of the room. All in all it had been a profitable night. I now had more money than I had arrived with and I'd received a right royal buggering. My arse was sore, my mouth was like a glue factory, my pocket was bulging and I'd learned an important lesson. I found Johnny and roused him, putting my hand over his mouth.

He came out to the kitchen with me and we spoke in whispers. I implored him to come with me but he shook his head sadly. "I like it here. And I don't have a lot of time." I didn't understand. He showed me a handkerchief which he held to his mouth and then opened it up for me to see the blood smears. I stuffed some notes into his hand and fled. I did not know how to react to something like this.

But as I walked back toward Central railway, the world did not seem such a bad place after all and I whistled so that folk in the street smiled and said 'good morning' or else avoided me as if I was a mad man.

CHAPTER NINE

~

A STING IN THE TAIL

I knew the money wouldn't last forever and set about finding lodgings within my price range. I'd heard about a house in Pyrmont that would suit a gent such as myself but the more I heard of it and the harridan named Mum Doreen who ran the establishment the less I liked the sound of it. Eventually I found a clean boarding house in Darlinghurst, off Oxford Street, so it was near the trams into the centre of the city.

It was a depressed inner working class suburb but beggars can't be choosers as I told myself frequently. I spent half my day pounding the streets looking for work and the rest at the GPO where I would pick up letters from mum who was writing daily. I would also sit and compose letters to send back home although my news was usually less than happy. Naturally I did not explain what had happened to me on the night I arrived and painted a much rosier picture of city life than I found it.

There was despair and hunger all around although those people fortunate enough to have jobs saw little enough of it. I saw young women forced into prostitution by circumstances and young men who turned to lives of crime just to survive or support their family. I sometimes wondered if prison might not be a better bet.

I haunted doctors' surgeries asking for any information on a Dr. Button but no one seemed to have heard of him. There was nothing to say he had remained in the city and it was more likely he had gone to the suburbs in the east or the north where the moneyed folk lived. He was not likely to want to mix with the down and outs of the inner city, although I did walk over to Pyrmont to seek out a French doctor who had a similar sounding name but the doctor was out on call when I arrived and I was told to come back by an old woman who was kindly but insistent.

By this time I had learned about Pfahlert's, a bar for gentlemen who liked other gentlemen, and it seemed my type was in demand. You had taught me citified manners, Damien, and tried to talk me outa, out of, speaking so rough that it labelled me as soon as I opened my mouth. But I found it helped to speak like a rustic sometimes. Some men liked it. A lot.

Most of my nights I spent listening to the radio, listening to how cultured people on the ABC sounded. I tried to imitate them but it just sounded stupid from my mouth. What I learned was pronunciation. To stop leaving the 'g' off the end of words. I didn't want to sound like a toffee-nosed prat but I did want to speak good. I bought a dictionary and looked up the words I heard that I didn't understand. I wanted you to be proud of me, Damien.

Sometimes I would get lonely and I would find myself a friend for an hour or two at Pfahlert's and I would sneak him into my room or, if it was after sunset we would creep into a park and have a bit of fun there although the ever vigilant vice police often put a dampener on our trysts. I came close to arrest on quite a few occasions. Sometimes I was offered money and if the gentleman was presentable I wasn't too proud to take it. A few left cash, unbidden, on my dresser when we'd finished. But I was surviving by being frugal.

It was a boring afternoon when I had nowhere else to look for you Damien that I ended up at Pfarlert's again. A gentleman approached me, I could tell he was after a bit of fun, he was an older chap about your age Damien, I think that's what attracted me to him. He felt my thigh under the table while we drank. He was on his lunch break and had to get back to work shortly. We'd swapped a few personal details, just enough to keep up a conversation, although not enough for blackmail. You can see that I'd learned a thing or two since I'd arrived in the Big Smoke.

He wanted to see me after work and asked where we could meet. I told him I was unemployed like so many others and looking for work.

"What sort of work?" he asked.

I was about to say 'anything' when I remembered what trouble that had gotten me into last time.

While I paused, he said. "You look like a strong lad, not too fussy about physical work."

"I was a coal miner so I know what hard work is," I said proud of my heritage.

"They make good money, why did you give it away?"

I tapped my leg. "Accident."

"But you can walk?"

"Only a bit of a limp," I said.

He downed his beer in one gulp and told me to hurry up; he might have an opening for me. We looked at each other and laughed out loud. The people in the bar must have thought we were pissed. Or mad.

"Josh, mate, how bad you want a job?" Will asked as we walked down toward George Street.

"Pretty bad." I knew where this was leading. "Who's dick I gotta suck?" I asked.

"You don't beat round the bush, do you, mate? You come right out and say it."

"Yeah, so whose dick is it?"

"The foreman's."

"How many times a week?"

"Once to get on the payroll. After that he's usually too drunk. My advice, don't be too good at it. Use your teeth a bit too often but not enough to do damage, just enough so he thinks you're new to the game and he's forcing you."

"Got it," I said.

"You owe me," he smiled.

"And you I won't be pretending to like," I squeezed his arse quickly and he squealed.

Will introduced me to the big fat greasy German who was the foreman of the team laying wooden blocks along George Street in The Rocks. The whole commercial centre of the city right up to Kings Cross and down to Broadway and along to Dawes Point was paved with wooden brick-shaped blocks made from Australian hardwood. The blocks were laid in a stretcher bond pattern, the same as brickwork in a wall, and then top-dressed with tar, pea-gravel and sand for a firm surface and to stop slip. I knew similar road paving in England and America had failed because of the softer wood and their tendency to rot. Sydney had originally tried sandstone but it wore too easily and cracked.

Laying the wood blocks was a filthy job and most men didn't last long. The most recent to quit had done so that morning telling the fat German where he could stick his blocks and his greasy cock.

The men who lay the bricks consider it bone-breaking work and envied the men who washed them down every night with disinfectant to stop disease. But they reserved their contempt for the 'sparrow starvers' as they were called, the men who cleaned the streets picking up rubbish and horse droppings, depriving the sparrows of the undigested seeds in the manure. This cushy job often led to a career on the city council.

I learned a lot of these facts as they rolled off the German's tongue while his balls rolled off mine. He was not someone I would have chosen as a mate but times were hard, and so was he. I'd done the act, telling him I needed the job to support my sick mother. He, in turn, had asked what I was prepared to do to get the job, after all, *there's a Depression on*.

As sexy as I could I said, "Anything."

The German played casually with the outline of his cock in his trousers so that no one could accuse him of being too provocative. "You really mean anything?"

"I'll do anything to get this job," I repeated. I had a bet with myself the preliminaries were taking longer than it would take him to spend his seed.

"How about you get down on your knees and show me how much you'd like this job," he said.

I looked shocked but he was already forcing me to my knees.

"I've never done that before. I don't know if I can," I pleaded.

"Oh, you can," he said. "And you will. If you want the job."

He undid his fly and unfurled a thick uncut sausage that would easily scrape my teeth because I had never seen one so big and thick let alone sucked it.

"Open up, boy," he said as he poked it at my face. It was only semi-hard so I licked it like I wasn't really sure what I was doing. I'd come a long way from that naive country boy who landed in the big sinful city a matter of weeks ago. As soon as he was fully hard he grew tired of my ice cream licks and wanted to stuff it all in my mouth. I choked, I really choked. There was no pretending, I can tell you. He was good practice and that's all I let myself think while I was doing it. He had a big pot belly and he sweated in the heat but I blocked it out of my mind. I concentrated on his cock and bringing him off quick as possible.

Pushing my mouth as far as I could manage along the shaft until I sensed he was enjoying it, he muttered a few German phrases and I picked up speed. It was a matter of minutes before he pushed his cock as far into my gob as it would go and I felt him squirt his spunk down the back of my throat so I didn't have to taste it.

He let me up and I wiped my mouth with the back of my hand. He didn't even bother putting his cock back in his trousers as he handed me a card and told me to report back the next day at 7am with it filled in and ready to work.

Back outside the small van that acted as his office, and harem, I gave Will a wink and wiped my mouth again. He dragged me along to meet the crew that I would be working with the next day, all nice guys, and then we made arrangements to meet later for tea at one of the cheap workers cafes dotted around the city. It was a given we'd be heading to Darlinghurst and my room for Will to get his reward. I gave it to him three times before he had to catch his tram back to Bondi.

The German, for all his gross application methods, turned a blind eye to our frequent rest breaks. We didn't make a welter of it, but in the sweltering sun of summer, all we wanted to do was strip off our shirts and let the breeze cool our bodies. But that was strictly verboten as he kept telling us. On really hot days he allowed us to shed our shirts provided we wore our singlets.

Will and I became occasional lovers but he preferred variety. He also told me he had every intention of settling down one day to marry and have a few kids. He was surprised when I told him my desire was to find you Damien and set up house together. He'd never heard of such a thing. It had never entered his head.

So the months passed. I never heard from you and I wondered whether you had gone to Melbourne or Brisbane purely to put as much distance between us as you could. I began to question whether you'd been trifling with me. I always gave you the benefit of the doubt. But as the weeks became months I knew I had to get on with my life. I couldn't stay in this awful state of limbo.

I may have let it go on a little while longer but for a fortunate accident. We were paving a part of Castlereagh Street that had worn badly although the blocks had lasted a good five years. We were laying pitch when a car seemed to lose control and ended up embedded in the tar, the wheels stuck fast. The chauffeur cursed his luck and attempted to reverse out but just succeeded in spraying the sticky substance all over the street.

I noticed in the back seat a young mother with what was obviously her daughter, they looked so alike, in obvious distress. Their combined weight, small as it was, plus that of the chauffeur were stopping the car from being moved. I quickly tied two of the wooden blocks to my feet by means of rags we used to wipe excess tar from our hands. It was a laborious task but I made my way to the car and opened the back door motioning to the woman to hand me the young girl. At first she didn't understand.

"I'll carry your daughter across to the footpath if you'll permit me," I said in my best voice. "Then I'll help you and the men may be able to free your car."

I piggybacked the young girl, pretending to almost drop her on the short trip to the side of the road. She screamed delightedly every time I let her slip a little. It seemed the right thing to do to make it an adventure. I went back for the woman and slipped my arms around her and carried her to the pavement like a young bride. A few bystanders clapped my gallantry. See, Damien. My vocabulary has kept pace with my experience.

With the help of the chauffeur we managed to free the car but the morning's work had been ruined. The young woman thanked us profusely; some of my workmates wishing they had been the ones to carry her like a blushing bride. She was attractive but, as my appetite does not lie in that direction, I thought no more about it.

Will clapped me on the back for my derring-do after the small fracas was over and asked me, "Did you not recognise her?"

"Should I have?"

"Oh boy. You don't read the social pages do you?"

"Parasites, the lot of them." I was still my father's son in some respects.

Just prior to knock-off time in the afternoon, another car, much grander, pulled up alongside the work site. The window wound down and a handsome foreign-looking gentleman called us over.

"Are you the crew that helped dig my car out of the predicament it was in this morning?" he asked.

When the men recognised him they quickly donned their caps and nodded. He asked us to come forward and handed each a crisp pound note. The men could not believe their luck and they bowed and scraped their appreciation.

"Which one of you men carried my daughter and my wife."

The men all pointed to me expecting that I might receive more of the stranger's largesse, for I had no idea who he was, and share it with them.

"Have you finished your work for the day?" he asked.

I told him I had. He tapped the chauffeur who immediately got out of the car and held the door open for me.

Will pushed me and I stumbled against the car.

"Please, won't you get in, Mr. Um"

"Carter," Will yelled for I was much too tongue tied to answer for myself. I had never seen a car with such a plush interior.

"I'm afraid I'm dirty," I said by way of an explanation for my tardiness.

"No matter," he said. "It's from a hard day's honest toil."

He held out his hand and helped me climb in. I sat back in the luxury as the driver sped off leaving my work mates gaping. I had no inkling where I was being whisked off to. Of course, Damien, you've already guessed that it was Enzo and the woman I'd carried to safety was his wife and the girl his daughter.

He showed me around his home, you could have put our whole weatherboard cottage at Seaspray in the dining room of his house. He asked me what I thought of it and, without thinking, I told him I thought it was very 'woggy.' I saw the look of horror on his face and realised I'd made a mistake.

"What do you mean by that?" he asked.

"It's very Italian. Full of style and good taste." That wasn't what I meant at all, I meant over the top with gold and old-fashioned furniture that you'd be afraid to sit on in case it broke or you dirtied it. But he smiled after I said what I did. He clapped me on the shoulder and said, "We Italians don't like that word, Josh, it's rather offensive."

I apologised and grovelled and that pleased him too. He invited me to have a meal with him, nothing fancy, just the two of us. He asked about my life and I'm afraid I blurted out about you, oh it's all right, I didn't mention any names. He liked the idea I was queer and before the night was over he asked me if I wanted a job, looking after his wife. He could trust a queer, whereas he'd had a few normal guys make advances to her.

The money he was offering was enough that I'd be able to do all the things I wanted to do for mum finally. I'd have money to spare. I'd been so broke I didn't even have the money for a present for Danny and Eileen for their wedding. Mum added my name to the card from her and dad. He almost blew a gasket when he found out.

I didn't go back. I'm finished with that town forever. Mum knows.

So I thought it over for a few days. I told Will and he filled me in on the background of who Enzo was but with some of the bastards I'd met he didn't seem so bad. I didn't know about the razor gangs then. Or the drugs. So, I took the job.

I enjoyed it. It was easy work. I liked Victoria and little Deborah. We all got along famously. Victoria knew what her husband got up to and didn't really care. She knew she would have to produce a son and heir but she expected little trouble doing so.

I slipped into another routine. Things changed when I accidentally opened the double doors to his sitting room the night of the party for that vaudeville singer, what's her name Valerie something or the other. I had a request from his wife so I knocked and went in.

I couldn't believe my eyes. Enzo is a real ladies man. He's always getting freebies from the girls in his stable. I wouldn't have been surprised to see a girl down on her knees sucking away at his dick but it was a bloke. I nearly shit myself and backed out as fast as I could. He told me he wasn't queer but just wanted to see what all the fuss was about. I was to keep my mouth shut.

But things have been going bad lately. Enzo's been on edge. He told me to be extra vigilant when I was out with Victoria. Well, we were ambushed. The true gangs don't attack the wives and kids of other gang members. It's unheard of. But Victoria and me got surrounded and they went for her. I did my best to protect her and got myself carved up in the process. Luckily some of the boys were nearby and came to the rescue.

* * * *

When Josh had finished I just wanted to wrap him in my arms and take him away from all the pain and the heartbreak we'd both been through. But I knew it was too soon. He was still weak from his ordeal and needed rest. He would best get that in the security of Enzo's mansion where I could visit every day to check on his progress.

I did that for another two weeks until one morning as I opened my surgery Josh was seated in the waiting room, chatting with Mum who was treating him like royalty.

"Josh! What are you doing here?"

"I thought I'd come and see you at work. Just like the old days, eh?"

I shook his hand gently because it still caused him pain and ushered him into my consulting room. It was there that he concluded the story you've read above transcribed as accurately as memory allows, other parts of which he had imparted to me during his recovery, almost as if it the telling of it had been keeping him alive.

I was sitting on the edge of the desk, holding his hand. I dared to kiss him briefly on the lips. We had never discussed our future during his recuperation although I had let it be known very early on that I had no encumbrances. Josh, however, had been more circumspect.

I could scarcely breathe after he'd pulled away from the clumsy advance I'd made. He must have seen the look on my face because he said, his eyes downcast, his voice choking, "I already have a boyfriend."

CHAPTER TEN

~

THE WORLD TURNED UPSIDE DOWN

For several minutes I was too stunned to speak. Josh had a lover, a 'boyfriend' he called him. In all the weeks I had nursed him back to health that had never seriously crossed my mind. I wondered whether it would have been better not to have found Josh at all. Did I regret saving his life only to hand him back to another man? That was too petty and beneath me; I did not want to go there.

"What did you expect, Damien?" Josh interrupted the creeping silence, a gap that threatened to engulf us both. "You left me there without a word. How do you think I felt? And for weeks I hoped you'd write and tell me where you were. Nothing! What was I supposed to think?"

I withered under the onslaught. He'd obviously bottled it up, now allowing his months of bitterness free rein. There was little I could do but protest. "What was I supposed to think when you didn't come back to my cottage? I waited hours for you. I only left because some of the miners threatened violence if I stayed. And then..."

I didn't want this fight. I still loved Josh. I didn't want to cause him pain.

"And then?" Josh asked.

I changed the subject. "Do you love this man?"

He hesitated slightly. "Yes."

"But not like you love me?"

"I will never love anyone again like I loved you."

I noticed Josh's use of the past tense.

"You won't leave him?"

Josh's response was telling. "I can't."

"Can't?"

"I owe him."

I was fighting for my relationship. "Does he love you?"

Josh couldn't look at me. "In his own way."

"That doesn't sound like a good basis for a relationship."

"It will just have to do," Josh shrugged his resignation.

I was powerless to argue at that stage. I was sinking into despair and self-indulgence. I was afraid I would lash out, so I spoke quietly. "I don't expect you will believe me now but Danny told me you'd changed your mind and were going to stay in Seaspray."

"You said you'd rather die than leave without me."

"And I would have. There was a lynch mob outside my cottage ready to tar and feather me. I gave Danny a note to pass on to you with my contact details in case you changed your mind."

He looked surprised. "Danny never said."

"No, I suppose he didn't." I wasn't sure if he believed that or not.

"And later, when I didn't hear from you, I poured my heart out in a letter I sent to your old address at Seaspray. I hoped you'd read it and know how much I love you. If you'd left, I hoped your mum would send it on."

We were at an impasse.

"Why didn't you try harder?" Josh asked.

I could have tossed the accusation back at him but there was no point. I could also point out that three rejections were about all my heart could take. "Perhaps I should have."

"Yeah."

"Will I see you again?"

Josh looked me in the eye; he was no coward. "I don't think so. It would be too painful. For you." Then his bravado must have failed him. "For both of us."

There was nothing left to say. I pushed my finger nails into the palm of my hand to keep my control. "Just remember, Josh. I never stopped loving you. I will always love you. I wish you every happiness. I just wish it had been with me."

I uttered the last words as he quietly closed the surgery door on hope. I sat, heartbroken, closing my eyes to my shortness of breath and the constriction across my chest. I knew I would not die from this feeling because I'd had it before. I could turn to alcohol, or drugs, or even sex, to try to kill the ache. But nothing, no one, could ever numb me enough. Yes, the ache would dull over time but it would always be there. Especially now, knowing that if I'd tried a little harder, if I had just waited another minute, another hour, in my cottage, I would be sharing my life with the man I love.

By tomorrow my despair would turn to anger. It was a process I had to go through. Had I not experienced it before, I would hate Josh and it might kill my affection, as surely as he had managed to suffocate his feelings for me. I did not want to hate him. I was genuine in my wishes for his happiness. I wondered about the man who had won his heart although the manner in which he described it, his new relationship did not sound like it was based on love but rather on debt. My mind conjured up so many fearful variations of his boyfriend, I just wished it would shut up. I had to trust Josh and his innate common sense.

A knock at the door, which meant I had another patient, shook me out of the doldrums. I called "Come in," and Mum Doreen stuck her head in. She took one look at my demeanour. "Did it not go well, love?"

"He has a lover," I said a little too curtly to make her mind her own business.

It worked. She announced there was someone to see me then ducked out as Valerie swept in as regal as any royalty, totally ignoring the squalor around her, a rose among the thorns.

"Was that the young man who almost died? The one you brought back to life?" she greeted me as she made herself comfortable in the patient's chair.

I nodded my head hoping this conversation would be short-lived.

"His recovery is remarkable. Little short of miraculous."

I interjected. "What brings you here today? Are you ill?"

Valerie looked at me oddly, as if trying to work out why I had cut her off, particularly as she was praising me. She knew I was as susceptible to flattery as any man, even more so when it came to my medical prowess. But she did not allow her inquisitiveness to over-ride the reason for her visit. She rarely came to my surgery, normally sending a message or a minion if it were urgent that she wanted me to wait on her at home. We had become fast friends and I always enjoyed seeing her.

"This is a social call, Damien," and without further ado she held out her arm and wriggled her fingers in my direction. It was magnificent. Provided the diamonds were real, and knowing Valerie they would have to be, the neat little diamond-studded ring was equal to what it would take me a year to earn. I came from behind my desk to admire it.

"Unless he's a thief, the lucky gentleman is very wealthy indeed." I leaned over and kissed her on the cheek. "Congratulations, my dear." I sat on the edge of the desk and held her hand, happy for her.

She egged me on. "Go on, ask me."

"Who's the lucky gentleman?"

She snorted. "I don't know that he'll be all that lucky. He's getting me, after all." If it was one thing for which Valerie was not noted, it was her fidelity.

I laughed with her. "Stop teasing."

"Cecil."

I hoped I hid the shock. "Cecil, whose dick you wouldn't suck even if poked through a hole in the wall?"

"You so much as breathe a word of that and I'll have your balls on a chain." She was only partly serious.

"What changed your mind?" I knew there had to be a very good reason.

She sighed theatrically. "Oh, I shall miss Sydney."

I jumped up excitedly. "You've received an offer from London?"

She nodded, scarcely able to contain the glee. I lifted her out of her seat and hugged her tightly. It was her dream.

"It's nothing to write home about," she said modestly. "But I promise I will. It's a revue in the West End. With Noël Coward. Tim, you remember Tim? He was my leading man in *Oopsy Daisy*. More like my leading lady. Anyway he headed off to London and met Noël at a party and, well, one thing led to another. Tim was always an incredibly handsome man. And naturally he and Noel, well, I don't have to draw you a picture. Noël and his boyfriend shared poor Timothy until he was, let's just say, run ragged. That was his entree into London society and the theatre elite. So when Noël was looking for just the right sort of vulgarity for his next revue he asked Timothy and he, bless him, remembered me. I did him a favour once when he was in a jam."

"What sort of favour?"

"A bit of trouble with the law. You know, soliciting in the toilet on Wynyard station. I took the stand and swore under oath that my Timmy was the most virile of men and couldn't abide pansies or anything to do with those sorts of men. In fact, I suggested demurely, he was so much the man that he had me on my back day and night when we weren't on stage. Oh, it was the performance of a lifetime."

"And the judge and jury bought it?"

"That, and the judge was an old acquaintance of Timmy's and virtually called the police liars and instructed the jury to acquit."

"It's good to have friends in high places."

"Don't be like that. I would do the same for you."

"Unless the world changed irrevocably, you will never find me soliciting in railway station toilets."

She smirked. "But I've gone one even better." She fidgeted through her handbag and triumphantly handed me an engraved envelope. "Here is your personal invitation to my engagement party. I expect you to be there. No excuses."

"I wouldn't miss it for the world."

"There will be plenty of boys like you at the party so you may arrive on your own but a man with your good looks is certain to go home accompanied."

A short stab of pain clouded my face.

"What is it?" she asked. "Here I am going on with all my wonderful news. But you are unhappy. How can that be? Mum tells me you have found your young man. Oh, is that it? Of course, you may bring him to my engagement party. I would love to meet him. He must be very special indeed to capture my Damien's heart."

"You have already met him." I sat back down behind the desk, my head in my hands. When I looked up, my cheeks streaked with tears, I saw Valerie's look of horror.

"The young man? The one who was here before me? The one whose life you saved? That is your young man?"

I groaned that he was. Valerie was out of her chair, kneeling in front of me clutching my hands gazing into my face.

"Oh, Damien. I'm so sorry. If only I'd known."

"He told me he has another lover."

"And one who is not likely to want to share his affections," she said seriously, handing me her handkerchief.

"You know who he is? He seems to have some sort of hold over Josh."

"Better you don't know in case you stir up a hornet's nest."

"Is he totally lost to me then?"

Valerie paced the room. "Damien, what's say I persuade Cecil to stake you a ticket to London on the boat with us. Not first class, but still comfortable. Leave all this behind." She waved her gloved hand around and I took her meaning to be not only the mess with Josh but the disreputable company I kept and the seedy circumstances in which I lived.

"That's very kind, Valerie. But I have to face up to my demons. It's about time I tackled them head on."

"You won't do anything foolish, will you?"

"No, I'm not that far gone," I said.

"I know you're too strong a person for that. What I meant was his lover."

"I will try to win Josh back. I know he still loves me."

"No, Damien. It's too late. Too dangerous."

I was becoming impatient. "Don't tease me like this. If there is something I should know, then tell me."

She exhaled audibly, playing nervously with her gloves. "You have to promise me that what I am about to tell you will go no further. If you breathe a word of this to anyone and I find out, I will deny everything and I will turn my back on you forever. Is that understood?"

"Of course. If I give my word, I keep it. You should know that by now."

"I do." She seemed to be gathering the strength to tell me. "I just needed to reiterate the seriousness of what I'm about to reveal." She looked me square in the eye. "Josh is lost to you, Damien. You must give up all hope of recovering his love. His lover is Enzo Fabrini."

I could not have gasped more loudly than had I been in an onstage melodrama. Foolishly, I had assumed Josh's boyfriend would be a lad of his own age and class, never would I have envisaged a relationship between Enzo and his wife's bodyguard, although little things should have been a warning.

Enzo's more than paternalistic concern for Josh's health during his near demise. Enzo's gradual estrangement from me and our brief sexual interludes. Once Josh recovered Enzo was absent more times than not when I called to check his girls for disease and even when he was home my attempts to give him oral relief were rebuffed without explanation. Enzo had also recently sent his wife and daughter to Italy for six months, ostensibly to meet his parents and to accompany them back to Australia, at which time he was hoping his wife would be rested and ready to produce more offspring, preferably a son. But while she was away, Enzo had free reign in that large mansion to have his way with Josh.

I had seduced Enzo into queer sex only to see Josh become the recipient, and the prisoner, of his insatiable appetite. I cursed myself for my behaviour.

"It's not well known outside Enzo's immediate circle of friends, and even then it's only hearsay. He can't afford for rumours to get out. His empire depends on it remaining a secret. He's lucky insofar as he's already established a reputation as a womaniser, and has a wife and daughter, so that for the moment he can laugh off any suggestions otherwise. But it would be very dangerous for Joshua if the whispers became more insistent. Or if anyone came between Enzo and Joshua."

I smiled weakly. "London is beginning to look all the more appealing."

"That reminds me," she said rummaging through her reticule. "Ah, here it is."

She handed me an advertisement from the *Sydney Morning Herald*. It was for a residence and medical practice in the heart of the city's most prestigious precinct for surgeons and specialists. Josh and I had often talked long into the night about living in an apartment that overlooked Sydney's verdant Royal Botanic Gardens with its majestic Moreton Bay Figs and the colony of flying foxes that filled the night skies with their migratory habits seeking fruit and the nectar and pollen of the eucalyptus trees farther south in the more spacious Moore Park and Centennial Park.

It would remain a dream outside the scope of any means I would be able to scrimp together. Besides, I would not be the sort of society doctor that was likely to be given the green light by other occupants of the building.

I attempted to keep the disappointment from my voice. "A wonderful opportunity, I admit. However, the hurdles are too great at this time."

"You can be such a sour puss sometimes, Damien. What hurdles?" Valerie was always unrelentingly upbeat. Sometimes irritatingly so. This was one such occasion.

"For starters," I thought she was being particularly obtuse if she could not see from the requirements spelled out in the advertisement itself, "I would require references to my character, ability, etc. And they would need to be from the highest pillars of the community. Look around. I don't believe a recommendation from Mum Doreen, as highly as I would regard it, would go far with the toffs who live there."

"How about these?" Valerie produced a bundle of envelopes and unwrapped the red ribbon she had around them before handing them to me.

I recognised the names of a number of prominent judges, three QCs, a conservative MP or two and any number of gents from the social register. "But I don't know these people," I complained.

"Agreed, but it's amazing what a little gentle blackmail will achieve, especially when done with a smile and a kiss that promises a little more." She stood and leaned over the desk as I sorted through the glowing references. She tapped her finger on one signed by a judge. "Smith, B.A.," she said. And another. "Smith, Sir D.L." One after another she tapped the sheets and gave me the pseudonyms they had used in my surgery.

"You cunning woman," I laughed.

"Most of them were happy to sign these documents. After all, how much easier and less stressful if they have a Macquarie Street specialist within walking distance of their chambers. No more having to skulk across the Pyrmont Bridge to the less salubrious Pyrmont to wait in disguise in Mum's kitchen."

"I see your point and I thank you for going to the effort. Provided these gentlemen are in agreement I would appreciate being able to keep these for later use. They'll come in handy."

"Oh, they'll do more than that, Damien. If you take them to the bank, whose name and address you will find at the bottom, they will open the vaults to welcome you. The manager is Smith, J.B."

Had I known my clientele at Pyrmont was so illustrious I may have charged a great deal more than I did. I had to laugh at how Fate deals the cards. What it gives with one hand, it takes away with the other. As much as this was all I had toiled for, my heart was just not in it. Call me old fashioned, but I was never one to work for myself. I always thrived best under the approbation of a special friend.

Valerie must have read my mind. "You will find him some day, Damien. Someone will see all the goodness in you, all the kindness. Until then, think of all the good you can do from such a position of power and privilege. Draw attention to the plight of the workers in the factories. The parliament will take no notice of a humble GP from Pyrmont. But they will sit up and take note when a Macquarie Street specialist speaks his mind."

"It's a big step," I fudged.

"Of course it is. Nothing worth seeking is not a big step."

"I'm scared."

"So am I, Damien. I may look confident about my chances in London, but it's all unknown. I may go over a star, but I'm a parochial star. London is the centre of the theatrical universe. I may shine brightly or I may burn out. But better I venture and try than remain here and wonder."

"I'll think it over," I said, and meant it. I would discuss it with Mum and Eric and a few close friends. They wouldn't steer me wrong. They had treated me with kindness when I most needed it. I would give them the courtesy of involving them in my decision.

"Meanwhile, the offer to accompany us to London is still open, and I would love to have a friend along, even just someone to talk to instead of Cecil." She rolled her eyes. "But he's a good old stick. He will look after me. Pay the bills. Be there when I come home from my tragic love affairs. Oh, yes, the marriage is one in name only. Purely platonic. But he's happy with that."

I walked her to the door and kissed her affectionately, promising to be at her engagement party. I watch her carriage disappear down Harris Street before going back inside to tell Mum the good news.

CHAPTER ELEVEN

~

OTHERWISE ENGAGED

$\mathcal{M}$um was 'lairy as a two-bob watch' – entirely floral, of course. I was worried that she would stand out in what society would consider her rather vulgar working-class apparel. I wasn't such a snob that I was embarrassed but I hated the idea that Mum would be the butt of cruel jokes. She wasn't going as my guest; she had received her own invitation and had invited Eric as her escort. She had beaten me to the punch.

"Don't worry, Damien, you can share with me," he said which set Mum off, cackling like a chook about to lay her eggs. "I don't think me plumbling's right for what you two boys want."

Yes, she'd said 'plumbling.' She'd had a few courage enhancing beverages to make the evening pass less painfully. Mum was shy when not in her own domain and at Valerie's engagement party she would be so far out of her depth that she wouldn't see the shore. With a few brandies under her belt she was so lively that nothing would sink her now, oblivious to everything, including pain.

Eric arrived and got Mum to twirl round in front of him. "Magnificent," he gasped. "You'll most certainly be the woman with the most class at the party."

I looked at the ceiling to show my displeasure while Mum giggled and turned on me. "He said I looked common." She poked her tongue out at me.

Then she noticed the large box that Eric had brought with him. "What's that?" she asked, her eyes pleading that it be for her.

"Just a little something for you to wear to the party this evening," Eric said mischievously. He removed the lid from the box and I heard Mum gasp in amazement. Even I was taken aback. I had never seen anything like it.

"It's only for a lend mind," Eric said as Mum rubbed her fingers across the exquisite flawless fur stole.

She was scarcely remembering to breathe. "Ooh, that's much too grand for me boys."

Eric placed it around her shoulders and she hugged it as if it were a dream from which she would wake up at any moment. Waltzing into her bedroom to admire herself in the full-length mirror, her euphoria was short-lived, and she came back very down in the mouth.

"It's much too good. It makes my best dress look so shabby."

She was right of course but, without putting too fine a point on it, a bath mat made her dress look shabby. My heart went out to her. Eric had, with the best intentions, crushed her spirit.

He went to her and danced around the room. "But it looks so good on you, doesn't it Damien?"

He signalled to me to agree with him. I did as enthusiastically as I could but my heart just wasn't in it.

"Please forgive me, Mum," he said humbly. "I should have asked what you would be wearing. What do I know about ladies' fashion? I didn't realise that things could clash. But..."

Mum looked up expectantly.

"Our good luck. The woman in the shop asked me what my lady friend was wearing as the fur stole only suited a particular style. When I said I had no idea, she said it was just like a man. Then she insisted just in case the fur clashed with my lady friend's evening wear that I take a dress to match. So..." Eric went to the box again and under a layer of tissue paper took out and held up a plain, but stylish, black dress that would not have been out of place at Buckingham Palace. He thrust it into Mum's disbelieving hands. "Go on, try it on."

"Well, it's not my usual sort of thing but it would be so nice to go out all la-di-da for once in my life. And with a real fur stole." She hurried into her bedroom to change.

"You sly bastard," I smiled, slapping Eric on the shoulder. "I had no idea how to get her to change. Not that she would have anything as elegant as what you chose. I didn't want her to be a laughing stock."

"Nor did I," Eric said.

"I don't suppose there's a pair of shoes in that box of yours," Mum called, sticking her head round the bedroom door.

"Coming right up." Eric took the box and passed in to Mum. "Now you hurry up or we'll be late."

When Eric came back I kissed him affectionately on the cheek. "You're a good man. John is very lucky."

"Please tell him that next time you see him please."

"Is something wrong?" I would hate to hear of my two best friends having problems. They were the only certainties in my life.

"He goes through this every now and then. The lack of time alone together. It does put pressure on us. We've applied for positions in the same house together but people look askance when we say we come as a double or not at all. You can almost hear their tiny minds screaming 'perverts.' John lets it get him down."

"You just hide it better." I gripped his arm in sympathy.

We didn't have time to go into it further because Mum emerged from the bedroom like a butterfly leaving the cocoon. It was amazing what difference a simple black dress with sensible black shoes made after seeing the nightmare in floral that she had once been. A simple strand of pearls was the perfect finish to Mum's couture. It did something for her. It gave her confidence, poise, making her eyes sparkle with the joy that she would get to live her dream even if only for one night. She would be on her best behaviour.

Wrapping the fur around her shoulders she sailed majestically down the corridor and out the front door to the waiting cab.

The party was at Cecil's and it was a good forty-five minutes before we joined the queue of vehicles crawling slowly up the pebbled driveway to disgorge their passengers at the front white marble entrance to the mansion. Mum was all impatience, mainly to show off I suspect, and wanted to jump out and stride the last few yards on foot. Eric had to physically restrain her, telling her it would be considered bad manners, that she would make more of an impression arriving with two eligible bachelors, one on each arm.

Make an impression she did. Eyes turned as our party was announced. I thought for a moment Mum had forgotten who she was when her real name was called to the milling assembly. It was the unfamiliar name that caught people's attention but it was her striking dowager-like appearance that had them wondering. As we entered we were welcomed by Valerie who cooed over Mum and her fur, somewhat enviously I thought. Cecil seemed totally taken with Mum who still had enough of her working-class charm to captivate.

Cecil shook my hand and seemed genuine when he told me how good it was to see me and told me to come and chat with him later in the evening. We passed into the crowded ballroom where a small orchestra was playing softly until it was time to dance. Pockets of men stood about while their partners were studiously ignored. It was an Australian tradition that I never understood. At social gatherings, high and low, men congregated together and women were left to their own devices until the dancing began. Even then it was sometimes difficult to prise the men apart: it had nothing to do with queerness.

We circled the room, nodding to those whom I knew by sight and stopping to chat to those whom I knew well, introducing Eric and Mum, now by her proper name, allowing her to shine. She had an opinion on everything, and if it wasn't always well thought out, she delivered it with a conviction that belied her currently polite exterior. Scratch the surface and she was still Mum.

I'm afraid I almost came undone when I saw him. Josh was standing among a group of men huddled around Enzo Fabrini. He stood a little to the side and to the back of Enzo, obviously guarding his boss, looking a little lost and uncomfortable but he had been suited out by experts who had emphasised the bulk and muscle of his body. He looked magnificent although he seemed completely unaware of the effect he had on women as well as men.

He was acutely attuned to danger, glancing around the room at intervals until he covered every nook and cranny. Eventually his eyes alighted on me. He hesitated, cast a glance between me and Mum and then to Eric. He couldn't stop the twinge of jealousy that appeared on his face for a matter of seconds, but I saw it. Eric was a heart stopper as well. A man I could easily fall for myself if my heart hadn't already been reserved. Josh tried reading my face but I'd already overcome my initial surprise and had assumed a neutral demeanour.

"My God, Damien, is that him?" Eric leaned into my ear to whisper. Josh's face froze as I nodded and smiled at him. "He looks so different all dressed up."

"That's him."

"My, what a beauty. I think I just saw a flare of jealousy, did I not?"

"I pray you did. Where there's the little green monster, there's hope."

"Is that your Josh?" Mum asked, squinting across the dance floor.

"Mum," I said brusquely, laying my hand on her arm to prevent her racing across to speak to one of the few people she recognised. "I need to ask you a very big favour."

"You mean not to mention to Mr. Fabrini that Josh is your long-lost love because it may cause trouble." Her smile was a mix of cunning and innocence. "Don't worry, dear. I'm discretion itself. You should know me by now." And before I could say anything she'd set off with Eric in hot pursuit.

While I was deciding what course of action to take I felt a presence beside me and felt a light breath on my neck as someone leaned in to whisper in my ear.

"Valerie said you were a beauty but she didn't do you justice."

I was about to turn to see who had been so complimentary but he stopped me. "No, don't turn around, keep looking straight ahead. I've been watching you for months now, Dr. Bouton, and I'm very impressed. Here, give me your hand. Discretely. That way you can see how impressed I am." I put my arm behind me and the young man moved his crotch against me so I could feel his erection through his trousers.

Just then Eric and Mum broke away from the conversation they'd been having with Enzo and his entourage. They were dragging him and Josh back toward me. The young man's crotch disappeared and I was alone when I turned around. He'd disappeared into the crowd.

"Ah, Dr. Bouton," Enzo said clasping my hand firmly. "Just the man I wanted to see. Can you spare me a moment?" I nodded, too tongue-tied to speak as I gazed at Josh. We moved off but Enzo turned to his shadow. "Josh, you stay here and keep Mum company, she was one of the angels who saved your life, coming over every day to nurse you while the doc here caught up on his sleep."

Josh looked less than enthralled by the prospect of spending time with Mum and Eric as Enzo steered me to double glass doors that led outside. We walked down into the garden, careful to avoid any shrubbery that could be inadvertently hiding other partygoers. He was not afraid of violence, but of gossip.

"How is Josh's health these days?" he asked.

"I don't know," I said honestly. "Joshua has stopped coming to the surgery. Is something wrong?"

"You've not seen him in—"

"Five or six weeks. What's happened?"

"That's around the time it started," Enzo confided. "Did you give him some bad news at your last examination?"

"No, exactly the opposite. I told him he was doing remarkably well for someone who had almost died."

"Would you know if he was keeping something from you?"

"It would be easy enough to disguise an ailment that I was not looking for. What are his symptoms?"

"It's nothing I can put my finger on." Enzo sounded genuinely concerned. "It's just, and I know this may sound silly to a medical man, he seems to have lost his spirit. He's not the Josh of old."

"It was a very serious injury he sustained. That's sure to knock a man down a peg or two, even one as strong as Joshua. That's without taking into account the effect on his mind."

"His mind?"

"It takes a while for a person's mind to heal as well as their body. Perhaps Josh is mulling something over in his mind." I was hoping it was me.

"I see." He thought about it for a moment. "Would you talk to him? As a favour to me?"

"That will only work if he wants to talk to me." Josh had left me in no doubt that he did not.

"I will instruct him to do so." Enzo had the subtlety of a tram.

"No. That won't work. If he's coerced into conversation with me he'll be on his guard. If you'll permit me, I'll attempt to draw him out over the course of the evening and, if he's amenable, try to get him to reveal his concerns. That's if he has any. It may be just your welfare that is occupying his mind. Now that your wife is holidaying in Italy, I hear he is your personal bodyguard."

"I doubt it could be that. No one would dare harm me. It would bring down the wrath of the angels."

"Josh owes you his life," I said, digging for information that might help me understand the sway Enzo had over him.

"If he owes anyone, it's you."

Just then, Valerie appeared on the balcony, calling us. Enzo waved to her, and then he squeezed my arse, "I missed you."

I didn't believe him for a minute. It had been a calculated move on his part to get me on side. "Me too," I replied, attempting to summon up as much sincerity as would make my words ring true. "I'll see what I can find out. Meanwhile, one thing you could do to help. Instruct Joshua to attend my surgery once a week for follow up on his injuries. If I'm not successful in sounding out any problems he has tonight, then I may later on."

"Thanks, doc. You're a pal."

Back in the ballroom, Mum was nowhere to be seen while Josh was in earnest conversation with Eric. He looked up when Enzo clapped him on the shoulder. "You're here to enjoy yourself not tag along behind me like a guard dog. Go. Dance, flirt, have a good time. Just don't get drunk."

The orchestra struck up and couples glided on to the dance floor. I noticed Mum and Cecil made an unlikely couple but he seemed totally captivated and they were chatting like old friends. Valerie came barrelling toward me; grabbing my arm she dragged me away leaving Josh and Eric together again. I watched as they headed toward the open door and I was stabbed with jealousy. I wanted to go and eavesdrop on their conversation but Valerie had other ideas.

I was pulled to the centre of the dance floor where Valerie clung to me like, well, like Mum's fur did to her shoulders until we'd arrived at the party and even then it had to be prised off her; she would have been content to wear it all night. As we waltzed, Valerie whispered about the men dancing with their partners. She was giving me a crash course in character, telling me stories from personal experience.

If it could have, my hair would have stood on end. I had enough ammunition to blackmail half of society. I was left in no doubt that Valerie had proof stashed away should that rainy day ever appear.

"Why are you telling me this, Valerie?" I asked.

"With this information no one will ever be able to best you. A quiet word here or a hint there and most people will come to your aid. These men are powerful. They can help you. But they can also be implacable enemies so use your knowledge sparingly. I've persuaded them to be on your side. Most of them already were because of your absolute discretion in the surgery. Did you apply for the Macquarie Street premises?"

"Yes. And I must say the references were a great help. I met with the building's body corporate and they were not inclined to even accept my application until I thrust the names of the referees in front of them. That got their attention."

"See, it's already working. Now don't be coy. These men will not hesitate to contact you for favours so tit for tat."

She swept me over to where Cecil and Mum were nattering away like old friends. Valerie cut in and we changed partners. "Enjoying yourself?" I asked Mum.

"Who would have thought your old Mum would ever go to a ritzy party like this? Look at me. Done up to the nines. And I've got you boys to thank. Don't think for a minute I don't know what youse both did to get me out of that old floral print dress of mine. I would have looked a right berk, and that's a fact."

"We only wanted you to have a good time."

"That I flaming well am. You know, that Cecil is a bit of all right. I could go him one."

I laughed out loud and couldn't help but notice Cecil kept looking over his shoulder to watch Mum. He seemed to have found if not a soul mate at least someone he could talk to at Valerie's incessant parties. I wasn't surprised when he tapped my shoulder seeking another dance with her. I was happy to relinquish as she was much too strenuous a partner for me.

I went to get myself a glass of punch, or something stronger if they had it, and was much delighted with the number of men who approached me to give me their business cards. They invited me to dine with them or else asked me to let them know when I moved to Macquarie Street. To them it seemed a fait accompli. I knew from experience these men got things done behind the scenes. I'd already been offered financing for the new surgery if my application was successful. I'd also been approached by tradesmen willing to supply the furniture I needed to kit out the premises and pay on the never-never.

If only my luck had been good in all departments.

I found myself a Scotch and soda and looked for Eric. He was dancing with a young woman with stars in her eyes. I hoped he would let her down gently. He nodded behind him and I glanced in the direction he pointed. Josh stood like a shag on a rock, not knowing where to look or how to stand as he was barraged by men trying to surreptitiously pick him up and by women wanting to dance with the handsome lug. He was keeping an eye on Enzo who was with a young beauty, hanging off her every word. There was only one reason for a man like Enzo to listen to the prattle of a young debutante. If she was a virgin, she wouldn't be by morning.

That explained Josh's woeful appearance. I grabbed another Scotch and soda and made my way over, pushing him out onto the balcony that led down into the garden. "Here, drink this, it might cheer you up."

He took the drink and sipped it. "Where are we going?" he asked suspiciously.

"Where I would like to go is home to bed."

"Damien..."

"It's all right, Josh. It's a dream. I just thought we could get some fresh air. You looked, uh, uncomfortable in there and I was rescuing you. As a friend."

We sat on a cement bench beneath a statue of some leering Greek or Roman god that I could not identify in the semi-darkness. We sat quietly for a moment listening to the crickets making their infernal racket. Josh placed his hand on my thigh.

"I'm so mixed up, Damien."

"Is it something Eric said?"

"He's a good man. I wish I had a friend like him."

"He can be your friend as well."

"No."

"He won't report back to me anything you say. He's not like that." I put my hand over his.

"I know."

"Then what is it?"

"I'm sorry." He tried to disguise a sob.

"What for?"

"I wrote to mum."

"How is she?"

"She asks after you. She knows we met again."

"Send her my love."

"I will."

Josh was silent for a long time. "I told her what you said about leaving me a note and sending me a letter. She took it into her own hands and marched straight down to Danny and confronted him. On his own. She gave him such a tongue lashing he broke down and admitted you'd left a note for me but he certainly wasn't gonna deliver a poofter's love letter. He also admitted that he'd bribed the postman to give him any letters addressed to me that were sent to Seaspray and he told her there had been one from you."

He squeezed my leg. Hard.

"I fucked up Damien. Really fucked up."

"We both did."

It was all out in the open now so why did we feel so wretched.

"What does Enzo have over you, Josh? You don't love him, do you?"

"He looked after mum when dad died."

"I'm so sorry. I didn't know your dad had passed away."

"Enzo saw how the worry about mum losing her cottage was troubling me so I couldn't sleep. He drove me up to see her. She didn't take to him at all. Thought he was too slick by half. But she was still grateful that he helped her out with the mine bosses. Threw his weight around a bit, some cash changed hands, and hey presto, mum's got the cottage for life or as long as she wants to stay there. That's why I owe him big."

"I can understand owing him your loyalty. But..."

"I think I told you I caught him getting sucked off by a bloke one day when I burst into his office."

I laughed. Josh looked at me as if to query what was funny.

"Remind me to tell you a story one day, Josh."

"After threatening that he would kill me if I ever told anyone what I saw, Enzo started looking at me funny. Every day I'd catch him staring at me. He started inviting me in to talk to him even though it was my job to look after his wife and daughter. One day he just spat it straight out, 'What's it like to be a queer?' I didn't know what he meant so he started asking questions and I answered as best I could. And he started getting excited. I could tell from the way he was breathing. And, well you know what a good looking sort he is."

"A very handsome man," I agreed.

"He wasn't you but I sucked his dick anyway. Then he buggered me. He wasn't gentle, but I didn't care much. He said he'd look after me. That's all I needed to hear."

"That doesn't explain why you're still with him."

"At first it was the sex. I got it mixed up with love. And he told me he loved me often enough but I'd heard him say the same things to the girls he fucked. And he fucked them twice as hard and twice as often now that he was doing me too. Like he was trying to prove something to himself. Sometimes he ignored me for weeks on end. I got horny. One day one of the other blokes in the gang tried it with me. He'd suspected me and finally got up the nerve to ask. Enzo had never said about others so I didn't see anything wrong with it. He found out. That bloke just disappeared off the face of the earth. Then Enzo made it very clear I was his and there was to be no touching."

"Can't you just leave?"

"He knows where mum is."

I could see his dilemma.

"You know the awful part?" he asked softly.

"No, Josh, what is it?"

"I love you so bloody much it hurts. I can't help it. I tried to hate you, to get you out of my head, but you won't go away. You're always in there."

I put my arm around his shoulder and he felt good against me until he shrugged me off. "Don't. You'll only put yourself in danger."

"Josh. Enzo sent me out here to find out what's wrong with you. With your permission, I'm going to tell him it's a slight mental disorder associated with your injuries and that I can cure it with hypnosis. He's also going to tell you to come back to my surgery for further check-ups. Will you do that?"

"What's the use? It will just make it harder."

"But at least we can see each other and maybe come up with a plan of action. All right?"

"I don't deserve you." He dropped his head and I smelled his hair and kissed him on the top of his head. He stood up to go back inside.

"Josh." He turned back to me. "Never forget I love you."

He went back into the house with a happier gait than I had seen all night.

CHAPTER TWELVE

~

THE END OF THE ROAD

I confess my heart was lighter for the remainder of the party even though I could see no way out of the impasse. If Josh and I were to run off to Melbourne to start a new life, Enzo would take revenge on Josh's mum and it would be comparatively easy to track us down. I found it strange that a man like Enzo who had a wife, a harem of working girls, plus Josh, could possibly get jealous. Perhaps the more one had the more possessive one became.

"You look happier," Valerie said. We were dancing together again after I had saved her from a death worse than tedium – a group of Cecil's cronies who had set out to prove they were a better alternative than her fiancé.

"Josh and I had a chance to talk openly and, at least now, we know what the odds are stacked against us."

"Impossible?"

"Let's just say daunting."

The remainder of the evening passed off without a fuss. Josh and I spent an inordinate amount of time smiling shyly at each other across the ballroom. We didn't get another chance to speak privately before Enzo whisked him away, promising to send him to my surgery for regular check-ups. Eric had taken Mum home earlier because he had to get up for work the next morning and, besides, he had found himself a tasty chorus boy morsel to snack on back at Mum's. I told them I would be fine and hop a lift with someone heading back toward the city, or else use one of the cabs that were hogging the mouth of the mansion's driveway in expectation of a fare.

As I watched the revelry dispassionately, I wondered whether I had done enough meeting and greeting, enough dancing with eligible young women, taken enough propositions from eligible young men, when the seductive voice once again whispered in my ear.

"Now that your young friend has departed you are all alone and in need of company." It wasn't a question. I felt a finger run up the arse crease of my trousers and I shivered. Of course, I would have preferred Josh but he would be back in Potts Point with the end of Enzo's delicious prick embedded in his backside or in his mouth. The thought of it excited me as well as repelled me. If Enzo hadn't been so damn attractive...

I leaned back against my admirer and felt his cock, rampant under his clothing, pressed against me.

"Care to join me for a cigarette, Dr. Bouton?"

"I don't smoke," I answered truthfully.

"Ah, but I do. Shall we say the same bench on which you and Mr. Fabrini's bodyguard shared such a romantic tête-à-tête early this evening? Five minutes, Dr. Bouton."

I tensed. I thought Josh and I had been so careful but someone had obviously seen us and overheard our plans. We were vulnerable to blackmail, or worse. My head ached at the thought of my career once again being in jeopardy. I got myself a stiff drink and, impatient for the five minutes to be up, headed to the garden as outwardly calm as I could muster. How I wished Eric was there to confide in. He would know what to do.

I strolled toward the seat. A young, well groomed lad about Josh's age sat smoking nonchalantly. I looked about to see if there was anyone else hovering. We were alone.

"Do sit down, Dr. Bouton. I won't bite." His smile was dazzling. Like that of a shark, I suspect.

I sat at the farthest edge of the bench. He laughed at my reticence.

"I'm not here to blackmail you, sir. Please relax. I have no intention of using any of the information I overheard accidentally between you and Fabrini's henchman."

He short-circuited my attempt to speak. "Yes, I reiterate accidentally. I was not following you, nor was I attempting to overhear your personal conversation. It was just unfortunate for you that I was engaged in relieving my bladder, the bathrooms inside the house being put to other uses at the time."

I relaxed visibly and examined my companion. Slim, brown hair, a moustache of the type common to bright young things of the era, a seductive smile, oh yes, he knew that smile of his was fatal. And he was turning it on me.

"Inside you suggested there were a few activities that you might like to perform upon my person," I said.

"Oh, very definitely. I hope you would wish to return the favour," he whispered.

"I would be delighted."

"Rodney Buchan." He offered me his hand, his grip firm and, I must say, arousing.

I was startled. "Not—"

"Please don't utter that awful cliché, 'Not the Rodney Buchan.' If you do I will be obliged to admit to it and you will immediately flee back to the protection of Cecil's bourgeois castle. So let's just pretend I'm just an ordinary everyday Rodney Buchan."

"I would certainly not seek to flee, as you put it, from a man whose work I have read with much interest, although not always agreeing with the arguments you have put forth."

He was genuinely surprised. "You've read my pamphlets?"

"I particularly admire your writings about the plight of factory workers for CSR in Pyrmont and Chippendale."

He ground his cigarette stub under foot and stood abruptly.

"Let's get out of here, shall we?" He held out his hand, pulling me up into his arms when I took it, and planted a strong, slow kiss on my lips. I didn't fight him even though we were in view of any partygoers standing on the mansion patio. When he released me, he said simply, "My place, I think."

He would not allow me to walk back into the party with him, suggesting rather that I follow after a suitable interval to make my farewells and then meet him at his car which was parked in the driveway. I dawdled after him and made a round of the ballroom to wish people goodnight, while watching him laughing and joking with Valerie. After he'd gone, I made my way over to her and Cecil who were holding court among a group of young people. They walked toward the vestibule thanking me profusely for coming to the party and I could honestly tell them I had a wonderful time.

I thanked them both for their friendship and the amazing contacts I had made that night.

"I think you'll particularly admire the attributes of young Mr. Buchan," Valerie said, patting me on the arse.

I jumped. "You don't miss anything do you?"

She smiled sweetly and kissed my cheek. "He's much more interesting than his reputation." Then she and Cecil walked back to their guests.

He had to be as his reputation was as a communist, and a rabid shit stirrer among the working class. He was the Sydney newspapers' whipping boy. They blamed him for everything from dock strikes to the bad weather and anything dire in between. The workers loved him, the bosses despised him and he'd suffered at the hands of hired thugs on many an occasion. It didn't pay to be seen with him.

However, even though he came from a privileged upper middle class background, he laboured diligently on behalf of the very folk I saw on a daily basis, the men and women who suffered incredible deprivation and disease because of the appalling conditions in which they worked. I had attempted to intervene on behalf of a number of my particularly brutalised patients but, in a period with rampant unemployment, factory owners essentially could do what they liked. I was pissing against the wind most of the time.

Rodney was waiting for me in his car, a nondescript vehicle that had broken windows and various dings to the doors. I knew it had little to do with his driving skills and more to do with his political activity. Was I afraid to be seen with him? Not in the slightest. Was it wise for me to be seen with him? Had I thought it through I would have said, 'No.' But with no solution to my 'problem' with Josh in sight, this man was excitement enough to help keep my mind occupied.

He lived in a rather luxurious house in Edgecliff, not all that far from Cecil although definitely on the wrong side of society's tracks. His home was a mass of papers, pamphlets, books and journals. He had one of the most extensive libraries I had ever seen and, yes, it contained the works of Karl Marx, George Bernard Shaw and other Fabians, plus Bertrand Russell and Nietzsche, scattered about his living and dining rooms. I only learned this later because his first objective was to get me straight away to his bedroom, a tidy and clutter-free oasis.

"Take your clothes off," he commanded me. "Let me look at you."

I did as he asked, standing naked and vulnerable before him. He ran his hands over my body admiringly although from what I could tell, his was the superior physique. He seemed in no hurry to undress himself, dropping to his knees, fully clothed, to lick the head of my cock which was hard and jutting against my stomach.

Squeezing my buttocks while running his finger into my arse crack, he sucked off the pearl of sperm on the head of my prick, and swallowed. He was quite a sight, this attractive young man, worshipping my masculinity, taking me into his mouth and then withdrawing so I could watch the penetration. Before I knew it he had his face buried to my pubic hair and I felt his throat contract around my shaft as he tried not to gag.

He was an expert at orally servicing me and I had to push him off otherwise I would have exploded much too soon. Standing reluctantly, he kissed me, his tongue slick with my pre-ejaculate. He attempted to stop me undressing him and it was only after I'd removed his shirt that I saw the reason for his reluctance. His upper left arm was red from where he'd been burned. I ran my fingers over it and he shuddered, probably from the memory of the injury rather than from pain, before I moved to his chest and pinched his nipples sending a very different sort of shudder down his body.

Now that I had seen his scar and accepted it, he shucked his trousers quickly and we fell naked on to the bed. Impatient with preliminaries, Rodney turned me over and I heard him fumble in the bedside table before I felt a cold salve invading my arse. He speared two fingers inside, liberally coating my hole. Kneeling behind me he slid slowly inside, hesitating lest he hurt me. He was of average size and the invasion was pleasurable. Once I had opened up sufficiently to accommodate him easily he pulled out. I turned over and he pushed my legs back for better penetration so I could watch the concentration on his face as he slipped back inside me.

Unlike Josh, he was an expert lover, beginning slowly and building up force. I watched him intently, the sweat trickling down the sides of his face from his hairline, biting his bottom lip in concentration, pure joy crinkling the sides of his eyes. After he had coasted for a while, fucking me smoothly, wanking my cock until I pleaded with him to stop or I would come too soon, he picked up pace and rammed harder forcing my body further into the mattress. As he leaned over to kiss me, hard, his cock battered my arse. I clenched each time he pushed into me, attempting to milk his prick.

He was unable to hold off and about ten minutes after his initial assault on my rear he shot his spunk inside me. I felt his cock twitch as it spewed its seed. I held him, feeling his heart thudding against my chest.

His recuperation was swift, he was younger than me, and after pulling out he insisted we swap positions as I had not as yet ejaculated. We repeated the experience, this time with me on top but I was much too excited and barely lasted five minutes before I returned the favour and dumped my load inside his inviting warm hole.

We fell asleep in each other's arms to wake when sunlight cascaded through his large bedroom windows to repeat the experiences. We fell into an easy camaraderie as we bathed and he made breakfast all the while keeping up a running commentary on his political work. I was genuinely interested and managed to get in a few perspicacious questions. He offered to drop me back in Pyrmont, an offer I gladly accepted, but not before he honoured me with an invitation to inspect his inner sanctum.

It was a locked room in which he kept his books, his notes, and his own writings on human sexuality. He had an encyclopaedic knowledge of queer history and queer lives. He showed me one of his prized possessions, a letter from the German sexuality pioneer, Dr. Magnus Hirschfeld, of whom I knew little. The brief tour over, he invited me to make use of any of his material, including his bed, at any time. I would be more than happy to take him up on that offer.

Our schedules didn't allow for meeting more than once a fortnight, always at his home. I enjoyed his company and his conversation. He never attempted to influence my political opinions, in fact we never discussed party politics, but we were as one on the dreadful conditions that some workers were forced to endure and sought ways to alleviate their suffering through medical and legal channels.

Another reason for the infrequency of our trysts was that I still had Josh on my mind. I'd taken the liberty of discussing him with Rod, as I now called him, but he could shed no light on a plausible course of action. He had an uneasy truce with the gangs who left him alone because he did not impinge on their entrepreneurial activities and his union work often helped their working class family members who toiled as manual labourers.

Josh's weekly visits, ostensibly for a check-up, were painful because he would not give in physically, worried that Enzo would know if he had made love with another man although I did manage to suck his cock on a few occasions and he reciprocated on a few more. We spent a lot of time in each other's arms, kissing and swearing our love but getting no further in our dream of one day living together. He was on edge all the time and seemed ready to explode at the slightest provocation. I prescribed pills to calm him down but he refused to take them saying they made his reflexes sluggish.

More concerning was the increasing rumours of disquiet among the gangs whose skirmishes into one another's territory were threatening to escalate into all-out warfare. I dreaded to think that Josh was in the thick of it and would bear the brunt of any assault that occurred.

I missed talking with Eric, having his own problems with his partner John who was buckling under the strain of their enforced separation because of their awkward working hours, to the extent that he was thinking of taking up an offer from Cecil to accompany him to London as his valet. Unfortunately, they did not need a cook, John's area of expertise.

Valerie was busy too, packing for her imminent departure for, she hoped, fame and fortune in the West End. I would miss her dreadfully. The only person who still managed to be bright and cheery day in and day out, was Mum, although even she was slowing with the advancing years.

It was about six weeks after Valerie's engagement party that Bert came to see me at the surgery. Mum brought him in. By his ear. She had a grip of iron on his lobe and forced him, shaking and terrified, into the patient's chair of my surgery, then stood, a mountain of impassable flesh, to prevent his escape.

"Go on, tell him." Her tone brooked no argument.

Bert, whose girlfriend, Kitty, I had helped when I first arrived in Sydney, looked sullenly at the floor. He'd promised he owed me in the wake of Kitty's recovery, but I'd never expected to collect. Mum seemed to think he had some information that was of vital importance.

She clipped him across the back of the head. Hard.

Reluctantly he shifted in his seat and his masculine pride returned. He faced me and pleaded, "Doc, you gotta swear on your life that this goes no further. I dunno what you can do but there's real lives at stake here. It involves your young man." He'd seen Josh at Mum's often enough now to know we were a little more than doctor and patient.

The blood froze in my veins.

Mum became more threatening. "Go on."

"There's to be an ambush." Bert paused, reconciling himself to the fact he would not be allowed to leave this room alive without spilling the beans. "Tilly wants Enzo Fabrini out of the picture once and for all. He's got too big for his boots, so she says. Always horning in on her turf. She's gonna put a stop to it." Tilly Devine was his boss and the underworld overlord of the patch of territory at Woolloomooloo.

"How?" I asked.

"She's arranged a meeting. Neutral territory in Darlinghurst. Fabrini and Tilly. Sitting down to discuss how they can combine for a bigger share of the market. So she says. And so he thinks. But it's a trap. She's scoped it out. Fabrini and his gang will be wedged down an alley when they get there. They won't stand a chance."

"Is Fabrini stupid enough to fall for it?"

"He's got so arrogant he thinks he's untouchable, particularly with that bodyguard of his. Your mate's already got him out of a couple of near misses. He's marked for the chop as well."

Josh earmarked for murder.

"I gotta tell ya, doc. I'm shit scared. If it gets out I ratted, I'm as good as dead. But you did right by me and Kitty, and I owe ya. I tried to get Mum to pass on the message but..." He looked at the woman who currently towered over him.

"I'm grateful, Bert. Very grateful," I replied.

"But I'm between a rock and a hard place, doc. If I don't tell ya, it's him that's dead. If you tell him, it's me that'll sleep six foot under at Rookwood. And I don't feel me time is up just yet."

I cared little about Bert's final resting place. "When's this meeting scheduled?"

"Day after tomorra. It was done quick so there'd be no fuck ups." He cringed expecting a blow from Mum for swearing. But she was too pre-occupied to notice.

"Thanks, Bert. I promise I won't tell Josh. I'll find a way out of this that doesn't involve you."

"Off you go," Mum said and Bert scampered from the room. "And keep your trap shut!" she shouted after him.

"You think he's telling the truth?"

"Yeah. Bert hasn't got the imagination to be fanciful."

I clasped my hands and rested my chin on them thinking hard for a solution.

"You gonna tell Josh?"

"Not unless I have to. I know I promised Bert I wouldn't, but when it comes down to it, I'd swap Bert's life for Josh's any day. I hope it won't come to that. If I tell Josh, he'll feel honour-bound to tell Enzo and that will lead to an all-out gang war."

"I'll leave you alone to think. But you know you can count on me for anything." She came over to ruffle my hair, her gentle way of showing affection. "You boys are like family to me. I don't want to see anything happen to you."

I sat at my desk a few minutes longer after she left. For the life of me, I had no idea what to do. I ventured out into the hall to enquire if any patients were waiting to see me. There were none so far that day. I found Mum in the back yard poking sheets into the vast bubbling copper with a long wooden handle; it was wash day. The evidence of her earlier labours were already flapping on the line in the lazy breeze.

"There's no one waiting, Mum, so I thought I might have a lie down," I told her. She knew I did my best thinking lying on the lounge in my darkened sitting room.

"All right, love. I'll tap if anyone comes wanting you. If it's not urgent, I'll tell 'em to come back this afternoon."

The cool front room was usually conducive to resting my brain but this morning, as I napped, I was visited by nightmares of the most horrific kind, all ending with Josh, bloody and lifeless, face down in a narrow laneway in Darlinghurst.

CHAPTER THIRTEEN

~

TAKEN FOR A RIDE

*T*here was feverish activity at the door to the surgery. Normally, Mum Doreen would knock lightly and let me know there was a patient in the waiting room, her kitchen, where she would regale them with a 'cuppa tea' and a good gossip. This time she crashed through the door without so much as a by-your-leave.

"In here, boys," she shouted. "Quickly. Quickly."

It had to be urgent for her to disregard even the few social niceties I'd attempted, mainly unsuccessfully, to instill in her. I didn't mind so much, she was a good old chook. I stood up from my desk ready to give a hand with whatever catastrophe was coming my way. Two burly brutes from the wharves half dragged, half carried a battered and bleeding body into the room. In the blink of an eye, I recognised Josh and my stomach clenched.

"Where do you want him, doc?" one of them asked as they manhandled him into the surgery.

I bit back my alarm at seeing Josh in this condition and assumed a professional demeanour. It would do no good to come unstuck in front of these men.

"Up on the bench, lads. Careful."

Josh moaned in pain. At least he was still conscious. Mum had already bustled off to the kitchen for hot water to wash the blood from his face. I examined him quickly, noticing as I did so that he looked much worse than he actually was. Someone had done an impeccable job.

"What happened?" I asked as I examined his cuts and abrasions.

The lads removed their caps and shuffled about on their feet as if they wanted to be anywhere but here.

"Well, sir," the older of the two said. "We work on the wharves and there's a bit of a to-do at the moment. You may have heard about it."

"Yes, a lot of your fellow workers are my patients."

From my own experience, ministering to the men who loaded and unloaded the ships, I had learned of the miserable wages and terrible conditions under which they worked. Slave labour in all but title, their jobs eagerly sought by the thousands of unemployed in the worst depression in memory. Plus, there was my friendship, and bedship, with socialist and union organiser, Rodney Buchan. His influence was strong.

"Well, this young lad was walking by and got himself caught up in the melee when a group of scabs were tryin' to enter the wharves."

"It were over as soon as it started," the younger of the two added helpfully.

"No one were hurt but then we saw this lad lyin' on the footpath—"

"Blood everywhere."

"We thought he was a scab at first but Mr. Buchan—

"He knows everyone."

"He says that he's no scab, he was just a innocent bystander."

"He got one of the lorries to drop us up here with the lad. Told us you was all right as a doc. So—

"Here we are. We know no more."

"And no less."

The story had been beautifully rehearsed.

"No witnesses?"

"Not a one." The young man shook his head gravely, then rather spoiled the whole effect by winking at me.

"Police been called?"

"It was urgent we got the lad to medical treatment. It will be up to him if he wants the cops involved."

"Thanks, men. I know where to contact you if I need you." I winked back at them as a way of telling them they had done a superb job. Out of sight of Josh I examined their hands, their knuckles skinned and grazed. I cleaned the abrasions but did not dress them as it would single them out in a crowd. "Go see Mum Doreen in the kitchen. I'm sure she'll have a nice cuppa and a few biscuits as a reward for being good Samaritans."

They mumbled their thanks and left the room jostling. Mum came in shortly after with a basin of hot water. "Is he all right?"

"He'll be fine," I assured her. "There's a lot of blood but no permanent damage. He might need a few stitches. And he'll certainly have a black eye or two. That's about the full extent of the damage that I can see."

Josh groaned, attempting to get up off the bench. The exertion opened up one of the cuts above his eye and blood oozed, blinding him briefly.

"What the fuck?" He was annoyed at his incapacity, wiping the blood on the back of his hand, merely smearing it across his face.

"Lie down, Josh," I insisted. "You are in no fit condition to get up until I've dressed your injuries. Now, they're not life threatening, but they are serious. The sooner you let me attend to them, the sooner you'll be back up on your feet again."

Not too soon, though, I hoped, because tomorrow was the big meeting between Fabrini and Tilly Devine, the meeting at which Josh and his boss would be ambushed and slaughtered. I had not slept in days, trying to come up with a plan to save Josh's life. I cared little for Fabrini, although I did not treat human life lightly. Yes, Enzo Fabrini was a charming man: I had sucked his cock and been buggered by him on more than one occasion. But, as well as being Josh's lover, he ran brothels, trafficked in narcotics, and was responsible for not a few murders. Oh, he never got blood on his own hands; he had henchmen to do that. And take the fall. I had no doubt that would also be Josh's fate when Fabrini tired of him.

I could not tell Josh about the planned ambush, he would be honour bound to tell Fabrini. That would lead to an all-out gang war. I could not go to the police because, at the very least, Josh would be arrested. The most heinous result would be the police would allow the ambush to go ahead and then arrest the killers. That way, they would get the best all-round outcome as well as the front page of *The Daily Mirror*. If the arrests came before the event, it was likely those arrested would all be back on the streets in a matter of hours with little more to show for it than a rap on the wrist from a judge on their payroll.

I had gone to Rodney with my dilemma. Multiple dilemmas really.

As he pushed me back on the bed and hoisted my legs over his shoulders, positioning his cock at my arse entrance, he asked, "Do you trust me?"

"Implicitly." I grimaced as he sank into my bowels. His cock was big enough to sting pleasantly for a few moments. It was worth it for the right royal buggering he delivered almost immediately my sphincter relaxed.

"All right. Leave it with me. But you have to promise me one thing."

"What is it?" I asked as he increased his speed.

"I'll save Josh. As a bonus I'll get rid of Fabrini from his life."

I was about to object when Rodney put his hand over my mouth.

"Best you not know what I'm going to do because Fabrini is an implacable enemy. Just trust me and go with the flow."

"What do I have to promise?"

"That if, after all this, Josh still rejects your advances that you consider my offer to take his place. Agreed?"

"Agreed."

It would not hurt to humour Rodney on this point. He had been at me for ages now to become his permanent lover, to the extent of asking me to share his home as well as his life. It was tempting. I genuinely liked him. I admired his courage and his convictions. He was damned good in bed. We had a lot in common. But he wasn't Josh. And I didn't love him. I knew, though, I couldn't keep pursuing Josh forever. I had a life of my own to lead. If he simply was not interested in a future together with me then it was time to let it go, time to consider Rodney's offer. Or Valerie's, to accompany her and her husband-to-be to London where I could start afresh.

I had to assume that Josh's bloody injuries were the result of Rodney's scheme to save him. I was grateful. Earlier in the day, I'd just about given up hope, lingering over my examination of Josh when he'd attended for his weekly check-up. It had been on his way back from that he'd been attacked.

His face was puffy and at least one of his eyes was closing up. I'd stitched up one of the wounds, which was deeper and more savage than the others. The men who had worked him over had been experts. The cuts, made with razors, had been superficial but designed for maximum blood loss without actually harming him. This, coupled with his other injuries, would put him out of circulation for about a week.

Not that he would sit still for it for a moment. He was attempting to get up from the bench even as I was dressing his injuries.

"Lie still, Josh, or I'll end up doing more damage," I pleaded.

"You don't understand. I've got to be up and ready for tomorrow. Enzo needs me."

"Enzo will just have to go on needing you. You're in no fit state to go anywhere. By tonight, that eye of yours will be totally closed up. You won't be able to see a thing. And the second one doesn't look so hot either. You may have concussion." I was laying it on thick.

"I have to be there with him tomorrow."

"What's so important about tomorrow? Can't it wait a day or two longer? Even a week?" I had to pretend not to know what he was talking about.

"It can't be postponed. It would look suspicious. He's counting on me. I gotta be there."

"The only place you'll be tomorrow is resting in bed." He struggled against me and I was becoming exasperated. Rodney's plan was not working. "If you don't lie back and let me tend to your injuries, Josh, I'll be forced to give you a sedative."

He lay back down quietly but far from happy.

"What happened to you?" I asked.

"I was down near the Monty, you know, the pub near the bridge. There was a bit of a barney going on between a group of wharfies and some scabs. I was about to catch the tram across the bridge so I wouldn't get involved when some bastards jumped me and lay the boot in. Next thing I know, I'm down on the footpath and those two blokes were picking me up and half dragging me back here. What's the damage?"

"Cuts, bruises, lots of blood, a cracked rib or two. Nothing too serious that I've found so far. You could have concussion. You feel any broken bones?"

"Nah, nothing like that."

I knew it was pointless asking him. He'd say anything to get away from the surgery. It pissed me off, frankly. If he'd put as much energy into our relationship we might still be together. As it was, I felt distinctly second rate and, I'm afraid, it began to show in my behaviour. I was needlessly rough with him and I noticed his eyebrow rise in surprise but I was trying to think of another way of keeping him from returning to Enzo.

There was a knock on the door. It was Mum.

"How are you, love?" she enquired.

"Not bad, Mum. Not bad. Nothing that one of your nice cuppas wouldn't fix."

"My sentiments exactly, young man," she smiled. "I was about to bring one in but there's two gentlemen at the door for you, love. Come to take you to the hospital. There's an ambulance and everything."

Josh looked at me.

"I didn't call for an ambulance," I said.

"Tell them to go away," Josh said. "I don't need an ambulance."

Two men pushed their way into the surgery. "Your benefactor would not be pleased to hear you say that, lad. He's spared no expense getting you the very best medical treatment money can buy. Beggin' your pardon, doc. It's no reflection on your obvious ability."

"I take no offence," I said, grateful for their intervention. Enzo could have sent them, though I doubted he would have had time to hear of Josh's injuries let alone organise anything like this. That left only Rodney. It had to be part of his plan. Either way, it appeared likely Josh would be out of action on the morrow. Unless, of course, Enzo suspected a plot and wanted a second opinion as to his bodyguard's condition. I was getting paranoid.

"Who's my benefactor then?" Josh demanded.

One of the strangers tapped the side of his nose. "The gent in question prefers to remain anonymous. He is someone very concerned with your well-being who wishes you a speedy recovery. He knows you will be eager to get back on the job but understands you will need a few days to get your strength back.

"Enzo," Josh sighed.

The strangers did not correct him. I noticed they had couched the description in terms that could apply to just about anyone. Even Rodney. But, it calmed Josh right down and he was meek as a lamb as they stretchered him to the ambulance outside around which had gathered quite a motley collection of locals come to gawp.

"Is he dead, mister?' one of the local kids asked, disappointed when I said he wasn't.

"Crikey, look at that shiner," another boy whistled as Josh was placed carefully in the back of the vehicle.

The driver handed me a card with the name of a private clinic. He added, "You're expected around four."

Mum had been fussing over him, making him comfortable, taking his mind off the unusual nature of the attack and the even stranger subsequent events. I told Josh I would be along to see him later this afternoon as the back door of the vehicle closed.

When they'd left, she nodded after the disappearing ambulance. "You think he's safe now?"

"It looks that way," I replied, "although I won't be happy until another thirty-six hours have passed. Enzo could prove unpredictable."

And so he did, although not in the manner I expected. When I arrived at the private clinic and was ushered into Josh's room, it was ablaze with flowers, so many in fact it looked for all the world like a florist's. It was Enzo's method of not only letting Josh know he was missed but also that others should keep their hands off. However, it wasn't the flowers that grabbed my attention but rather Josh's leg. His bad leg. It was wrapped in a plaster cast from his thigh to his toes and elevated by means of a pulley system over the bed.

"What on earth happened, Josh?" I rushed to the bed.

"Ah," a voice emanated from somewhere in the foliage. "Dr. Bouton. Punctual, I see."

A man in a white coat approached me with outstretched hand. "I'm Dr. Delaney. Thanks so much for coming. I was just attempting to find a power point to plug in an old radio for Mr. Carter, but the jungle has taken over. I should not be surprised to find a pygmy tribe living under the bed."

"I'm bored shitless, Damien."

"I'll get a nurse to come and plug you in, Mr. Carter. Perhaps, you would accompany me, Dr. Bouton."

I quickly shoved my meagre little get-well gift at Josh. It was so puny in comparison to Enzo's extravagance. But I had neither the money nor the lackeys to do my bidding.

I followed Dr. Delaney down the pristine corridor to his office. He sat down, not behind the desk, as I would have expected, but in a chair alongside me.

"It's a real pleasure to meet you, Dr. Bouton. Your reputation precedes you."

I laughed. "Good or bad?"

"That would depend on which side of the political divide you favoured. Me, I have an affinity with the likes of our mutual friend, Mr. Buchan. I see you smile."

"I was unsure who had organised the ambulance that appeared from nowhere. I'd believed it to be Mr. Buchan but there was always the slight possibility it came from Enzo Fabrini."

He screwed up his nose in distaste. "The horticulturalist."

We both laughed at his little joke.

"His leg?" I was curious.

"Very effective," Dr. Delaney said with a superior smile. "It stopped Mr. Fabrini in his tracks. He followed his gaudy floral tributes by about thirty minutes and immediately began to throw his weight around, though to little effect here. He was under the impression he could take Joshua home with him. A contingency we had not overlooked. Thus the very theatrical cast on his leg, and enough medical obfuscation on our part that Mr. Fabrini was quite convinced by the time he left that young Mr. Carter may never walk again."

"How long will he be here?" I asked.

"At least a week, and then I have instructions to release him into your care. After that, the cast is to remain on for another two to three weeks. We are not suggesting that his leg is broken, just that it was injured in his fall and that as a result it may do untold damage to his original surgery leaving him unable to walk without a cane. Both Mr. Carter and Mr. Fabrini bought the suggestion."

"I don't know how I can possibly repay you, Dr. Delaney. You can't possibly know how much this means to me." I was becoming emotional.

"Perhaps there is something you could do, if you wished, but there is no compulsion as Mr. Carter's stay with us has all been taken care of."

"Just name it," I said.

"How would you feel about spending one day a week, helping with the patients at the clinic? You will be amply rewarded for your labours. You would be doing me a great favour; I am spending less time with patients and more and more shuffling papers."

"As I think I am about to lose a most lucrative patient in the next few days, that would fill a gap nicely." The loss of which I was thinking was Enzo Fabrini and his stable of prostitutes whom I checked once a week for venereal diseases. It would be quite a step up to work with Dr. Delaney's prestigious clinic. Don't mistake my meaning: I am not a snob. But I would be more likely to meet wealthy clients here and thus subsidise my work in Pyrmont, which relied on payment on the never-never.

"Good. Good. Come and see me when this business is all over. I know only my part in the scheme of things—" he held his hands up to prevent my telling him anything at all. "No, Dr. Bouton, I don't wish to know. Please allow me to be as surprised as anyone at the manner in which it unfolds. I'm afraid I'm a dreadful actor. Now, off with you to your young man."

I didn't need to be told twice and made my way back to Josh's room. He was smiling broadly as he thumbed through a paperback I had brought. He looked up as I entered his room. "You're a lifesaver, Damien. Just when I thought I was gonna die of boredom you bring just the right thing for me. I can't believe you remembered what I liked to read."

"Of course, I remembered. Paperback westerns and that confounded new woman and her Belgian detective you're so fond of."

He patted the bed beside me, inviting me to sit. He took my hand. "I know the doctor talked about me. Is it serious? Will I be able to walk when they take the cast off?"

He looked so concerned I just wanted to fold him in my arms and reassure him everything would be all right. But I had to play my part. If only because something could go wrong. "There is some concern that you injured your bad leg and it may lead to complications and a more pronounced limp and Dr. Delaney is taking no chances."

"That's a great big cast for a few little complications."

"Better safe than sorry."

Josh looked concerned. "Enzo was none too pleased I can tell you," he confided.

"It's only for a few weeks. Surely he can do without you for that length of time."

"Damien, don't say anything, but big things are afoot and I was to be part of them. Now I'll miss out and I'm not sure he'll ever forgive me."

"I'd forgive you anything, Josh."

"Don't. You know we can't."

I sighed and he let go of my hand.

"I'm not sure Enzo would have believed I'd been injured if it had just come from you. He was highly sceptical."

"Of what?"

"I can't say, Damien. Don't ask for more details. I told him you had just patched me up and someone else had sent an ambulance to bring me here. He pretended it wasn't him. Dr. Delaney calmed down his suspicions."

I stayed an hour and, to entertain Josh whose second eye was beginning to close from the beating, although not as badly as the first, I read aloud to him from his westerns. He lay back and my heart ached with love for this beautiful young man. Occasionally my affection caught in my throat and Josh would glance at me strangely. I threw myself into my reading and was well satisfied when Josh began to snore. Kissing the top of his head I left the clinic and, in a daze, walked back through the city and over the bridge, my mind a swirl of possibilities for the future.

No matter what happened tomorrow, I would have to make decisions I had been putting off for far too long.

CHAPTER FOURTEEN

~

RIDING THE WHIRLWIND

*A*ll hell broke loose the next day. There was little I, or anyone, could do but hold on tight and ride the whirlwind. By that evening the main storm had passed although the ripple on effects were still being felt, and would be for weeks, if not months to come. The whole affair is a blur in my mind now although at the time each new piece of information was seared into my brain because of its immediacy and the hopes I had riding on its outcome.

For me it didn't happen in an orderly narrative like in a novel. It was delivered to me piecemeal, like a jigsaw puzzle that I had to put together myself. I spent the day in jitters scarcely able to perform my duties, sending away all but the most serious cases. Mum, too, usually as stalwart and reliable as the weekly dunny cart men, paced the kitchen enough that she'd wear a groove in the kitchen's linoleum if the tension lasted more than a day.

I was due to visit Josh at the clinic late in the afternoon, by which time the afternoon papers would have printed their final editions. If there was any report on Enzo and Tilly Devine it would be on the streets before I reached the hospital. It was unreasonable to expect the outcome might be kept from Josh. I had no contingencies worked out on how I would approach the news in his presence. I would adapt to the circumstances. The situation was so fluid that it changed more regularly than the tides.

Just after lunch, news began to trickle in. First was a runner from Rodney Buchan, followed shortly by word from Bert, who had managed to escape with a minor injury. I was able to patch him up reasonably well in my small surgery and the insufficient seriousness of his wound meant that I did not have to report it to the police. I could not afford to get involved to the extent it would bring down police action on my medical practice.

A little later I received word that Josh had been moved, for his own protection, to another private hospital the name of which I would learn when I visited that afternoon. I was not to do anything irregular, as Dr. Delaney believed that the clinic was being watched, by whom his note did not specify. Realising I would be impatient for information, all he would impart was that Josh was well, although he had been attacked in his bed at the hospital, and that he was in no immediate danger, at least not from his injuries.

I duly turned up at the clinic around four o'clock, frantic for news but keeping my composure, with much difficulty, until I was in Dr. Delaney's office. The questions tumbled out of me, one after the other; I was gabbling, making little sense. He allowed me to continue uninterrupted until I had exhausted myself and sat quietly, catching my breath.

"Feel better?" he said smiling, in case I took it as patronising.

I took a few deep breaths. "Much better."

"What you need to know, first and foremost, is that Mr. Carter is well and in fine spirits, if somewhat bored, but that seems to be his usual state. We moved him for his own safety. Unfortunately, he was attacked here, in the clinic, early this afternoon by a visitor. In checking with staff and with reception, they confirmed the man arrived in an extremely agitated state demanding to see Mr. Carter on a matter of utmost urgency. The visitor threatened the woman at reception with physical violence so she gave him directions. She then went in search of an orderly to tell him what had occurred. By the time he arrived at Mr. Carter's room, the assailant had his arm around Mr. Carter's head threatening to cut his throat, while Mr. Carter was yelling that he didn't know what the stranger was talking about. In the confusion the wards man, a quick thinking lad, picked up a metal bedpan that was lying on a gurney just inside the door. His aim was quick and true and, voila, one unconscious killer."

"Where is he now?"

"We have the attacker locked in one of the padded rooms until we decide what to do with him."

"I meant Josh."

"Oh, of course. His exact location is a secret. It will be divulged to you in due course. I apologise for the secrecy but it is necessary, as you will see soon enough. Now, if you will excuse me, I have much to contend with today."

I was distracted and far from happy with the obfuscation but had to content myself with the knowledge that others with cooler heads than mine were guiding the day's events to a satisfactory outcome.

As he showed me to the door, Dr. Delaney handed me a sturdy walking cane with a heavy metal bauble atop the handle. "It would be to your benefit, just for today, to avail yourself of this walking stick, Dr. Bouton. It is not valuable so were you to lose it or otherwise dispose of it, it's of no concern. I'm sure we will meet up again soon."

He disappeared down the corridor, leaving me frustrated and flabbergasted in his wake. I clutched the stick, finely balanced and plain but beautifully hand carved mahogany. I suppose I was stupid not to realise its significance; I can only plead my confused state of mind. I learned soon enough. As I stepped out into the quiet street that served as the entrance to the clinic a group of men appeared from nowhere and set upon me. They took me quite by surprise so that it was a few moments before I could make an impression with my cane. I whacked a few heads and cheeks with it, knocking one lad to the ground. I knocked him unconscious and managed to clip the knee of another sending him screaming in agony on top of his mate, before somebody grabbed me from behind.

I was outnumbered; inevitably, at the mercy of a large group. They manhandled me roughly and thrust me up against the brick wall of a terrace house abutting the laneway; hands gripped my throat pressing me on to tiptoes. The cane was confiscated, snatched from my grasp and held threateningly in the air.

"You put up quite a fight for an old bloke," he said.

I spluttered indignantly, more hurt by the accusation of being an 'old bloke' than by the lack of oxygen to my lungs.

"Now, granddad," he continued. "What have you done with Josh?"

I attempted to squeak an answer, signalling that I was unable to breathe let alone speak. He relaxed his grip, allowing me to stand more steadily. One of his offsiders opened a mean looking razor.

"Don't attempt anything or you'll be sorry," he warned.

I straightened my collar and tie, smoothed down the front of my coat, and looked the leader square in the eye. "If all you'd wanted was information, all you had to do was ask. There was no need to rough me up."

He shrugged smugly. "The lads do like their bit of fun. All in a day's work. Now, where's Josh?"

"Even if I did know, which I don't, I wouldn't tell you." I was not happy with this turn of events.

The thug raised his fist level with my face, holding his arm back, cocked like a spring.

"You can threaten all you like, but I don't know."

"Aren't you his doctor?"

"I'm his GP, but he needed specialist care for his leg, the one that was injured in the mining accident. The reason why he's banged up and in a cast."

He lowered his fist. "Why'd they move him?"

"That I do know," I said co-operatively, hoping to buy time if not my freedom. "Sometime early this afternoon, as Josh's specialist tells it, a bloke rushed into the clinic and attempted to slice open Josh's throat."

"Who was it?" one of the men asked.

"Should give him a medal," another harrumphed.

"Look, I wasn't here when it happened; I just came to visit. All I know is some man attacked Josh and they've moved him for his own safety. His doctor hasn't told anyone, including the staff where he's been taken."

The leader grabbed me by the throat once again and I was marched back into the clinic, nurses scattering before us, wards men shadowing our movements, kept at bay by the razors.

Pre-warned, Dr. Delaney came out of his office to greet us.

"Gentlemen, what can I do to help you?" He smiled warmly, showing no fear.

"You can tell us where you've taken Josh," the leader said.

"I'm afraid I can't do that. Patient confidentiality and all that." He kept his voice chatty and non-belligerent.

"I don't know about patient whatchamacallit but I do know that the doc here," he indicated me with his thumb, "will get himself mighty cut up if you don't tell us what we want to know."

"Oh? I don't think that will change my mind," Dr. Delaney said calmly. I wished I had his confidence. I had a sharp razor at my throat and felt blood trickle from where it had grazed me already.

"Why's that?" the leader asked, clearly puzzled that Dr. Delaney did not show more fear.

"Because the man you're holding is of no concern to me. You can only blackmail me into revealing information by holding someone about whom I care. That man is of less concern to me than one of my patients. You can do what you like with him. I'd rather you did it outside however, as the cleaners complain about blood on the floor." So saying, he turned and began to walk away, to the consternation of my attackers.

"I mean it," the leader bellowed.

The doctor turned, steel faced and determined. "If you mean it, then do it! I have sick people to attend." He turned away, then, as if he'd forgotten something, turned back. "I think it only fair to warn you, to give you a sporting chance, that if you make any further cuts to my colleague's throat and you and your men will, in turn, be cut down and killed. If you care to turn around you will find this is no idle threat."

One of my attackers must have done just that for he swore violently. "Shit, he's not kidding. They've got guns."

The man holding me spun us both around to face the threat, a short way down the corridor a number of men aimed pistols at my captors.

"Now, gentlemen, if you would be so good as to hand me your weapons, we can sit down and discuss the situation calmly." Dr. Delaney was standing beside us now. One of the men reached over to grab him as a shield, a bullet whizzed through the air tearing into the palm of his hand.

"Do as you're told," the leader said reluctantly. Dr. Delaney and I relieved the attackers of their razors and knuckle-dusters, before handing them to one of the fake wards men. A nurse took the injured man away for help.

"Now, gentlemen, if you would be so kind as to join me." They followed him meekly along the corridor, probably planning how to turn the tables, until he stopped abruptly in front of one of the rooms. He slid aside a panel in the door and beckoned me forward. I shook my head I had never seen the man before. Then he invited the leader of the assailants to look inside.

"That's one of Tilly's gang," the leader said, the other members of his group crowding around the peep window to see for themselves. They all confirmed his identification.

"Is that the bastard tried to top Josh?"

"Yes," the doctor said.

"What are you going to do with him?" the leader asked suspiciously.

"We haven't decided yet," the doctor said.

"Josh is all right, ain't he?"

"He's perfectly fine." Dr. Delaney then surprised us all. "Would you like to see him?"

"Yeah," the leader said. "That's all we ever wanted to do."

"Well, you went about it the wrong way." Dr. Delaney laid down some ground rules. They would be taken to Josh's new location but only if they agreed to be blindfolded. Secrecy was paramount to Josh's safety. "Of course, your companion who has been shot will remain here and you can pick him up upon your return."

"How do we know this is not some sort of trap?" the leader asked reasonably.

"You have my word. If we meant you any harm, we could easily have shot you down in the corridor and claimed you had stormed the hospital, armed and dangerous. After one near fatal attack this morning, we could say we were not prepared to take any further chances and when you threatened

Dr. Bouton here, we cut you down in self defence. No judge or jury in the land would convict us. That, gentlemen, is my final offer. Take it or leave it."

There was much grumbling but they reluctantly agreed. "Dr. Bouton will come with me but he, too, will be masked." I made a pretence of grumbling which placated the other men who were led away. I followed Dr. Delaney to his office where he sat down behind his desk and phoned a number of instructions to various people. Then he called for afternoon tea to be brought to his study. He asked me to join him in the book-filled room that opened off his office. It was light and calm and we seated ourselves in plush leather armchairs beside a small antique table.

"Refreshments will be along in a moment. I also took the liberty of ordering a few sandwiches." He leaned over to examine my neck. "Superficial. A little blood. We'll get that cleaned up before you go. Best leave it for now."

I kept looking at the clock wondering when we were going to start off, but Dr. Delaney seemed unperturbed. About half an hour passed and I was getting increasingly restless when there was a knock at the door.

"Ah, it's time," he said as he stood up. We walked out and farther into the hospital wards until we paused in front of a door marked with the patient name, Neil Wilkie. It meant nothing to me. The doctor handed me a mask. "Here, put this on. The others will be here soon."

"You devious bastard," I laughed as I tied the mask at the back of my head. I heard the others stumbling along cursing and jostling in frustration. I greeted them as they reached the door and Dr. Delaney knocked before we were ushered into the room and told we could remove our masks. I remembered to rub my eyes at the light.

Josh was startled to see us all congregating in his room. He barely glanced at me before launching into questions of his gang mates. He motioned to a newspaper he had been reading. "Is it true?"

"They got Fred," the leader said, sitting on the side of the bed. He seemed to have a rapport with Josh, who made the right guttural sounds at Fred's demise.

"I told Enzo not to believe that cunt," Josh said. I was shocked at the term but had to agree it fitted Tilly Devine. "I knew she couldn't be trusted. I done a recon on the meeting place and it was all set for a trap. I told him. Silly bastard wouldn't listen."

"Fred went in first. Didn't stand a chance. It would have been you, Josh," the leader said.

I shuddered at the thought.

"I got more sense than Fred. I woulda been more careful."

"Doesn't matter how careful you woulda been, you woulda ended up dead."

"Don't underestimate old Josh, mate," he said.

"Enzo put some men on the roof of the building opposite but the Loo mob were already staking it out. Standoff. That's where Leo and me was," the leader said.

Leo chimed in, "Jack here got two of them before we heard gun shots from the street."

"We raced downstairs fast as our legs would carry us," Jack, the leader, continued. "But it was all over bar the shouting. Tilly didn't even show up. They threw a dress on one of the gang, an' a big hat, to pretend. We got the bastard, but Enzo copped a slug. We dragged him away. He was calling for you, Josh."

"Fuck, no. I wasn't there." He rocked back and forth in the bed, hugging his arms around himself. "I shoulda been. I coulda saved him. I shoulda been there."

Jack placed his hand on Josh's shoulder as a sign of solidarity. "No, mate. You couldn'ta done nothing. Nobody coulda done nothing. We was cut orf. An' outnumbered. They only let us go so we would spread the news. A warnin' to anyone tryin' to muscle in on Tilly's turf. They had you marked, Josh. They said they was gonna come after ya."

"Yeah," Josh said, his voice cracking. "They sent Spud. He woulda got me except one of the orderlies caught him. Knocked him out with a bed pan."

The men laughed, but it was hollow.

I cleared my throat. "I'm just going to step outside to discuss Josh's medical condition with Dr. Delaney."

"Sure. Go ahead,' Jack said; obviously relieved they could talk in private.

Dr. Delaney joined me as we stood guard outside, watching through the little window in the door.

"Do you think Mr. Carter will seek revenge?" Dr. Delaney asked.

"I hope not," I replied. "It will depend on whether they leave him alone."

"You're welcome to spend the night."

"Here?"

"I'll warn the staff."

"Let's see what Josh thinks of the idea first."

After an orderly led his gang mates away blindfolded, Josh warmed to the idea that I would stay with him until the following morning. I, of course, wanted to spend as much of the time in his bed as I could, while he seemed more attuned to my company to relieve his boredom. But first, he wanted to talk about Enzo. He needed to get it out of his system, so I kept my tongue checked as he heaped praise on the man who blackmailed him into staying in an abusive relationship.

Occasionally, I would intervene when he became too maudlin or too effusive in his praise to remind him that he could be the one lying dead at this very moment.

"That would be the best result all round."

"Not for those who love you," I said pointedly.

"There's damn few of those," he replied. Had he forgotten how much he meant to me? I'd noticed his manners and his language had coarsened while in Enzo's employ and I didn't like it. When he got weepy over Enzo, I hugged him until he'd sobbed himself dry, then he pushed me away as if I were a stranger intruding on his grief. When I attempted to discuss whether we had any chance of a future together, he looked at me repulsed that I could bring up the subject on the day his boyfriend died. He was not happy when I reminded him about the lopsided nature of his relationship.

In the end, I did not stay the night. It was too painful. Josh seemed to have totally forgotten our earlier relationship, had cut the feelings out of his heart. Foolishly, I had hung on to them. It had brought me nothing but pain.

With Dr. Delaney's blessing I took Josh's assailant back to Tilly Devine to negotiate a truce for Enzo's requiem mass at St. Mary's Cathedral, the impressive Gothic church on the eastern edge of the luxuriant Hyde Park. Ironic that the cathedral faced Boomerang Street to the south, and the

Archibald Fountain in the park to the west, both notorious night-time areas frequented by queers.

I also took it upon myself to negotiate a truce over Josh, assuring Tilly that there would be no repercussions or revenge attacks. She had already absorbed half of Enzo's gang members, the other half having scattered to the Kate Leigh gang in Surry Hills. Tilly offered Josh a prominent position with the Loo gang if he ever felt the urge. I laid it on thick about his leg, injured in a mining accident and now injured again in a vicious unprovoked attack by the wharf scabs.

It took all my energy, and far too much of my time, to smooth things over but for Josh's sake I had to try. I visited him daily but there was no sign of the former spark we once shared. I helped him to attend the mass at St. Mary's where the cream of society mingled awkwardly with the cream of the underworld, Tilly and Kate Leigh battling for the most histrionic attack of the sobs. Josh was a focus of attention as he hobbled down the centre aisle, taking his rightful place in the front pew. I sat a few rows back and watched as he hung his head and watched him mouth what looked like a request for forgiveness but as he was neither Catholic nor religious, it was probably my romantic imagination.

At the wake, he was friendly to his former criminal comrades, both sides of which attempted to win him over to their new bosses. He refused to be drawn, saying he needed time to think, but that he was more than likely 'gonna chuck it in.'

I was there when the Will was read, leaving him a small stipend which was too large to be mere appreciation but not small enough that it wasn't for 'other' services rendered. Enzo's wife remained in Italy not returning for the funeral although she had his body shipped back to his home country where another more dignified requiem mass would be said in his honour. His luxury home was put up for sale and nosy gawkers traipsed through the gilded hallways pawing the statuary and the silverware, pocketing souvenirs when no one was looking.

I was there, too, when the cast was finally cut from Josh's leg and Dr. Delaney gave him the all clear.

The following day he disappeared.

CHAPTER FIFTEEN

~

DANNY'S REVENGE

"*O*f course, I can't tell you where he's gone," Dr. Delaney said.

"Patient confidentiality," I parroted, just before he said it. He'd already given me the same answer a dozen times before. Still I persisted. I was frantic to know what had happened to him. I needed to know before I could get on with my life. Truth be told, I could see no life for me without him. No, I wasn't contemplating self-harm, though I could understand people who did.

Rodney Buchan was pushing me to throw my lot in with his, and I could do much worse. Valerie was also adamant that I should come to London with her and Cecil. Both offers were tempting. So I was considering putting my hands around Dr. Delaney's neck and throttling the information out of him. He must have read my mind because he chortled before he said, "You should know by now that physical violence gets you nowhere with me."

"I just want to know that he isn't dead."

"Damien, you're getting a definite whine to your voice. I can tell you on good authority that when he left here he was very much alive. He needed time to think, to be alone. None of his former mates had anything to do with his leaving."

That was more information than he'd revealed before. It set my mind at rest, if not my heart. Josh had been left a tidy sum in Enzo's will although not enough that he did not have to work. Jobs, however, were few and far between for an unskilled young man with a crippled leg.

It had been a few months since Enzo's murder and, naturally enough, the police and the public had lost interest. He had been a major crime figure and it was more or less a case of 'good riddance to bad rubbish.' The police maintained they were still investigating but no one believed them. They knew who was responsible and much as they would have loved to pin the crime on Tilly, lock her up and close down her gang, it wasn't going to happen any time soon unless someone ratted. The person who did would find himself at the bottom of Sydney Harbour in cement boots or else under the foundations of one of the new city buildings. He would never survive long enough to testify in court.

I had settled in to Dr. Delaney's clinic and become an accepted part of the routine. I enjoyed the work. It was a welcome break from the unrelenting hardship of working-class Pyrmont where poverty and serious illness were twinned. At the clinic, I encountered much more genteel illnesses, the diseases of the wealthy and privileged, psychosomatic illness that infuriated me to the extent I wanted to take the patient and rub his nose in the filth and grime and utter poverty of Harris Street.

Instead, I bit my tongue and pandered to their whims and fancies, their barely noticeable coughs they interpreted as consumption, their aches, which they feared were cancer, and their obesity they were convinced was hereditary rather than a result of their conspicuous appetites. These people had the luxury of making themselves miserable. To my normal patients, it was a way of life.

I went home to my room in Pyrmont from the clinic in a haze of despondency that the disparity in living conditions within a few short miles of one another was so chasmic. There were only two people in the world with whom I could share my thoughts. Mum would listen patiently then nod knowingly before sharing her wisdom, "It's like they say, love. Money can't buy happiness." Perhaps not, but it buys a much more comfortable misery.

The other person I could share with was Rodney Buchan, the popular press's favourite leftist whipping boy. Sometimes he would listen to my rants swatting arguments back and forth to force me to clarify my thinking and convey it more forcefully. Most of the time, however, I felt he thought of me as a lightweight intellectually, that I should be more frontline in my attacks on behalf of the proletariat. I was never one for jargon. I was never a foot soldier for internationalism. I was more of a backyardist. I would do what I could for those in my immediate vicinity and hope, like a ripple in a pool, for a knock-on effect.

Buchan was all for manning the barricades, dynamiting outmoded and unfair social foundations. I guess explosives always terrified me, but give me a hammer and a chisel... I also came to the conclusion he resorted to sex to escape the horrors he faced daily. I just wasn't sure I wanted to be his permanent shelter.

Mum always welcomed me home with a nice cuppa and a hot meal. I paid her handsomely for her time as my cook and cleaner, as well as rent for her front two rooms in which I lived very comfortably. We would sometimes spend the evening listening to her radio round the kitchen table while she welcomed the denizens of the night who rented her rooms for their clandestine assignations. Sometimes a friend would come over and I'd retire to my room and Mum would smile knowingly, perfectly content to listen to one of her 'boys' pour out his heart about his romantic problems. She was a good soul and I heard her sort out many a seemingly unfathomable dilemma to the satisfaction of all parties involved. It didn't always involve ideas that were legal or even socially acceptable.

One night, on my return from the clinic, she was eager with news and began flapping a letter in front of my nose as soon as I came in the door.

"You'll never guess who I received a letter from today."

I was tired; I didn't want to guess.

"No, who?"

"Come on, guess," she instructed.

She was a little too keen and suddenly my heart skipped. I offered tentatively, "Not Josh?"

"No, but close enough," she almost did a jig in the hallway.

"Who then?" I was interested now.

"His mum."

"Mrs. Carter?"

"Has he got more than one mum?" she snorted. "Of course, Mrs. Carter."

I made a grab for the letter but she held it out of my reach. I followed her into the kitchen while she retrieved her glasses and perched them on her nose. I sat obediently because she was obviously going to milk this for everything she could. I poured us both a cup of tea from the pot that had been stewing in expectation of my arrival. She took a sip and then, ahing her satisfaction, unfolded the correspondence.

"Blah, blah, blah, blah. Oh, here it is. 'Joshua has been home these seven weeks now and has sunk deeper into depression. He misses his Sydney friends although from what he has told me they seem a worthless bunch. Do pardon me, I don't mean that nice Dr. Button. He has always been the gentlemen, but Joshua now mutters about being led astray. It has to do with his friend Danny's influence. Joshua has even got himself a girlfriend, a nice young lass, a friend of his sister, who is new to the town and has not heard of the scandal of a few years back. But rather than make him happier it seems to have plunged him into worser depths of despair. Perhaps if you could persuade some of his Sydney friends, he must have had some nice ones, to visit him. There is a big dance held here on the last Saturday of every month. I expect it's nothing like your big city dances but I'm sure you would enjoy it and it would please an old woman to see Joshua smile again. I could possibly make room for about six or seven people as long as you don't mind sleeping rough'. That's all there is."

Mum folded the letter carefully, sliding it back in the envelope.

"Stupid bugger," I spat.

"There's no denying your nature," she said to me. "That's what's making him blue. He'll learn the hard way."

"How long have you known where Josh was living?"

"Since he left Sydney, love. It was never no secret."

"How did you find out?"

"I wrote to his mum and asked after him, saying his friends in the city missed him and hoped he would come back soon. Especially a certain young doctor who had lost his way since Josh had left."

I almost choked on my tea. I had been the subject of correspondence, a rather personal and private correspondence. Mum looked at me, a little fearful about what she had done, but I picked her up and held her in the air, dancing about with her until she wriggled and cried, "Put me down, I'm an old woman." I kissed her theatrically on the forehead. "You're not angry with yer old mum then?"

I was already consulting the calendar from the local butcher, which had pride of place on her kitchen wall because it had a biscuit tin scene of a lake somewhere unidentifiable. Sometimes she gazed at that picture for what seemed like ages, and then came back to the present with a start, saying wistfully, "I should like to have had a holiday in a place like that."

It was my long cherished hope that one day I would have the means to send Mum on a holiday to just such a place. That was another reason I worked at the clinic and was looking to get a foot in the door at Macquarie Street, although my enthusiasm for the latter had lapsed somewhat during the problems with Josh.

"Two weeks until the next dance. I think we could organise a little party to cheer up Josh, what do you say, Mum?"

"Go on with you. It's for young people, not for the likes of me. Besides, I can't leave the house. Who's to look after my boys while I'm away? Money doesn't grow on trees, you know."

I did know and I would have been a wealthy man if I'd a penny for every time Mum spouted that cliché or the one about there being a Depression on.

"What if I find someone to look after the house and collect the rent while you're away?" I teased her with the prospect.

"They'd have to be reliable."

"Oh, he is."

I asked Rodney a few days later. He'd spent the occasional night in my lodgings, particularly when he was organising on the wharves nearby, and had met and liked Mum Doreen. She was wary of his proselytising, believing him much too serious for me, but liked him none the less. When I explained that it would give Mum a nice break, he added sarcastically, "And it will give you another shot at winning back that coal miner of yours."

"I thought you would approve," I nudged. "You can't get much more proletarian than a coal miner."

I begged, cajoled, and blackmailed the group together and two weeks later we headed off in two cars. Valerie, never one to miss an opportunity, had rung the mine manager, organising to sing a few songs at the dance. The local newspapers picked up on her attendance and Mrs. Carter wrote that there was an air of expectancy about the event and that people from townships as far away as Wyong and Morisset were attending. It suddenly became the biggest event in the town's social calendar. Naturally, Valerie felt she had to live up to expectations, so packing along with a trunk load of costumes and casual wear, her own personal pianist who could also triple as her costume changer and hair dresser. He was a comely lad of about twenty-five, blond, slim, and devastatingly good looking. And definitely available to the likes of me. Young Ty, short for Tyrone, made it abundantly clear that I was a dish in which he was interested. If it hadn't been for Josh, I would have reciprocated. As it was, I had to straighten my erection so it was not too obvious after he had goosed me provocatively on that morning. They were in one car while I drove Mum, Eric, his lover John who had managed to inveigle the weekend off, a rare occurrence, in Rodney's vehicle, which he had loaned me for the occasion along with a lecture on taking care of his precious automobile.

It was a long, hot drive along the Pacific Highway up through the northernmost suburbs of the sprawling city, Hornsby, then Cowan before the winding descent to the pretty river hamlet of Brooklyn. We stopped there for lunch and made a picnic of it. Valerie had one of her many servants pack a basket for the journey and he had done us proud. There was wine, bread, cheese, sandwich meat, hard-boiled eggs, cakes and biscuits to suit all tastes.

Valerie was never abstemious, the wine flowed like the Hawkesbury River beside which we were parked and I had a little too much. If I were honest, I would say I had a lot too much. To the extent that I was unable to drive. Fortunately, Eric stepped in and took the keys from me before I could get behind the wheel to continue our journey. Somehow, Ty rearranged the seating and Mum found herself in the back of Valerie's car, while John shared the front of ours and I was suddenly face down in Ty's lap in the back.

The scent of heat and masculinity filled my nostrils as I felt my cock harden in my pants. In my inebriated state I thought it great fun to be among friends who would turn a blind eye or at least forgive my rather outrageously loose behaviour. I lay along the back seat, slightly cramped, with my head in Ty's lap as he stroked my face. It was a most pleasant feeling. It had been so long since I had felt this relaxed. My concerns that Josh would not be pleased to see me vanished under the expert ministrations of young Ty.

Valerie had warned him away from me but with the sort of bemused scolding that signified she knew it was a lost cause already. I hadn't known just how lost until he held my face and buried his tongue between my lips. Starved for affection, I gave in immediately. Rodney was a superb lover in the technical sense but what was missing when I was with him, I realised now, was the romance, the tenderness.

I kissed Ty eagerly wanting more of his softness. I felt his cock stiffen in his trousers as he lowered my head back to his lap and unbuttoned. I didn't know what Eric and John were thinking of me but I had been too much the buttoned down respectable city doctor of late. Too much the dour lovesick dolt living in a fool's paradise. Life was to be lived, not mulled over and muddled through. I needed to grab my life back with both hands. If I made a fool of myself then so be it. I would not go to my grave regretting what I had not at least attempted.

Feeling around in his underpants, I freed Ty's cock enough that I could lick the shaft and wrap my lips around the glorious circumcised head. In trying to free his balls from the confines of his clothes, I'm afraid I hurt him and he gave a little yelp. I kissed his slit to make up for it and he giggled.

Bugger what Eric and John thought of me. I sucked Ty's delicious weapon in an effort to bring him off but he stopped me. "Let me have a turn," he whispered although the two men in the front seat knew exactly what was going on. I sat up; my lips wet with saliva, and unbuttoned my trousers, tugging them and my underpants down to my ankles. I was totally naked from my waist to my socks.

It was a gloriously liberating feeling as Ty ran his hands over my stomach then up under my shirt to my chest. He tugged at the mat of hair on my pectorals before pinching my nipples, which caused a sharp intake of my breath. I did like to have them played with. With his other hand, he gently squeezed my balls and ran a fingernail up the shaft to the head.

"Very impressive, Dr. Bouton," Ty said.

Before I had a chance to repay the compliment he had leaned over and taken most of my cock into his mouth, his tongue flicking at the glans as he slid down. Much farther and it would hit the back of his throat. I didn't know how long I could hold off, his mouth was so pleasurable. I attempted to lift him but he was having none of that, increasing his oral ministrations until I could no longer fight it and shot my spunk into his throat. I shuddered slightly as two, three, four squirts filled his mouth. He swallowed, and then licked my prick clean. When he kissed me, I could taste my salty ejaculate on his tongue.

The car veered off the highway between two trees, in the heavily timbered area through which we were travelling. Eric manoeuvered the vehicle so that we could no longer see the busy thoroughfare. More importantly, we could not be seen either. He drove a little farther until he spied a small clearing and pulled over to stop the car.

"We thought you may like a little more comfort than the back seat of the car," Eric said. "We know we would."

"Watching you two has made us all hot and bothered," John added. "Lucky we brought the picnic rugs with us."

"You buggers planned this all along," I smiled.

"We had hopes," Eric admitted.

"Are you objecting?" Ty asked.

In reply, I grabbed him as he hopped out of the car in an attempt to kiss him again, but with my trousers around my ankles, I fell off the back seat and landed on the grass. Eric and John picked me up under the arms and I kicked my clothes off so I could stand unencumbered.

Ty had already found a spot as devoid of twigs and prickles as possible and spread out one of the rugs. He shucked off his clothes and lay provocatively on his back. I sank to the ground and embraced him like a man starving. Only peripherally did I register that Eric and John lay their rug alongside ours, also stripping ready for action. They, at least, had the good sense to come prepared, sharing the cream by placing it between the rugs.

I had no idea of their intentions. I had slept with both Eric and John in the past, individually and as a couple, enjoying their company but I was unsure whether Ty was inclined to such sexual escapades. They kept to themselves even while watching us closely. I worked my lips along Ty's shaft until I had him back to full mast before I flipped him over and prised open his arse cheeks, his pretty-pink hole a sight to behold and I pressed my lips against it to lick and softly bite it, making it puffy and ready for my entry.

I took a chance and pulled Ty on to his hands and knees doggy style. Covering my fingers with the cream, I slid them into his inviting rump and he threw his head back and gasped. That was my opportunity. "That's such a pretty mouth Ty; it seems a pity to let it go to waste. John, why don't you give him something to do with it."

John stood; his hard cock was at mouth level. Ty didn't hesitate to engulf it making John moan in appreciation. Eric lay on his back slipping under us and gulping Ty's prick into his wet mouth. While Ty was preoccupied, I prodded my slicked cockhead against his anal opening and pushed. I slid in easily although there was a gasp of momentary pain from the impaled youth.

All four of us were an integral part of a sexual frenzy. It was invigorating to thumb our noses at society. If we were outside the norm then we may just as well be way outside the norm. We broke so many conventions that afternoon we lost count.

I pumped my cock into Ty's tight arse until my balls were slapping against his butt, forcing his prick deeper into Eric's throat. At the same time, John was gagging Ty with his substantial dick plunging in and out of his saliva-slicked lips.

There was no way to co-ordinate our orgasms, besides which, Eric's prick had been neglected – for the moment. Ty shot his load first, into Eric's mouth. I knew because I felt his sphincter squeeze around my shaft until I thrust deep one last time and held his waist as I shot my sperm deep inside his bowels. A few moments later, John let out a howl of pleasure signalling he was dumping his load in Ty's willing gob.

I pulled out and Eric, who had yet to come, kneeled and took my place. He sank into Ty's pretty arse. I watched as he stabbed hard and fast until he began making those familiar sounds of the ejaculating male. Eric and John cleaned themselves up while Ty and I cuddled some more on the rug. It had all been over too quickly but I knew we would all team up again.

The sound of a horn, honking impatiently, forced Ty and me to dress quickly, still sticky from our lovemaking, and run for the car, carrying the picnic rugs smeared with our passion, and the tub of cream we'd used as lubricant.

We were all in a jovial mood as we caught up with Valerie's entourage on the highway just before the turn off to Seaspray Bay. The dirt road was difficult going but soon we peaked the hill and drove into the tiny village, posters adorning every tree and the church hall where the dance was to take place. I directed Eric to Josh's home, my stomach suddenly feeling very sick indeed, as locals came out to see who was making all the fuss. A few of them recognised me and whispered behind their hands as we parked.

Mrs. Carter came out, wiping her hands on her apron as usual, to greet us. She flung her arms around me in such a manner that my welcome was unambiguous. She whispered as she did so. "Don't let my boy make a terrible mistake. Take him away from here."

I introduced her to our fellow guests and she shooed us all inside. Her tiny dining room was cramped, but we managed to squeeze around the table while she poured the tea. Mum helped out, the two of them at home with each other as if they had been lifelong friends. Mrs. Carter was somewhat in awe of Valerie who did everything to put her at her ease. Eric and John fit in anywhere and Ty was like a young kid. Only Cecil looked totally out of place. It made me wonder how he would cope with married life to Valerie in London.

We were in high party spirits when Josh appeared at the back door. Conversation dried instantly, everyone glancing between the two of us before the shrieks of friendship rent the air. Hugs all around and a quick handshake for me. After we all had our fill of tea and Madeira cake Mrs. Carter suggested we take a stroll along the small beach. That would get us out of her hair while she and Mum Doreen washed up and had a good old natter.

Josh tried to walk with Valerie but she and the others did their best to distance themselves, leaving us alone. Finally, Josh relaxed and we began, tentatively, to claw back the lost months. "I missed you, Josh," I said.

He sighed.

"How are you getting on?" I wanted to keep my tone friendly, unthreatening.

"Not much to do in a small town. I miss the city."

"I was hoping you missed me." It was self-indulgent, and I shouldn't have said it.

"What do you want me to say, Damien?"

"You know what I want you to say, Josh. What I've wanted you to say since we left this place." He went to reply but I stopped him. "Let me finish, Josh, please. I love you now as much as I did then. Perhaps more. I lived, hoped, for the day you would say those same words back to me. But, if you can't. If you no longer care for me. Then release me, let me go. Say the words and I'll never bother you again."

"It's not right, Damien," he said.

"Who says so?"

"Danny has introduced…"

"I don't want to hear about Danny," I said a little too savagely.

"Danny is my friend," he snapped back.

"Do friends do what he did when he drove us out of town?"

"He was only thinking of my wellbeing."

That was just so patently ridiculous I knew I had already lost the battle. Josh confirmed it by walking away without another word. I went to sit on the grassy hillock at the end of the beach while Valerie shepherded the others away to a reception being held in her honour at the mine's offices on top of the hill. My heart shattered into a million tiny pieces, each a pinprick tear. I was determined I would not cry until I got back to the city. Why had I come back? The black memories of my time here blanketed my soul. I tried to remember the happy times but that only made Josh's rejection the harder to bear.

Even before he spoke, I knew whose shadow it was. "There's nothing here for you." Danny stood over me but I was not afraid of him.

"I had to try, Danny. But you wouldn't understand that."

"What I understand is you were the worst thing that ever happened to Josh. We were fine until you came along."

"No, Danny. I was the best thing that ever happened to Josh. You'll wake up to that fact one day. Just as you'll wake up to the fact of what you are one morning. I just hope you don't ruin too many lives before that day arrives."

"No hard feelings, doc. Josh is back with the people who love him. Where he belongs."

"You're fooling yourself if you think he'll stay, Danny. I'm not saying he'll come back to me but one thing I know for certain, you'll never be able to keep him here."

I got up and walked away, frightened Danny's poison would find its way into my veins.

He called after me, "See you at the dance tonight, doc."

It was a miserable and dispiriting affair although everyone but myself seemed to be enjoying it, even Mum and Mrs. Carter sat watching the fun and I nudged each of them into dancing with me while they professed that it had been years. I also partnered Valerie when the locals left her alone, Cecil having no talent for dancing. He spent most of the night chatting happily to the old women who populated the chairs around the walls of the hall. Eric and John danced with some of the local girls but it was Ty who threw himself wholeheartedly into the party mood. I must say Josh looked no happier than I did and when I saw him leave the hall via the back door, I escaped out the front and intercepted him at the side of the building.

He just looked at me, frightened. Before I could say anything, he grabbed me tightly, pulling me to his chest. He planted a kiss so tender I almost melted in his arms. I never wanted it to end. I felt his excitement swell in his trousers. His breath was ragged. I reached up to brush his hair out of his eyes.

"There you are, Joshua, I've been looking everywhere," a female voice said. "Danny said I might find you out here. Hello, I'm Carol."

"Damien," I said, staring at the raven-haired, freckle-faced girl, not much more than eighteen years old, who then linked her arm with Josh's.

"Come inside, I want to dance," she whined, as she dragged him away.

Back inside I watched them. It didn't look as if Carol was going to let him out of her sights again so I tried to enjoy the evening as best I could. Most of the men gave me a wide berth but some of the women were keen to dance with me. About an hour later; Danny got up on stage and hushed the band.

"Ladies and gentlemen," he attempted to make himself heard over the din. When he was unsuccessful, he put his fingers in his mouth and let out an ear-shattering whistle. That did it.

"Ladies and gentlemen. And distinguished visitors. Before we get to tonight's entertainment, the incredible Valerie Sweet all the way from Sydney, I'd like to take this opportunity to make a very special announcement. It's with great pride I announce that my best mate; Seaspray Bay's own Joshua Carter, and that new little lady in town, Carol Patterson, tonight announce their engagement. Let's hear it for the happy couple."

As Danny led the applause, he looked directly at me; smug and self-satisfied in his victory.

CHAPTER SIXTEEN

~

A CHANGE OF PARTNERS

*T*y found me on the beach, the whoops and cheers of joy over the news in the hall still ringing painfully in my ears. Eric had sent him in case I was tempted to do something stupid although I was unlikely to do anything as downright dumb as Josh. Engaged to be married, for God's sake!

I was angry. Damn right! He was throwing his life away. He was queer. I could just about accept if he no longer cared for me and chose another man's love instead. Painful, but understandable. But, no. He'd allowed Danny to hector and cajole him into bartering his love for acceptance and respectability. In my career as a doctor I had seen the cancerous effect this had on many men's souls. They put a gun to their head, or jumped from the cliff top at Watson's Bay. Others, too frightened of God's, or society's, opprobrium regarding suicide, merely became careless around dangerous machinery. The result was always the same.

By the time Ty joined me, my anger had gone through despair, murderous thoughts, to resignation. Ty had been delayed in order to play piano for Valerie's requested vocalising for the happy couple. She admitted later the lyrics tasted like sand in her mouth.

I couldn't take any more. My life had been marking time for too long in hope of a reconciliation some day with Josh. My love, regardless of my other sex partners, remained constant. I wanted to believe he had been the same. I had concrete proof now I'd been mistaken.

Ty sat beside me quietly, both of us gazing out to sea, except I saw nothing but the bleak and bitter future ahead. I appreciated his company. And his silence. I broke it finally. "Can you drive me to Gosford?"

There was no argument, no excuses, just the squeeze of my hand and a simple, "Okay."

It was a long drive and we did it without speaking until we reached the outskirts of the town. Ty allowed me the time to wallow, not even reaching over to give me a supportive pat. He was a gem of a man. Perhaps, in time, I could get to appreciate him more fully, but not while my emotions felt as if they'd been scrubbed with a wire brush.

"Will you wait on the station for the first train in the morning or should I pull up outside an hotel?" he asked.

I opted for the hotel. I was exhausted and needed four walls of privacy to release my howl of frustration. He waited in the car as I tried a number of establishments, until I found one that was not overly suspicious of my lack of luggage or the extreme lateness. I was barely containing my tears when I shook Ty's hand warmly, holding it longer than customary to let him know I treasured his generosity of spirit, and went in to sign the accommodation book. The publican waived the paperwork, explaining I could do it in the morning, and showed me to a spartan, but comfortable, room with the only thing I needed at that moment: a warm, inviting bed that would embrace me unconditionally.

I grieved momentarily for the long, lonely drive Ty would have back to the mining town which in turn reminded me, all too painfully, of Josh's betrayal. I cursed the day I had ever set foot in the wretched coastal hamlet of Seaspray Bay. It bred hearts as cold and black as the deposits the miners dug out of the ground.

My sleep was spasmodic and troubled so I took the opportunity of leaving early to catch the first train south, the publican dismissing my concern about signing the register; pocketing the cash I paid as a tax-free perk. I was back in the city by mid-morning and back to the welcoming embrace of Mum's Pyrmont abode and Rodney's arms by lunch time.

He was a good enough friend to merely embrace me, my distressed and dishevelled appearance enough to give him pause in questioning me. Instead, he made me an ample breakfast and the ubiquitous pot of tea, and while I was eating regaled me with tales of the characters who'd hired rooms for the night at Mum's boarding house of the bent and socially unacceptable. He made me laugh; he made me forget my problems. Later, when I looked back on this period with more clarity, I marvelled that we humans can make such mountains of such trivialities. Of course, they don't seem trivial at the time but in comparison to the problems of poverty, factory injuries or the paucity of concern for our fellow humans, they need to be put in their place. And I determined to set about doing so.

Rodney sent me to bed after my late breakfast, having added a sleeping draft portion of spirits to my tea. It did enable me to get a few hours, uninterrupted. I bathed in the late afternoon, symbolically washing off the dust of Seaspray Bay and, more reluctantly, Josh's hold over my heart. The latter, however, would take some determined scrubbing before it would relinquish all traces. I had made a start.

I joined Rodney in the kitchen, the heart of this tiny terrace universe. "Give it time, Damien. It's a cliché, I know, but it's true nevertheless for that." He neither pushed me for information on what had occurred to precipitate my early return from the coast, nor for an answer to his suggestion that we become a couple. He was patient, it was one of his most endearing traits, and he knew he would get his response in good time. Pushing for it when I was at my most vulnerable would be madness on his part.

He headed off not long after. I told him I would look after the house until Mum's return, although he offered to stay, encouraging me to go out and get pissed, get fucked, or both. I didn't feel inclined to either so I spent the early evening writing a letter to Mrs. Carter apologising for my rude behaviour in running out on the weekend visit.

I made several attempts to explain my actions as delicately, but forthrightly, as I could without giving offence, during which time I took rent and doled out keys to various callers, stopping occasionally for a longer chat with one or two of the regulars after they'd gone about their business, and were leaving. I was putting the finishing touches to the epistle when there was a cacophony of laughter and general bonhomie which dried up the moment the two carloads from the country entered the hallway. I was hurt that they could be so joyous while I was riddled with so much pain but forgave them when I realised it was unreasonable to expect other people to take on my grievances.

There were too many to fit in Mum's rather tiny kitchen so I opened up my sitting room and they piled in there. Valerie helped herself to my somewhat meagre ration of spirits, pouring a generous brandy for Cecil. She was already three sheets to the wind and the other more subdued members of the party were attempting, unsuccessfully, to get her to tone down her exuberance in front of me.

Eric had already excused himself to make tea and sandwiches, instructing Mum to take it easy for once. I thought it politic to join him as I was just dampening the mood of revelry. "Don't think too badly of them," Eric said. I stood alongside him at the table while he buttered the bread.

"I don't," I said honestly. "Life goes on. I can't expect people to share my misery."

"We do though. We're just too impotent to do anything about it."

"I hope you don't think me foolish," I said.

Eric put down the butter knife. "We all still hold you in the highest regard. It's Josh who's being foolish but he's being manipulated by that friend of his..."

"Danny," I said.

"Yes, him. Even Josh's mum flew at him over the sudden engagement. She knew nothing about it and told him point blank to his face that it was a mistake and he would live to regret it. Both of them said things they'll wish they hadn't. She stuck up for you. Good as told Josh that he was never likely to find another friend like you, that he was throwing his life away if he married, and I use her exact words here, 'that snivelling excuse for a brainless trollop' Carol. Seems most of Seaspray has had her at one time or another. You were right to come back when you did."

"I thought so."

"It did take a little of the gloating out of Danny's triumph." Eric handed me the butter knife while he made the tea. He paused, as if considering the repercussions of what he was about to reveal. "Although you did miss Ty's moment of one-upmanship."

"Oh?" I tried not to sound too interested.

"He was ingratiating himself with Josh to the extent that we were wondering if he was going to make a play for him." Eric paused to see what effect his words were having. I admit, I did freeze, my blood ran cold at the prospect of Ty claiming my former boyfriend. "But it was all a ruse, I'm pleased to say. He carried it off with such aplomb we were convinced we had a traitor in our midst. He showed such concern for Josh's feelings, even siding with him against us. We underestimated him. While we were getting nowhere telling Josh he was a fool, that he would regret his behaviour, and all those other judgmental arguments we were bringing to bear with little chance of success, Ty took the other approach, encouraging Josh in his willful pursuit of the impossible dream, extolling the virtues of his life in Seaspray with a wife and kids. Josh's look of horror as it began to sink in just what he'd signed himself up for was priceless, but heartbreaking."

"Poor Josh," I chuckled.

"That was just the half of it. Once he had Josh hooked, he went for the kill. He mentioned that he shared a moment of passion with you on the journey to Seaspray and that he'd found it so superior to any other man he'd ever been with that now that Josh had no claim on you then Ty was going to be a more than willing substitute and that you had certainly given him every reason to be hopeful of a long-term relationship, especially now that you were heading up in the world with your Macquarie Street practice.

"He managed to sound both eager and mercenary at the same time. I thought he'd gone too far and you could see most of the group were buying his performance. Then he delivered the coup de grace. He said that he had sought you out on the beach after Josh's engagement had been announced and that the two of you had made very special love in the sand and that it was one of the most romantic trysts he'd ever had. He went into so much detail of what you did to him it was bordering on pornographic. Just as we were getting uncomfortable, Josh grabbed him by the throat, so red in the face I thought he would explode, and shouted. 'You leave Damien alone you bloody little slut!' Josh shook him a few times before he let him loose and ran out the door.

"That boy has a future in the theatre. It was the performance of a lifetime."

"You don't think he's serious?"

"Do you want him to be?"

"I don't know," I answered.

"It wouldn't take much to turn him that way. He would be quite a catch." Eric placed the teapot and cups on a tray. I followed in his wake with the sandwiches; cheese and tomato on one plate and ham with mustard on the other.

Back among the travellers I thanked them for their support, hoping they would not think it remiss of me if I went to bed because I had a full surgery tomorrow and I was exhausted. They all said the right things and Mum told me to use one of the spare rooms because they were all partying in my living-cum-bedroom, reluctant to leave. I took the key to the room farthest upstairs so I wouldn't be disturbed by their conviviality, stripping off my clothes, slipping naked between the sheets. I had no energy or inclination to bring myself off although my cock was hard, whether from thoughts of Josh or from Ty I could not be sure.

There was a quiet tap at my door about a quarter hour later and I mumbled an invitation to enter. I saw from the light in the hallway that it was Ty. I made no protest when he removed his clothes and climbed into bed alongside me. He pulled the sheet and blankets down to my waist so that he could stroke my chest.

"Thanks for what you did," I said quietly to break the silence.

"Eric told you?"

"Yes."

"Big mouth," Ty said.

"Big dick, too."

We both went off its fits of giggles, each setting the other off. It went on for so long, first one then the other, there was a tinge of hysteria to it. It did me good. I clasped Ty close to me, kissing him feverishly. When I finally released him, he leaned on my chest his face inches from my own. I knew he must be studying me in the dark.

"I was serious," he said so softly I almost missed it.

"I know. And I'm flattered."

"It wasn't meant to flatter," he said.

"Can I have time to consider?" I asked.

"As long as I can continue to visit to show you what is on offer."

"That would please me," I said.

I thought he would be eager for a repeat of our initial experience but, instead, he held me closely, caressing my body until I fell asleep. He must have crept out during the night for when I awoke the next morning I was alone but his warmth and concern had been the morphia blanket I'd needed to regain my equilibrium via an untroubled slumber. I was ready to tackle what the world threw at me once again, although with a little less enthusiasm.

By concentrating on my medical practice I managed to keep the fearful demons of longing and jealousy at bay, aided by undemanding interludes with Rodney and Ty. Neither pressured me while offering solace and a comforting embrace which left me satiated if not totally satisfied. For the moment, it was enough.

When I went downstairs, Mum was bustling about the kitchen as usual, preparing breakfast for her favourites, including Eric and John who were bemoaning the fact it would be weeks before they had a day off that coincided. While I commiserated with the cruelty of their situation they did, at least have the consolation of each other.

I ate with them as Mum went on excitedly about meeting a kindred soul in Mrs. Carter, Josh's mum. They had formed a friendship over numerous cups of tea and the loneliness of two elderly women. To everyone's surprise Mum took to spending time at Seaspray in Mrs. Carter's small cottage, returning to the city refreshed and reinvigorated. She restricted the news about

Josh to the observation that 'he's not happy, Damien' and left it at that. She left me in charge of her lucrative accommodation business and I was pleased to handle it for her even though it meant I was chained to the Pyrmont terrace during her absence unless Eric could take over for me. On the occasions I was temporary landlord Ty would call in to keep me company provided Valerie wasn't monopolising his time. Even then he would try to get back to me after a recital.

It would be true to say he was successful in keeping my thoughts from Josh and he was amiable company indeed. We stepped out together socially to the envy of both sexes who saw us together. So many people assumed we were a queer couple that I'd almost begun to think of us that way as well. I hadn't heard from Josh and no one seemed to know much about his state of mind except from Mum's monotonous updates of 'he's not happy, Damien' which is all she ever revealed. If it were code for something else I never cracked it.

Much of my time was spent preparing my application for residency in exclusive Macquarie Street. It had long been my dream and the applications had been culled to four or five prospective interviewees. I was surprised I had survived the slaughter as I'd been informed through unofficial channels that some major surgeons had not made the cut. I guessed that I had my superior references to thank for my inclusion.

I didn't expect to actually be selected for the third floor living area with surgery attached but I was determined to give it my best shot. It would be good practice for later applications when I believed I would stand more of a chance. The reason for my pessimism was not that I was much younger and less decorated by initials after my name from prestigious universities but that I had one stalwart enemy on the board that was engaged in the selection: one Sir Michael Cycledes. He was a surgeon in his fifties, his wife Lady Myrtle having produced two sons and a daughter now spent her time meddling in the boards of numerous social charities, while he worked out of the nearby Sydney Hospital, an acknowledged heart specialist, not a field in which I was any competition, so it was difficult to understand his antagonism toward me.

Rodney offered to dig up any dirt in his background but I warned him off. I wanted to get this position on my own merits; I was not in the market for blackmail, tempting though it was. My one concern was that I could not lug my second-hand furniture into Macquarie Street. There was a regulation snobbish grandeur to uphold and that required a ready supply of cash. Most members of the doctors' chambers had a steady supply of old money, courtesy of the family. Mine would be new money, courtesy of the bank.

The day of my interview, I was dressed as bright and shiny as a new pin. I had prepared as best I could under the circumstances. All I could do was speak the truth. As it turned out, I also spoke my mind. Sir Michael Cycledes baited me beautifully, drawing me into his sophisticated trap until it snapped shut trapping me in my own opinions and biases.

The interview had been going quite well until then. The questions were convivial; probing without seeming to, until I believed the board was on my side. After outlining my background and my experience, particularly with regard to my work on factory injuries, which had been extensively published, Sir Michael sniffed as if the mere speaking of such matters was akin to a dirty smell assailing his nostrils.

"The working classes are all very well," he huffed, before adding, "In their place. And no civilised man has anything but the highest regard for the worker. They are the foundation of this country's wealth. Without them we would not exist."

"I couldn't agree more," I said, sensing he had a lot more to say on the matter.

"But, let's be frank, they are not the sorts of people we particularly want turning up at our offices here. We are among friends, so I must say I have heard on good authority that these working class people actually...smell."

"True," I said, scarcely restraining my anger. "They smell of perspiration. They smell of poverty. They smell of rotting teeth because they can't afford a healthy meal let alone the price of dental care. They take to their own mouths with pliers to relieve the agony of toothache. They smell because they have suppurating sores that they can ill afford to treat."

Some members of the board were non-plussed by my unvarnished truth.

"Gentlemen," I continued. "I thought we swore a Hippocratic Oath to treat the ill and the injured. I must have missed the section that specified they had to be of a so-called superior class to warrant our attention."

Sir Michael snorted at my audacity. "I'm told these people have their own doctors."

"Indeed," I was quick to add. "And I am one of them."

"I can only assume you will no longer indulge in such unseemly behaviour if, and I must stress 'if' so that you do not get your hopes up, we were to offer you the vacant surgery."

"Then you assume wrongly," I said, leaving it at that.

"But we can't have people like that mixing with the likes of our important patients in the foyer," one of Sir Michael's supporters sniffed.

"I will continue my Pyrmont practice but I reserve the right to treat any man, woman or child that I chose from the premises here." There was a murmur around the table. "I will not be dictated to with regard to my patients."

"I would find it very difficult to be caught on the stairs with a person who was not at least a gentleman," Sir Michael continued. "Would they even know the protocol for whom goes first?"

"Provided they knew who you were I'm sure they would give you all due deference."

"Of course they would know who I am. Everyone knows who I am," he was quite red in the face.

"Excuse me for saying so, but I have no idea who you are apart from your title, your name, and the alphabet soup after it on the board downstairs." That wasn't quite the truth because I had asked around about him and the more I heard the more I knew I would dislike him. My initial reaction was proving all-too-prescient.

"A gentleman would," he chided. "Are you a socialist, Dr. Bouton?"

"Not as such," I replied, "although I have a certain sympathy for some of the tenets of their beliefs."

"There would be anarchy in the streets if they ever got power." Sir Michael was itching for an argument.

"That is merely cant. The worst sort of argument put forward by those who do not wish to see the status quo disturbed. While some people sit in their ivory towers, there are people out there starving to death or dying because they cannot get proper medical care. I am not prepared to sit idly by and watch that happen."

Sir Michael stood abruptly, signalling the interview was at an end. "I don't think, Dr. Bouton, you are our sort of people."

I stood as well, gathering up my papers. "I am proud to wear that accusation, sir. I abhor the wood-panelled, plush carpeted, gilt-edged hauteur of your interrogation. Your inflexible and inviolate opinions fossilised into dogma by privilege and position sickens me."

I thanked the remaining members of the board for their time, some of them shaking my hand, others smiling slyly in their whiskers, and exited into the bright Sydney sunshine. I took a deep breath, savouring the fresh air which revitalised my spirits after the stale ideas that had atrophied one or two of the brains upstairs.

I gave my application to the Macquarie Street chambers no more thought. After my weeks of preparation I felt as if I had my life back again. My medical practice in Pyrmont, if not exactly thriving, was none the less supplying me with a liveable wage. My part-time work at Dr. Delaney's clinic provided much-needed mental stimulation, while my friendship with benefits with both Rodney and Ty provided succour for the soul.

Content for things to continue as they were, I determined I would apply for positions whenever a realistic opportunity presented itself without compromising my beliefs or betraying my friends. I would not try to be something I was not. I would find a permanent companion sometime in the future and, while regretting it would not be Josh, I would rejoice in whomsoever won my poor battered heart. It would not be Ty either; for he had grown tired of waiting for my answer and had thrown his lot in with Valerie, taking my place on their planned sojourn to London. There, I was sure, he would be gobbled up by a society eager for such a talented and beautiful Antipodean boy.

I had learned, too, that although Rodney was a consummate lover, any man who desired him would always play second fiddle to his political activity. I related to many of his concerns but I was loathe to share a man with a cause. I relished both their friendships while acutely aware that my future happiness lay elsewhere.

CHAPTER SEVENTEEN

~

SUCCESS, BUT AT WHAT COST?

*N*aked to the waist, I was seated in Mum's backyard soaking up the sun's rays trying to turn my vampire pale skin a light chestnut. I never had that tanned look that is so appealing to men of my persuasion and many a joke was made at my expense when I removed my shirt. Not at the condition of my body which is muscular and sporty, but at the paleness of my skin. I had rubbed a brand of coconut oil into my arms and chest, while Jack, whom I had met the first morning at Mum's all those years ago firmly rubbed my back. I had never succumbed to his clumsy attempts at seduction because of my regard for George, his long-suffering boyfriend. Jack was a trollop, his sexual appetite prodigious and his taste in male flesh indiscriminate. Still, he was good-hearted, often pitching in when Mum needed a hand with an odd-job or a message run.

I had seen Jack on a number of occasions for sexual diseases of the anus. A few days later George would turn up for much the same problem in his penis, the result of loving a promiscuous boyfriend. George never lost his sense of humour and I marvelled at his resilience. You can probably put up with a lot when you actually have a physical relationship with the man you love. But is any relationship better than none?

Jack was gossiping about his latest conquest, I only ever half listened, allowing the murmur of his voice to lull me into relaxation. He tried taking liberties, pushing his oily hand down the back of my trousers to my arse or, even worse, attempting to grope my cock and balls. Often I would find his lips tantalisingly close to my own or else feel him brush his fingers across my very sensitive nipples.

He was at it again. He'd turned his attention from my back to my chest and stomach and sat astride my lap, all the better to apply the lotion. His constant movement was causing friction to my groin and arousing interest where it should not have been aroused. I was in danger of giving in to his insistent demands and my breath was coming out of my throat ragged and short. Jack knew the effect he was having, so began to massage my chest while grinding his arse against my cock. It was so pleasant I thought I would allow him the liberty.

I had no patients scheduled for the afternoon which is why I was sunbathing, at the ready, however, should there be an emergency or a patient wandering in off the street. Jack wiped his hands on my arms and reached down to the buttons on my trousers, fumbling at my waist and eager to have my fly undone. He would have succeeded had it not been for the pounding at the front door. Jack cursed and I couldn't help but thank Providence for the timely interruption.

As I wiped myself down in preparation for donning my work clothes I sent Jack to let the patient in asking him to seat them in my surgery until I was ready to see them. However, Jack came out into the backyard with a telegram. "I signed for you, doc. I hope you don't mind."

It was difficult to stay annoyed or angry with Jack for long. He hovered in order to read over my shoulder. "I wonder who died?" he said, perpetuating the cliché. The working class rarely used telegrams except as a means of sending news of injury or an imminent death. This turned out to be neither. "Well, I'll be buggered," he chortled. "I ain't never to this day seen good news in a telegram."

He was more chuffed by that fact than by the incredible news it imparted. After giving due consideration to all the applicants who had applied for the vacant surgery in Macquarie Street, they had decided that I was the sort of person they were looking for. I learned later that Sir Michael Cycledes had been the one dissenting voice, preferring instead, a colleague who worked with him at Sydney Hospital. They asked that I make myself available the following week to sign the necessary papers in front of a solicitor and that payment was required by bank cheque.

This was news of life-changing fortuitousness and I had no one to tell. Ideally, I should have celebrated with Josh. In his absence Ty or Rodney would have done but one was in Melbourne playing the piano for Valerie, the other was fronting a picket line on the wharves. Mum was in Seaspray Bay visiting Mrs. Carter on what was becoming a monthly sojourn.

"Jack, my lad," I said, taking him by the arm, "I have just been handed the most wonderful news and I have only you to celebrate it with. Come inside and we'll get shickered together."

He was eager to join me, in expectation, I suspect, that if he got me drunk enough, I might allow him to suck my cock. I probably would have, too, I was so euphoric. In the end, though, he passed out before I did. That's how John found us later that afternoon when he turned up to look after the terrace while Mum was away. It was his turn and he was hoping that Eric may have been able to get a free day. No such luck, as it turned out.

I lied, telling him I had drunk myself into oblivion to forget Josh and that Jack had kept me company. It was not as ridiculous as it sounds as Jack was well-known for his love of alcohol. John ministered to us both and I supplied aspirin for the headaches that were going to cripple us shortly. There was a reason for not revealing my good fortune, not least of which was my superstitious fear that until everything was signed, it could all evaporate like an illusion in the desert.

It was difficult keeping the extraordinary news to myself, particularly after I had told my friends how disappointingly I thought the interview had gone and about the personal antagonism of one particular board member.

The following Wednesday, armed with my bank cheque, and all the necessary paperwork, I presented myself at the chambers where Mr. Gralt, a solicitor who was one of my supporters, smiled broadly as I attached my signature to the contract. He patted my back warmly, moving his hand somewhat lower than was absolutely necessary for the task at hand, but I was not going to reprimand him for the liberty. He was one of the fraternity. Sir Godfrey Seaton welcomed me on behalf of the Board, assuring me that I had given an outstanding account of myself at the interview, that there had never been any doubt and that the delay had been purely because of the tactics adopted by Sir Michael in an effort to thwart my acceptance.

"He gave in at the end with his usual lack of good grace," Sir Godfrey said. "And for heaven's sake just call me plain old Godfrey, I only ever use the Sir when confronted with the police or particularly recalcitrant public servants."

After the contracts were signed and the bank cheque notarised, we celebrated my acceptance into the hallowed residence by raising a glass of sherry to the portraits of the founding fathers of the establishment which adorned the walls of the room reserved for residential business. I drank it down although my palate has never been particularly fond of sherry. Give me a good brandy or a single malt any day.

At the conclusion of the short ceremony, it was a business day after all, I walked out with Mr. Gralt, pestering him with questions about my rights and privileges in the building. He understood that I was unfamiliar with many of the legal terms and conditions and, after warning me never to sign a contract in future without fully comprehending what I was getting myself into, offered to take me through the document at a convenient time.

"Would this afternoon at three suit, Dr. Bouton?" he asked.

"That would suit marvellously, Mr. Gralt. I will see you then."

I had a few errands to undertake and completed them to my utmost satisfaction, took lunch at Pfahlert's where I longed to jump on the bar counter and announce the wonderful news to my fellow travellers. Good news only becomes wonderful news when you can share it. I had bottled it up for so long I was in danger of exploding.

At three o'clock I was shown into Mr. Gralt's office where he very thoroughly, and in terms comprehensible to a lay man such as myself, explained everything to my complete satisfaction. At the end of the ordeal, for such it must have been for him, I said, "I wonder, Mr. Gralt, if you would be prepared to undertake the task of being my solicitor if it is not a conflict of interest for you. I'm impressed by your preparation and your kindness."

He seemed startled and I was afraid I had insulted him.

"It's most unusual," he began, "for someone to ask for my services. I have to be honest with you, Dr. Bouton, I am but a mid-range solicitor. Oh, I hope to climb to the top, or near enough to, in my career but for the moment, most people usually prefer one of the senior partners to handle their affairs."

"In order that they charge at senior partner rates but while someone such as yourself does all the footwork," I said.

"Exactly so, Dr. Bouton, although it is worth more than my job to say so."

"Are you turning me down, Mr. Gralt?"

"Indeed, no, Dr. Bouton. I would be very pleased to have you as my client but I believe there are protocols to follow. Please allow me to make a few enquiries while you wait."

He disappeared out of the office, returning about ten minutes later with a much older man, elegantly dressed as a figurehead usually is, who bowed and scraped just enough to put me in my place and let me know where the real power resided. I was determined to reverse that. He was introduced as Sir William Feston, one of the two senor partners who had set up the venerable firm forty years before.

"Ah, Dr. Bouton," he said, extending a hand as bony and lifeless as his personality. "Young Mr. Gralt informs me you wish to engage us for your legal work. He also informs me you have just been accepted into the Macquarie Street residence. My hearty congratulations. I think I can say we are well placed to handle any dealings you may require. Now, I would recommend our Mr. Eagleton. A very senior solicitor with our firm." He scooped me toward the door, leaving Gralt, dismissed and ignored, in his wake.

I extracted myself. "Perhaps, Mr. Gralt did not make it clear. Or perhaps the fault was mine for not explaining myself well enough. I wish to engage Mr. Gralt as my solicitor."

"But Mr. Gralt is a mere junior. Mr. Eagleton has years more experience and expertise," Feston whined.

"And charges accordingly for his expertise," I said.

"Naturally. We assume you want the very highest legal minds on your business," Feston smarmed.

"Indeed, I do. Can you guarantee that your Mr. Eagleton will give my business his attention, or will he pass the work to menials who will then prompt him with a written response just prior to my next visit?"

Feston hedged for a moment before saying feebly, "That is the nature of the business."

"I'm quite sure it is," I said, not without a certain smugness. "So, if you will forgive my saying so, I wish to engage Mr. Gralt and only Mr. Gralt to handle my business. I prefer to pay the ventriloquist, not his dummy."

I thought Feston would have apoplexy on the spot, and was equally sure that Gralt would burst out laughing at any moment. In the end we all kept our dignity and I got my way. After he left the office, I got down to business with Gralt. I had a lot on my mind and wanted all the legal hurdles taken care of.

"You don't pull your punches, Dr. Bouton," he said, shaking my hand to cement our business relationship and, I hoped, our friendship.

"Damien, please. I need someone who is on my side and I trust you to look after my back."

"That you can, Damien," he replied. "Clement, though I prefer Clem."

"Right, Clem. To work. I have a multitude of questions."

By the end of office hours I had all my questions answered to my satisfaction, Clem was on to the paperwork and we had forged the beginnings of a real working partnership. I felt I had the measure of the man and was satisfied I could trust him.

As I left, I said, "I suspect if all goes well, you may find yourself offered a more senior position. Even if only that I may be billed at a higher rate."

"You're a cynic, Damien; however, in this case, I suspect you are one hundred per cent correct."

The next day I approached Valerie, who had returned from her triumphant conquest of the great southern audience in Melbourne, with my news. I'm surprised they didn't hear her in that distant city for she let out such a whoop of joy I thought my ear drums might be permanently damaged. I swore her to secrecy, allowing she might tell Cecil. She, in turn, took on the task of organising the gala event at which I would announce my good news because it would not remain secret for much longer.

So much can be achieved in three days so, by Saturday night, Valerie's palatial residence was a blaze of light as people from all walks of life turned up for the party. I had even inveigled Eric into demanding a night off from his far from happy employer just so he and John could be there; telling him it was of such importance he could not afford to miss it. Even Rodney took time off from his socialist activities to attend.

The whispers about the room were all to do with Valerie and her imminent trip to England. She looked like the cat that ate the canary all night, bursting to reveal the secret. She barely got through a number of songs in celebration of success and happiness and people were getting fidgety. She called me over and I took centre stage, or the centre of an elevated platform in her ball room where she performed.

"Ladies and gentlemen," I said, calling for quiet. "Yes, Mum, no need looking around, I meant you, too, when I said ladies." There was a roar of laughter from those assembled. "You are all the friends I have in the world, and I wanted to share my immense good fortune with you all, and I'm so glad to have the opportunity before three of the people dearest to me, Valerie, Ty, and Cecil..." Cecil looked so startled to be included in that list he almost spilled his drink but recovered enough that he raised his glass in salute.

"Many of you have known me since I first came back to Sydney and Mum took me in. I thank you from the bottom of my heart for your friendship, your patience when I had to negotiate those dark, dark days."

I knew if I didn't get to the news shortly I would lose their attention, so I just blurted it out. I expected many different reactions but not the one I got. Stunned silence, then a roar of approval, Valerie leading a sing-along rendition of "For He's a Jolly Good Fellow." If only Josh had been here to share my news. I learned later that he did experience it, second-hand, when Mum wrote to his mother in great detail about the night and how we had all raised our glasses to 'missing friends.'

I endured the back slaps and the congratulations as I went in search of Eric and John. They were as effusive as the rest, wary when I ushered them into the privacy of Valerie's library, something I had organised with her earlier.

They sat together as I made them a drink from Valerie's generous liquor cabinet. They were genuinely pleased for me. "You are two of my dearest friends," I began, unsure how to tackle this. They raised their glasses to that. "I know you have been unhappy in your employment for a long time, Eric." He nodded. "I would like to offer you a position at my Macquarie Street residence. I'll be in need of a manservant, especially one I can trust. You know what I mean. I can only afford to match your current salary at the moment but, given time, I should be able to afford more."

Eric shook his head.

John looked at him in horror. "Don't be a fool, love," he said.

"We swore we would never take another position without we both work for the same employee," Eric said.

John was excited. "But can't you see, this is the next best thing? You can ask for days off to coincide with mine. It won't be perfect but it has to be better than what we have now." John turned to me, "Thank you, Damien. That's very generous. He'll take it."

I laughed. They looked at me as if the happiness had affected my brain.

"You didn't let me finish," I said, ready to spring the surprise. "I also need a cook. I want both of you."

John stared at me as if he hadn't heard correctly, then a sob shook his frame and the tears rolled down his cheeks. He couldn't stop, the emotion was too much and I left the room quietly as Eric comforted his lover, mouthing the words 'Thank you' as I retreated.

Mum had been looking everywhere for me. She was an old woman, as she kept telling me, and was eager to get home. "I don't trust that old piss pot I left in charge of my boarding house." She seemed quiet, too quiet, as I walked her to the front door. "I suppose I won't be seeing as much of you any more, now that you've gone all la di dah."

"Why?" I asked. "Are you going to throw me out of my Pyrmont home? Or now that I'm a man of some importance are you going to triple the rent so that I can't afford to stay there anymore?"

She slapped my arm. "Cheeky." She stared at me. "You really going to keep Pyrmont open?" I nodded, and then she added, "There are a lot of people depend on you."

"I may not be able to spend every day there but at least once or twice a week and I'll get a telephone installed in case there's an emergency."

She was still shaking her head in amazement as I helped her into Valerie's car for the chauffeur to drive her home.

I stood in the driveway wondering why my success felt so hollow.

CHAPTER EIGHTEEN

~

THE ACADEMY SCHOOL OF DANCING

*J*ohn's sobbing did eventually subside, but it took days. He was prone to break out in tears for no apparent reason. Eric was still dazed by the events, although it had sunk in enough that he handed in his resignation the next day, giving his employers the bare minimum of notice without even the courtesy of staying on to train the new manservant. He believed he had been treated shabbily, so returned the favour on his departure.

It was a godsend in a way as I needed him to oversee the establishment of my new premises. I gave him full power because I had little enough time to concentrate on the minutiae and he was expert at that. John had a more difficult time extricating himself from his employers who were none-too-keen to see him go. They kept offering him more and more money to stay, his constant refusal spurring them on to increasingly ridiculous incentives. When they found no amount of bribery would induce him to remain, they turned nasty and made his final month there a living hell. If he hadn't had Eric for support and the knowledge that he was finally going to a job where he could live openly with his lover, he may have buckled under the pressure.

The month passed quickly enough and he soon joined Eric setting up the accommodation and, especially, the kitchen. The rooms had been allowed to deteriorate under the previous tenant and I was determined that I would have living quarters and a surgery that was as state of the art as I could afford. Other residents of the building took to popping in to watch the progress while Sir Michael Cycledes merely continued to complain about the disruptions to his patients with so many 'lower class' tradesmen in the building although he had no hesitation in asking one of my plumbers to have a look at his hot water system. I billed him for the impertinence.

In all, it took six weeks before I was able to move in. Eric had been living on the premises from the end of the first week, making do until John joined him a month later. They were too happy to notice the shambles which, to them, appeared as perfect as a palace. I envied their comfortable domesticity. If I couldn't have my own, then I would try to help others to theirs.

It would have been nice to have carried Josh over the threshold as I moved my life into my new residence. I had brought Mum with me for support as I knew she had a good eye for anything superfluous or out of whack with the surroundings. She announced herself pleased with my new accommodation. "More in keeping with the gentleman you are," she said proudly. I kissed her fondly on the forehead as we went to the kitchen to share tea and cake that John had prepared especially for the occasion. I'd also invited the others who shared offices in the building to drop in at any time during the day. Most of them took advantage of the offer if only to cast a critical eye over my improvements or to sample John's culinary skills about which they'd heard so much.

There's was something of a competition over who would warm my bed that first night but I slept alone, in sombre tribute to the man who should have been sharing my success. Subsequent evenings I was not as virginal, although it did not suit Rodney's socialist tendencies to be seen in such an advantageous address even though he was wealthy himself.

Slow to begin with, my practice began to improve once the social list who trekked to Pyrmont in disguise felt it easier and less socially unacceptable to be seen at Dr. Bouton's of Macquarie Street where they could plead a stomach problem, a nasty cold or some other imaginary ailment, instead of the clap. I was discretion itself and kept my files securely locked away, writing in code for any sexual 'disturbances' my patients suffered.

I preferred my own company to that of party crowds, usually spending my free time, what little there was of it for Wednesdays and Saturdays I was at Pyrmont, with Clem or Valerie and Cecil or with Eric and John. Often, when I finished my rounds in Pyrmont on a Saturday, I would buy fish and chips from the local. Mum and I would sit and eat out of the newspaper wrapping with our fingers, listening to the radio in between the incessant bed renting traffic.

All too soon, Valerie had packed up her costumes, laid covers over the furniture in her house, dismissed the servants, and headed for a brave new adventure in the Mother Country.

She played havoc with the pursers on the ship, many of them of the fraternity which she twigged to almost immediately. They worshipped her, and she had them doing everything but cartwheels for her. Ty would make short work of most of them on the voyage. There were also a number of attractive male pursers who were interested in women, and very interested in Valerie.

I almost regretted my decision not to accept Valerie's generous offer to accompany her but I knew Ty would put it to much better use. He would be happier in a big city like London rather than the parochial cultural backwater that was Sydney. We were sipping champagne in Valerie's spacious cabin, cramped with the number of well-wishers, when a sudden silence descended. I had my back to the cabin door but I knew immediately the reason. I heard Valerie shriek with delight before gushing, "I'm so glad you could make it. Grab a champers, you already know just about everybody here." I heard her flamboyant kiss on a cheek. Then another.

Ty squeezed my hand in support. "I'm here if you need me."

I turned, a smile frozen on my face. I was unprepared for the change in Josh. He was haggard, stooped as if he had the weight of the world on his shoulders, looking years older. Mrs. Carter saw me and smiled. She pushed her way through the crowd toward me, dragging a reluctant Josh behind her. He was looking for someone, anyone, to block his path.

"Doreen wrote to me about your new practice in Macquarie Street, Dr. Button..."

"Mum, I don't know how many times I have to tell you, it's pronounced Boo-ton."

"Actually, I prefer Damien."

"See," Mrs. Carter crowed. "No airs and graces on this one. Still the same lovely man that came to Seaspray Bay. Oh, we do wish you'd come back."

"You'd be the only one," I said, a little ungraciously.

"You'd be surprised," she said.

"Congratulations, Damien," Josh said, after a dig in the ribs from his mum's elbow.

Everyone in the cabin was watching while pretending not to.

"Why don't you show him the ship, Damien?" Mrs. Carter suggested. "I'm sure he'd like to see it."

"Mu-um." Josh was uncomfortable.

"Come on," I said. "It's getting a bit claustrophobic in here anyway."

I leaned over the rail and watched the lights of the city. Sure, Sydney was small in comparison to the major cities of the world like London, New York and Paris, but here there was room to breathe, room to grow. This was where I belonged.

"How's your fiancée, Josh?" I kept the sarcasm, the contempt, out of my voice.

"Don't," he said.

I realised the man standing beside me was a stranger. I didn't know him anymore.

"Your new boyfriend is very handsome," he said. He swallowed so hard I heard it.

"He's not my boyfriend, Josh. He's a friend, a very good friend."

"You slept with him though." Josh sounded petulant.

"I've slept with lots of men."

"Same here," he admitted.

"But there's only one that I want to share my life with."

"Who's that?" he queried.

"The man standing beside me now. I wish he could be there always."

"Don't," he said, more forcefully than he intended because he took my hand to show he hadn't meant it. "I spoiled it, didn't I?"

"Spoiled what?"

"Us."

"Let's take a walk, Josh."

He kept abreast of me as we walked silently past hordes of well-wishers spilling from cabins like confetti at a wedding, streamers and conical hats adorning their heads.

"Why are you here, Josh?"

"Mum dragged me."

"You're a grown man, you could have refused." I shot him a sideways glance. "Where are you staying tonight?"

"Mum's staying with Mum Doreen."

"And you?"

"I guess she'll have a spare room for me."

I grabbed his hand and pulled him toward the stairs to take us down to the gangplank and away from all the artificiality and forced bonhomie. I looked back to see Eric watching us from the railing. He would make our apologies and I didn't think anyone would mind.

We could have caught a taxi but it was a warm and sunny afternoon for walking.

"I'd forgotten how beautiful the city is," he said as he looked around him, reappraising an old friend.

"Its beauty pales alongside yours." I felt foolish saying something so sentimental, but it was true.

He stopped and turned to me. "Do you still have feelings for me, Damien?"

"I've never stopped loving you."

"You're smarter than me, Damien. Why do I see your face on the men I go with? Why do none of them satisfy me the way you used to? Why did I count the days until I could see you again at Val's farewell?"

"You don't need a reason to see me."

"I didn't know what you think of me."

"What I've always felt about you."

"I don't understand. Look at me. I'm a mess."

I couldn't disagree with that. "It's..." I was about to say 'Danny' but changed my mind. "It's that village of yours. It's unhealthy for you."

"Mum needs me," he said simply.

"No, she doesn't. I need you."

We walked in silence until we reached Macquarie Street. I knew, after the splendour of Enzo's home in Potts Point, my abode would still appear humble by comparison, but I wasn't out to impress. As we walked through the foyer I saw him glance at my name in gold lettering on the Directory. He stopped to admire it, running his fingers across the letters, almost as if he were trying to recapture the past.

I steered him to the lifts and soon we reached the door to my surgery, again with my name picked out in gold on the frosted glass. It would have been easy enough to take him in via the living quarters' entrance but I wanted him to see where I work. I unlocked the door, ushering him inside. It was the waiting room. I closed and locked the door behind us and took him into my surgery. The view over Macquarie Street to the Botanical Gardens was breath-taking. I could see he was impressed despite himself.

I patted my padded bench, the one I used to examine patients. "Drop your trousers. Hop up here for a second."

He looked unsure. I saw fear in his eyes.

"It's all right, Josh. I won't hurt you."

He must have been reassured because he did as I instructed. As he lay there, I pushed and prodded his body, paying particular attention to his crippled leg.

"You haven't been looking after yourself, Josh," I said.

I undid his shirt to examine his chest. As I touched his skin, I noticed his cock stiffen in his underpants. He tried to cover it with his hands.

"I'm flattered that I can still have that effect on you, Josh."

I got him to turn over which he did readily enough if only to cover his erection. I slapped his arse when I'd completed my examination, and turned my attention to his ears, eyes, nose and throat.

"Are you sleeping well?"

"I have bad dreams."

When I'd finished, I said. "You can get dressed now."

While he did so, I sat behind my desk and wrote a prescription, folding it in half and putting it in an envelope for him. "You're not well, Josh. I've written a prescription. Make sure you follow it to the letter and you should be back to your normal self in next to no time. But, I am worried. You seem to be suffering from exhaustion. Your blood pressure is very bad for a man of your age and constitution. Do you have a lot of worries?"

"My life's a mess," he admitted.

"Come inside. We can talk about it if you want."

I gave him a quick tour of the living quarters and watched his eyes widen in wonder. "You've come a long way, Damien. If anyone deserves it, it's you."

"Everyone deserves happiness."

We went to the kitchen and I found leftovers which made a palatable enough snack, eating it off trays in the living room. It was comfortable being with Josh like this. Almost like old times. I pictured him as a permanent member of my home, wondering if, as he looked about him, he was attempting to picture the same. I was about to broach the subject when I heard the front door open.

"There you are!" Mrs. Carter seemed delighted to find Josh with me.

"Sorry," Josh said.

"Nothing to be sorry for," she chided. "Eric saw you leave and I knew you were in good hands."

"Wasn't that a grand send off?" Mum sniffed, wiping her eyes with her handkerchief.

"Have you ever seen such a big boat in your life?" Mrs. Carter said in awe.

"Ship, mum. Not a boat," Josh corrected.

"Ship. Boat. Whatever it was, it was bloody big," she replied, sending Mum off into fits of giggles.

Eric mimed a glass to his lips. They had imbibed liberally.

"Listen, everyone," I said. "I'd like you all to be my guests tonight for dinner. No, don't look at me like that Eric, I meant dining out at Repin's or some such." I didn't want to make it too posh because the women would feel uncomfortable and out of place, but I wanted it to be better than they could afford themselves. "Then a spot of dancing afterwards."

"I haven't danced in ever so long," Mrs. Carter confided, looking as if she would cherish the opportunity.

"Where were you thinking of?" Eric asked, cocking an eyebrow.

"Black Aggie's, of course."

He nodded his head in the direction of the two women who were babbling excitedly about the opportunity to dance.

"Will there be any men who will want to dance with two old boilers like us?" Mum asked.

"Are you up for a bit of an adventure?"

"Count me in," Mrs. Carter said quickly.

"Me, too," Mum added. "Them three pissin' orf to the Old Dart has made me realise life is slipping by."

"Is this place suitable for my mum?" Josh asked.

"What do you think, Eric?" I winked at him.

"I think the ladies will be well looked after," he said, smirking.

As it was already getting late, the ladies went to freshen up. Josh bailed me up as soon as they were out of earshot. "Where are you taking them?' he demanded.

"Somewhere they'll have the time of their lives. Somewhere you might even enjoy if you learn to relax."

We were all dressed respectably if not fancy so we found a middle-range restaurant that was classy enough to impress but not cower diners of Mrs. Carter and Mum Doreen's taste. I told them to order what they liked without regard to price but they went for the old stand-bys. As a treat I ordered an extra serving of some of the more exotic items on the menu because I knew they would love to sample them but were afraid to order lest they not like the taste. I was right to do so because they positively fawned over the new tastes and textures. They left the restaurant with enough stories to tell their friends for weeks. It was a pleasure to see their enjoyment in such a simple pastime.

We walked the short distance from the centre of the city through Hyde Park to Commonwealth Street, an area of warehouses and Griffith Bros Teas. The discreet entrance to Black Aggie's was a plain wooden doorway identified by an old painted sign that swung listlessly from the awning; it had seen better days but still proclaimed *Academy School of Dancing*. In much smaller letters underneath it read, Proprietress: Agnes Stone. This was the famed Black Aggie's.

I knocked loudly, a panel in the door slid back, like in those Hollywood speakeasy movies. That had Mum and Mrs. Carter gasping in awe. The door swung open as soon as I'd been identified, to reveal a large coal black American woman, the proprietress acknowledged on the sign.

"Dr. Bouton, how nice to see you. And who are these lovely ladies you've brought with you tonight?"

"This is Mum Doreen and Mrs. Carter, who is in the city for the weekend and whom I promised to show the most sinful sites Sydney has to offer."

"Then you have come to the right place, ladies. Let me show you the way."

She went ahead of us, her stout frame blocking anyone from passing on the stairs to the first floor where the dance academy held its 'lessons.' Her size was a definite asset when the police raided, which they did on a regular basis. I had neglected to tell Josh or his mum about that aspect of the evening.

Upstairs, Linden tinkled away at the piano while couples danced in the centre of the hall and others sat around watching or gossiping. There was a palpable sexual tension in the air, the sort you expect in premises in which people congregate to pick up partners of either gender.

There were a few men dancing together and a female couple but otherwise the club was fairly deserted at that time. Later in the evening it would be packed to overflowing. I ordered tea for all of us much to Mum's delight. "I'm parched, love," she said. "All those stairs, not good for me at my age."

When the large pot of tea was delivered to the table, there was a strong smell of alcohol. Mum looked at me slyly and poured herself a cup. "Hmm, pretty piss weak tea, Damien. I wonder what they use for tea leaves?" She took a sip and coughed as it burned her throat. "That's one mighty strong cuppa."

"They don't have a licence," I explained. "That's why the teapot and the cups."

As I knew they would, they found it all very adventurous. Eric and John did the right thing and asked the ladies to dance. Josh watched his mum. She must have been quite the looker in her younger days and more than held her own against Eric's skill and dexterity.

I stood, holding my hand out to Josh.

"I can't, Damien. You know my leg."

I didn't budge.

"I have wanted to dance with you for years, Josh Carter, and I won't take no for an answer, even if I have to carry you on to the dance floor."

"I couldn't, not in front of mum."

As if to put the lie to it, Mrs. Carter looked over and beckoned us both on to the floor.

"If that isn't permission enough, I don't know what is."

Josh sighed as he stood up to join me. He took my hand and we swept out on to the floor. I moderated the steps to take account of his injury. He was tentative at first but as he overcame his shyness he cut loose. The next number was slower and he laid his head against my shoulder. We danced through a third number and then went to sit down. Eric and John were dancing together and Mrs. Carter was dancing with a likeable young man that I knew slightly. Mum was in the arms of a rather masculine woman who guided her around the floor with more panache than most of the men could ever do.

When they came back to the table they were flushed with excitement.

"What a cheek! She invited me back to her place." Mum's words belied the fact she sounded secretly pleased.

"What's it like to dance like that with a woman?" Mrs. Carter wondered.

"Just like dancing with a man, except there were no pointy bits."

The women roared with laughter.

Our pot of tea was 'getting cold' and I was about to order another when the shout went up. The loud banging on the downstairs door should have forewarned us, and then there was a shout up the stairs from the door man: "Coppers."

There was a scramble as men and women on the floor changed partners. Eric and John went into action, taking Mrs. Carter and Mum on to the dance floor with the skill of regulars. Aggie picked up a large baton that had lain across the lid of the upright piano, while the pianist thumped out a popular dance tune, as if those on the dance floor were learners. Aggie beat time with the stick.

"One, two, turn. One, two, three, one, two three, will the couple on the left keep in step. Two, three, one, two, three. Listen to the music. That's it. Glide, two, three, glide, two, three. Good evening officers, may I help you?"

The police knew what was going on and harassed the dancers as antagonistically as possible by taking down names and addresses, all of them fake, while the head of the squad was taken into Aggie's office for a spot of tea and a nice envelope of cash. Everyone knew the routine and played by the rules.

Occasionally, the cops would take away one of the more effeminate of the men and he would spend time in the cells at Surry Hills or Darlinghurst where he would be raped and bashed by those on duty. I'd done my fair share of patching up the cops' handiwork.

Their visit was over in ten minutes or so but it seemed a lifetime and it sent a pall over the evening. Even the fact that Mum had been accused of being a prostitute, over which she had a chuckle with Mrs. Carter, failed to lift our spirits.

"Is it always like this?" Mrs. Carter asked.

"Not always," I replied. "But it comes with the territory."

"Bastards!" she spat.

I thought any good news would be a cheery antidote to the gloom.

"By the way, I'm looking for someone to help at the surgery. Now, that business is picking up, I need someone who can handle patients. You were always good at that, Josh."

"Are you offering him a position?" Mrs. Carter beamed.

"Yes, I am. The money is good, although not great. There's on-the-job training. Free board and lodgings..."

"That's a very generous offer, isn't it Josh?"

He didn't respond, just sat there like a stone then unexpectedly he turned on me, his anger cold and all the more dangerous for it. "How dare you put my mum in a situation where she could have been arrested."

Eric jumped to my defence. "There was never any chance—"

"If you set out to impress, you did a lousy job of it," he said.

"Josh," his mother warned.

"You think this hotbed of perversion is a suitable place to entertain respectable women? Then I don't know you, Damien. You're not the man I once knew. Come on, mum."

He held his hand out to her. She sat without moving.

"You're making an even bigger fool of yourself than normal, Josh. Sit down. I'm not going anywhere. I'm enjoying myself. As for perversion. I don't see any. All I see is a lot of people who were having a good time until flat-footed coppers came and destroyed the fun."

Eric and John discreetly led Josh's mum and Mum Doreen out onto the floor leaving Josh and me alone.

"I'm sorry if you think this place is inappropriate Josh, but she seems to be having a good time," I said to placate him.

"I don't know what's wrong with me. I'm always losing my temper. With everyone around me." Josh sat with his head in his hands, miserable. "You know what that young guy you were seeing said?"

"You mean Ty?"

"Yeah. Funny, but he's a really nice guy. I can see why you like him. He really likes you, too. Told me at Seaspray. Also told me the reason I'm angry with everyone around me is because I'm angry with myself. How dumb is that?"

I would have replied except that a few thumped cords on the piano announced that Aggie was about to sing. She'd read the dispirited mood of the crowd and realised we needed cheering up. The dancers returned to their tables, Josh sat down and I moved my chair close behind him. As the lights dimmed and Aggie began to belt out the upbeat "Alexander's Ragtime Band," it got our feet tapping, our hearts pumping, and the joy flowing. It's amazing what a song can do to lift people out of the doldrums.

Aggie had a gravelly blues voice, full of cigarettes and pain, as if she'd spent her life with shiftless and faithless men. We could all identify with that. Well, maybe the lesbians in the room had to do a bit of transference. Tentatively, I put my arms around Josh and gently pulled his body against mine. There was no resistance. His hair was just under my chin and I ran my fingers through it, kissing it, stroking his face. He'd forgotten his mother was across the table from him. He sighed, releasing all his pent-up frustration, and hugged my arms around his chest. I saw his mum nudge Mum to have a look at us. She seemed well pleased.

Our spirits had lifted considerably by the time Aggie had finished her half dozen or so songs, and the venue was getting more crowded and much more boisterous. Reluctantly, we got up to leave.

"Sorry, mum," Josh said. "I can be a miserable sod sometimes."

"Just like your father," she said.

"I enjoyed meself tonight," Mum said.

"We have to do this again some time," Mrs. Carter replied. "Soon."

They went to do whatever it is women do in the rest room, returning open-mouthed to report that there was a man dressed as woman in there putting on his make-up and padding his chest. It surprised me that things I took for granted were such new territory to other people. Mum knew about female impersonation but I guess she never expected to find one in the women's toilet.

"Would you like to spend the night with me, Josh?" I asked when we had a moment alone. When he hesitated, I added, "There's a spare room if you'd be more comfortable there. That way Mum can rent out your room at Pyrmont." Mum was putting up Josh and Mrs. Carter free of charge for all the times she'd spent in Seaspray Bay.

That must have given him the excuse he was looking for. "Yes, I would like that."

I nodded to Eric who had already volunteered to take Mum and Mrs. Carter back to Pyrmont. Josh made arrangements to meet at Central for the train back home the next day, then he and I walked back along College Street toward Macquarie, passing by the Archibald Fountain at the northern end, already busy with painted boys attempting to earn a living, strangers looking for a quick liaison, and the occasional plain-clothes cop moving in for the arrest like some venomous spider.

Back at the residence I prepared the spare room, hoping he wouldn't use it. By the time I'd finished, Eric and John had returned after dropping off the ladies in a taxi. John prepared the four of us a nightcap and we sat in the living room, John in Eric's arms, Josh seated on the floor at my legs, leaning his head on my knees. We were the picture of connubial bliss, except that Josh and I weren't really doing any connubialing. Still, it was very pleasant to even have him by my side.

John and Eric went off to bed. Josh yawned and I knew it was time to relinquish my hold on him. "There's the spare room, Josh. Or, you would be more than welcome to share my bed."

He seemed tempted for a moment but settled for the spare room. I showed him the way, gave him a towel for the morning, and wished him a good night.

"Damien?" he said softly.

I paused and he came to me, kissing me lightly on the cheek. If I expected more I was in for a disappointment.

"Goodnight," he said.

I went back to my room, frustrated that I was unable to break down his stubborn reserve. I could tell he still had feelings for me but I was at a loss over how to get him to release them short of taking a crowbar to his heart. I lay awake in my bed, tempted almost beyond endurance to sneak to his room. I would get little sleep that night having him under my roof.

It was more than an hour after I had switched out my light, after attempting to read, that there was a soft knock at the door.

"Come in."

Josh peaked around the door. "Sorry to wake you."

"You didn't. I can't sleep."

"Me neither."

I turned down the blanket and sheet, and patted the bed. Without hesitation, he slid in beside me, his strong arms around me like he was frightened I would disappear. I held him as he lowered his head to my chest and within a matter of moments, he was fast asleep.

Now that he was in my bed and in my arms I tried to ward off sleep but to no avail. We woke up in virtually the same position in the morning. Eric knocked on the door early to say there had been an accident at CSR and they were asking if I could attend. Reluctant as I was to leave Josh I had a duty to perform. I dressed quickly and took the car. If it were an emergency then speed was of the essence. I would bathe when I returned. I asked Eric to pass on my apologies to Josh, asking him to stay until I managed to get back.

Given the circumstances, I did not get back until the afternoon, a poor wretch had caught his hand in a machine and it had to be dismantled in order to free him, to much grumbling from the overseer who kept muttering about lost production. The accident had only come about because the protective guard had been removed because it slowed down the work.

By the time I returned to Macquarie Street, bloodied and weary, Josh was long gone.

CHAPTER NINETEEN

~

PRESCRIPTION FOR HAPPINESS

I wrote to Josh explaining the circumstances of the accident at the CSR factory in case he believed I'd deliberately stayed away. I didn't think it would make any difference to our situation but I wanted the opportunity to thank him for spending the night, albeit virginally, because I now saw it as his parting gift to me. I appreciated the gesture as a final closing of the book. Yes, it hurt, but there was nothing I could do. I had given it my all, insipid as that may have been, and I was out of ammunition.

Danny had poisoned his mind. Unless Josh could break the influence he was headed for a life made miserable by the effect it would have on his family and friends. I no longer considered myself part of either. I had picked the scab and applied the dressing. It was only a matter of time before the scar healed over.

Fortunately, I had my burgeoning practice to help me keep my equilibrium, and the vitriolic contempt of Sir Michael Cycledes who never tired of complaining about real or perceived misdemeanours by me, my staff or my patients. I had tried being reasonable with him, even proffering the hand of truce, if not friendship, but it seemed the more determined I was to ignore his behaviour the more odious became the taunts.

As much as possible I avoided him but was forced to endure his rants at the building's monthly meetings at which we discussed ongoing maintenance issues, the general running of the chambers, or, in his case, diatribes against my methodology and my lack of class. It became so wearying and unreasonable that other members rallied to my defence, becoming friendlier than had he ceased his opposition to my residency.

One of the flashpoints was the number of working class patients I handled at the Macquarie Street practice, people who Cycledes believed should be neither heard nor seen. They had never caused a disturbance, most of them preferring to use the stairs than share a lift with their so-called social betters. No one had ever complained to me about breaches of decorum, they all complained to Cycledes it seemed, and then only anonymously. At first, the board was inclined to take them seriously until they became so unrelenting and so repetitive that the anonymity became suspicious. He was told that until someone was prepared to sign their name to a written complaint, and supply proof of their allegation, the board was powerless to act. Any further unsubstantiated accusations would be regarded as a personal vendetta against me.

I knew Cycledes would not let it rest and he would be scheming to precipitate a confrontation of some sort. I couldn't allow it to blight my life so I continued much as before, just a notch warier than most people would be. I was determined not to be taken completely by surprise.

The months passed slowly, but inexorably. I worked a lot, I played a little, I wrote to Ty and to Valerie about their beloved Sydney, their return letters full of their excitement and dreams. It would be no time at all before their correspondence slowed to a trickle and then became a card at Christmas as they adjusted to their new lives. Some nights, I wished it were me in London with them. They had hinted warmly that they would love to see me there. It was tempting but I would have to begin all over again and, quite frankly, I had no stomach for it at present. Perhaps in a year or two.

Mum continued her monthly visits to stay with Mrs. Carter but she resolutely refused to pass on any information about Josh. Not that I even bothered to ask. She did enjoy her trips north in the train. She was always met at Gosford, the coastal hamlet's nearest large neighbour, where she and Josh's mum had a cup of tea and a bun at a café before one of the Seaspray locals, in town to stock up on supplies, drove them back. They spent the weekend chinwagging, walking around the small village, shopping, and swigging copious amounts of tea. Mum was enjoying herself so much in this new-found friendship; she was beginning to neglect her 'rental accommodation.'

A few of her friends, including Eric and John, were becoming concerned at her absences. I didn't see that it was any of our business. I still enjoyed our Saturday nights around the radio listening to the serials. I would always bring a cake, a fancy extravagance from David Jones' or some upscale pastry shop. I was careful to eat the smallest of pieces and even though, in a mood of generosity, she might share the treat with her 'favourite boys', she was still careful to place the remainder in a tin and hide it under her bed to savour over the following few days.

It was one such night when Mum put down the saucer from which she'd been drinking her hot tea. "That coconut tart really hit the spot, Damien. You really are good to your old Mum." I made the usual sounds about it being nothing. It was a ritual we went through every week, only the name of the baked goods changed. That week she surprised me by deviating from the well-worn, taking my hand kindly, looking me in the eye and saying, "Josh still loves you, you know. He doesn't realise it, but he will."

I didn't want to hear that. It opened up old wounds. It gave me hope when there was none. Just as I was finally getting over my foolish feelings, here she was encouraging me again. I wanted to remonstrate with her about her particularly bad timing, to ask why she would say such a thing, particularly now. I got my answer but not in the manner I would have liked. Her hand gripped my arm with a strength that belied her age and gender. She had the presence of mind to mutter, "The cake tin, under the bed," before her eyes went back in her head and she gave the tiniest of gasps as she pitched forward, her face slamming onto the table. Despite it being such a surprise, I was up and feeling for her pulse but it was already too late.

I suppose I shouldn't have done it but I could not leave the woman who had been like a second mother to me, face down on her kitchen table, apart from the fact it was bad for business. I carried her into the bedroom to lay her out. Before calling the necessary authorities from the phone I'd had installed which Mum eventually insisted I lock away in my surgery because every Tom, Dick and Mary in the neighbourhood took to dropping in to use it, I rang Eric asking that he and John take a taxi to join me.

We turned away all new business that night. Most accepted with good grace, some asking to view the body one last time, while others kicked up such a fuss you'd have thought the world was about to end. Those we had no hesitation in slamming the door on. It wasn't as if other houses in the vicinity hadn't opened in the wake of Mum's success. Unlike her establishment, however, they gouged punters with their high cost of 'accommodation' charging more the next time if you complained about the bed bugs.

I found the cake tin under a loose floorboard beneath her bed. It contained her last will and testament, as well as about a week's takings. She always liked to have a little ready cash for 'emergencies' such as paying off the police and to lend to those in dire needs. I had no idea whether she trusted the banks, something people of her generation tended against.

The following weeks were a blur. My practice suffered although I handled the emergencies. It was only with the goodwill of Mum's real friends that we managed to give her a right royal send off. She'd expressed no religious convictions that I'd ever heard beyond the occasional, "Thank God for that." Still, I didn't think she'd mind that we buried her in the Church of England section of Waverley Cemetery where many of us endured a partisan ceremony as she was lowered into earth on a hillside that faced the glimmering blue sea. We knew she couldn't see the view but, I suppose, it made us feel happy.

We laid on buses from Pyrmont for those who wished to attend, plus transport back for those who were coming to the wake for which we'd purloined Mum's Pyrmont terrace. I'd been permitted to continue my medical practice twice a week from the premises albeit for a substantial increase in rent; previously I had paid a peppercorn amount. We had contacted Valerie, Cecil and Ty about the sad news not expecting they could attend but they did, however, send a beautiful wreath that would have made Mum proud. I reminded myself I had to stop thinking like that.

I was not surprised when Mrs. Carter turned up but was more so that Josh was with her. When he begged to be one of the pallbearers because, he said, he and Mum had formed a rather close friendship over the months she'd been visiting I had to tell him the positions had been filled. Rodney graciously elected to relinquish his place in the face of Josh's adamant refusal to be rejected. Mrs. Carter took me aside to explain that Mum had helped Josh through a very difficult time, and that I would be very grateful for her intervention. Busy with preparations, I had no time or inclination to ask what she meant by that, tucking it aside for later.

Eric, John, Jack, Bert, Josh and myself shouldered the coffin to the hearse which was to take it to the cemetery. Those who could not afford to take the entire morning off work or neighbours who just came to pay their last respects, or to gawk, lined the footpath. There was a real outpouring of emotion for a woman who had become an integral part of the area and who was never too proud to help out those in need.

The pallbearers crammed into two cars to follow the cortège through the city to the eastern suburbs. On arrival the nods and introductions were sombre, befitting the occasion. We took our places around the grave, the coffin sat atop wooden planks and strong canvas straps. The floral tributes covered the lid and I watched many covetous eyes wonder how they could get their hands on them when the service was over. The minister cleared his throat.

"If everyone is here, I think we should begin."

I looked about the assembled group, refusing to bow my head, much to the consternation of some religious mourners. Eric caught my eye and smiled at my defiance.

The minister intoned impersonally, "Forasmuch as it hath pleased Almighty God of his great mercy to take unto himself the soul of our dear sister here departed, we therefore commit her body to the ground; earth to earth, ashes to ashes, dust to dust..."

It was the other side of the world when I first refused to humble myself before a non-existent deity. Many soldiers lost their beliefs, as well as their mates, during those terrible four years, not least of all, me. I lost my innocence, my beliefs, and my beloved on the battlefields of France.

Fromelles was a disaster, although the British labelled it a success in their communiqué, because around one hundred and forty Germans were captured.

Our exchange? A complete rout of Allied forces, the near crippling of the Fifth Division and the loss of over five thousand five hundred Australian lives, including that of young Edward Gordon Teale, who had relied on me to save him. In the end, it transpired, I couldn't.

We had discovered a mutual attraction as well as a mutual secret early in our enlistment. About the same age, we became fast mates as well as clandestine lovers. He was soft and a little afraid, out of his depth in the all-male camaraderie, never made for the battlefield. There are some people, some men, who are not meant for the horrors of life, too fragile to survive. Ted was one such. I don't mean to imply that because he was queer he was a coward. Anything but. Many a queer soldier served his country well. It was only years later that I discovered that two of the wars most celebrated poets, Siegfried Sassoon and Wilfred Owen, were, like myself, queer.

Ted believed himself invincible because of my protection. He believed I was as close to a deity as the one he prayed to each night that he survive another day, but, in the end, God was either not listening or had His mind on other matters that day. Ted was mown down like so many others, his body trampled into the mud by fleeing soldiers, to be buried in anonymous pits behind German lines. I could have attempted to sling him over my shoulder and carry him back behind Allied lines but I knew he was dead. I could have lied and told them he was alive when I picked him up, but the Germans were retaking their lost positions and my life was in danger.

In case you think me callous, it was what we had to do to survive. Common decencies had little part in the war, not if you wanted to live. Much as my heart ached for my lost companion, instinct took over. Only much later did my betrayal prey on my conscience and it took years to finally lay my guilt to rest. Ted lay beneath the earth somewhere in France, in the embrace of his fellow soldiers.

Now Mum was being welcomed by that same earth as the coffin was lowered into the ground. My cheeks were damp but I didn't remember weeping. The flowers had been removed, except for Valerie's ostentatious tribute, distributed among the well-wishers at the funeral. The wreaths were left but others were taken to adorn front parlours and hallways. I thought it a good use.

The first thud of soil on the coffin lid brought the transient nature of life back to me. I didn't need any further reminding and walked away to an area reserved for a gathering of the nearest and dearest.

Mrs. Carter was dabbing her eyes as she approached. "I shall miss her," she said. "We became fast friends these last months." She left quickly, dragging Josh, who scarcely acknowledged me, with her to Eric's car as he was giving them a lift to the wake. I watched them climb into the borrowed vehicle with Rodney, George and Jack. Eric was leaving to get to Pyrmont before the general rabble arrived for the free food and booze, which meant a rambunctious and lively afternoon. I was not looking forward to it, particularly with Josh there.

"Damn and blast!" Eric said as he came back to me. "I've left two of the cakes at Macquarie Street. I'll need them if I'm going to feed all these people. Could you stop off and pick them up?"

I welcomed the diversion which meant I would get to Pyrmont later than anyone. Mum's friends could hold down the fort until I arrived, I had every confidence in the people travelling with Eric.

"Thanks," he said. "If you weren't my boss I'd kiss you."

I laughed. It was the first time in days. Eric had that effect on people. It was one, just one of many, of the reasons I was thankful to have him in my employ. He and John kept me level-headed and sane. They were fiercely loyal and very protective.

I watched the cars and buses leave one by one until I was left alone. I had no one to drive back, no timetable dictating my movements. I walked over to the gravediggers who were shovelling soil into the pit. They stopped and leaned on their spades as I approached. I looked down into the open maw of death.

"Thank you both; you've done a good job." It was a rather silly thing to say but the men seemed to appreciate the fact I'd taken the time to thank them.

They broke out their cigarettes, going so far as to offer me one. I shook my head and told them I didn't smoke but that they should go ahead.

"She must have been a good woman," the older of the two said. "We seen a lot of people put under the sod here. You can tell a person from their mourners, can't you, Keith?"

"Aye," Keith agreed.

"Your mum, was she?" the older asked.

"Yes." This wasn't the time to go into the intricacies of our relationship, and my reply was half truth.

"You see, them what has a lot of mourners are there because of genuine affection, like your mum's, or else to make sure the bastard is really dead as a result of being a mongrel all their lives."

He and Keith guffawed loudly.

"Beggin' your pardon for the language, sir," Keith said.

"No pardon necessary," I said, and they both visibly relaxed.

I stood talking to them while they went about their work, taking turns to shovel or to talk to me. The older man had served during the war, both of us relating our experiences while Keith worked.

"It gave me the feel for death. The smell," the older man related. "I don't have no skills of any sort. After I came home, I couldn't settle."

"Not uncommon," I said.

"I got to thinkin'. I seen so many young lads blown to bits, buried in large gaping pits. Germans, you understand. But human beings regardless of being Hun. We took better care of our own lads. A lot of the men couldn't stand the smell. But me? I didn't like it neither, but I got to thinking. As long as I could smell that smell, taste that smell, it meant I was alive. You get my meaning?"

I nodded that I did.

"That's why when I came back home I thought I'd apprentice to this bugger of an industry. Beggin' your pardon."

His swearing and his automatic pardon begging required no response; they were his natural way of speaking. He went through the motions in case I was offended. I wasn't in the least.

"I wanted to see the dead treated with a little dignity."

I extended my hand to them. They attempted to wipe the soil off on their trousers but I grabbed them before they could do so. I was unafraid of a little dirt.

They were startled that I would shake their hands at all. I strode away more confident than I had been in ages. The older man's simple, homespun philosophy was just as applicable to my situation; I had just been too blind to see it. The pain of loss I still harboured over Josh proved I could still love, that my heart was not dead to new emotions. Most of all, I was alive. I had been half-dead for so long I had forgotten joy, I had forgotten happiness, I had forgotten to appreciate what I had which was so much more than many who were living on the breadline day-to-day.

I would go to the wake. I would enjoy my misery and rejoice in the celebration of Mum's life, as well as mourn her death. On the drive to the city, I hummed so that, by the time I was back at my residence to pick up the forgotten cakes, I saw unlimited possibilities stretching before me. My euphoria was short-lived. When I entered my apartment I heard unfamiliar sounds of activity. Eric and John would have been at Pyrmont. There was no one else who should be there. I suspected a burglary, rather brazen in daylight hours. I quietly extracted a walking stick from the hall stand, holding it by the base so that I could bring it down heavily on some thief's skull if necessary.

Unsure where the sound was coming from I crept down the hallway, peeking into the semi-darkness ready to spring on the intruder. The kitchen was bare; no sign of anyone in the bathroom, Eric and John's room was pristine, as were the other bedrooms. The living and dining rooms were empty and I was beginning to think I had imagined the sounds or that they had come through the walls from next door. The third alternative was too disgusting to contemplate: that the city vermin had infiltrated my flat.

I lowered the walking stick and went to my bedroom to change. I was so startled that I screamed. Not a full-bodied scream but enough to startle the occupant of my bed who was, Goldilocks-like, fast asleep. He, too, screamed and sat up quickly, the sheet falling from his body to reveal he was naked.

"Josh, you scared the bloody life out of me," I said, my heart pounding in my ribs.

"That makes two of us," he said.

"What are you doing here?" I propped the walking stick against the chest of drawers. "Are you ill?"

He didn't answer. Instead, he took an envelope from under the pillow. "You once wrote me a script, Damien, when I was at my lowest ebb, telling me I should get it filled when I felt totally overwhelmed by circumstances. Is the script still valid?"

I looked at him closely. "That particular script is open ended. It will always be valid."

Josh unfolded the sheet that had been inside the envelope to read what I had written months before. "Prescription for happiness for Joshua Carter. Take one Damien Bouton daily for the remainder of your life. Side effects may include euphoria, bliss, extravagant protestations of desire, contentment, and just plain love. If symptoms persist keep Damien Bouton on hand."

He handed the sheet to me. "I've come to have the prescription filled."

I stared. I wanted to scream that I was not some second best whenever everything else went wrong with his life, that he had put me through hell, but I didn't. I hesitated.

"Relax. There are no cakes to be delivered to the wake. It was just a lie Eric cooked up to get you here."

"How many people know about this?"

"All your friends."

I removed my clothes slowly, wondering if I were doing the right thing as I slipped into Josh's embrace. He was ready for me, more than ready if I was to judge from what was prodding into my stomach. But I wasn't ready yet. He ran his tongue across my lips but I resolutely refused to open up for him. He said nothing. I turned over, leaning my head against his chest as he cradled me in his arms, his now impatient dick pressing against my back to remind me I had not taken care of it yet.

He ran his hands through my hair.

"You can't just turn up any time you feel like it and run off the next morning, Josh." There, I'd said it. "I can't do that anymore."

I went to move away, but he held me fast.

"Me neither," he said simply. There was a long pause before he added. "You were right about Danny."

"In what way?"

"He was sleeping with Carol behind my back."

Why wasn't I surprised?

"I'm sorry," I said, although it sounded totally insincere and inadequate for the occasion.

Josh snickered. "You don't sound it."

"All right, then," I snapped. "I'm not. You didn't love her. Her betrayal obviously did not hurt as much as Danny's. Am I right?"

Josh reluctantly agreed that I was.

"How did you find out?" I asked.

"He invited me over to see him about some new scheme he had for making money, he's always been one with a ready plan to get rich quick. I turned up early and they were in bed together. I think he set it up so I would catch them."

"Awkward." What else could I say?

"They both seemed delighted I was there. I hope you believe me Damien when I say I had never even seen Carol naked, let alone done anything with her, I was saving that for the wedding night. You see, I wasn't confident I would be able to consummate our arrangement. Now I found I was hard watching Danny on top of her. They noticed and Danny suggested I join them, make it a threesome. I was shocked."

I smirked. "A man of your experience?"

"No, I was shocked at my willingness to be involved."

I was jealous. "Did you?"

"I knew if I did, Danny would have control over my whole life. Still, I played along. I sat on the end of the bed watching, asking questions as if I was weighing up my options even though I had already made up my mind. I was cool as a cucumber. They revealed they'd been rooting around the whole time we'd been engaged and that Danny had every intention of continuing even after we were married. Carol could see no harm in it. It might even have worked if I'd been a different sort of man. I watched a little longer until I think they forgot I was even there. I let myself out and went home."

"Have you told your mum or your sister?"

"No. I won't either."

"But you won't go ahead with the wedding?" I was horrified to think he might.

"Does it look like it?"

"For all I know you could be here for one last fling to get it out of your system." His sharp intake of breath told me all I needed to know. "Or," did I dare say it? "You may be here because you love me."

"Have always loved you but couldn't admit it to myself. It's not your fault, Damien, it's mine. Can you ever forgive a stupid little bugger who didn't know his arse from his elbow?"

I wasn't sure I could forgive that easily, but I'd make a pretence of it. My mute reply was to lower my hand to his throbbing prick and wrap my fingers around it. They felt right at home and Josh groaned at their familiarity.

Handwork is all well and good but it's a poor substitute for the real thing. After I had worked Josh into such a state that he would have done anything for me, I slid down the bed to lick his balls, sucking them one at time into my mouth, lathering my spit and love on them to drive Josh wild in anticipation. He tried to move my head onto his cock but I resisted. I wanted to torture him a little. But the torture was mutual and I soon transferred my tongue and mouth to that glistening shaft, its excitement leaking from the slit. I had dreamed of this for so long, I wanted neither of us to be disappointed. Using my tongue to swab the head, I swallowed the pre-ejaculate, before sliding smoothly down to his balls, keeping my mouth and throat around his hardness until he gasped, attempting to pull me off lest he come too quickly.

I took pity on him and loosened my oral grip, kissing, licking and suctioning the shaft like picking at portions of a favourite meal. In between gasps, Josh croaked, "You're still the best."

It was unchivalrous of me to question whether I could say the same about Josh, particularly after the expert ministrations of Eric, Rodney and Ty. Let alone the other anonymous men with whom I'd shared my bed.

I lowered my tongue to the little groove that runs from just beneath his testicles to his arsehole. I bit it lightly as I ran my teeth along its edge, nuzzling my nose into his wrinkled hole before my tongue sought it out, pushing its way into the snug tunnel. He pulled his cheeks apart to welcome me and give me greater access. I licked and hawked a gob of saliva as I pushed his legs in the air. Josh got the hint and held them for me, spreading himself wide and vulnerable for my penetration. He seemed to sense that this initial onslaught would be free of any sort of artificial lubricant. It was a sad indictment on my personality, but I had to inflict pain. He must have guessed for he was stoic in his resignation.

He whimpered almost silently as I pressed my point home. I was not gentle. Once I'd breached his resistance I pushed all the way in. He gritted his teeth, a shadow of doubt crossing his face. Even then, I did not hesitate, repeatedly and cruelly ramming his arse. If I did not release this pent up hatred now it would simmer and fester, poisoning any relationship we might form in the future. I must confess I did not know if we had a future together.

He took me, uncomplaining. I looked him in the eyes and he unflinchingly returned my gaze. We searched each other for some truth, some semblance of the men we once were. If we couldn't find it then we would part in the morning and our lives would go along separate paths. I did not help him with his own relief, leaving his cock for his own hand if he so desired, but he didn't touch it. I grunted and spewed my spunk into his arse before collapsing on top of his body which had remained passive and limp during the onslaught.

While I was still exhausted, he flipped me on my stomach, licked two fingers and plunged them inside me. I was probably less tight than Josh because I'd had more opportunity than him. He must have cottoned on to that as well because he unceremoniously removed his fingers and positioned his cock. I gave him no help or resistance and he plugged me brutally with one thrust. I grunted into the pillow, biting off any cry of pain. He rode me swiftly and hard, repaying kind for kind. I wondered if we could survive such brutal behaviour.

He made very little sound as he came inside me. I felt his cock contract as he unloaded, and I felt his tears dropping on my back. He lay on top of me until his weight threatened to cut off my breathing. I scrambled out from under him. Neither of us dared look at the other.

"That's that then," he said sadly.

"It's not as easy as that, Josh," I said. "It will take a lot of repair work. We're both raw but I hope tonight got that out of the way. It may take weeks, it may take months, but I'm prepared to try. If you are, I'd like you to take that job I offered you. You can have your own room, you do not need to share my bed every night, but I at least hope you will want to share it sometimes. Ultimately, though, Josh, I don't want an employee, I want a partner. A partner in the business and a partner in life. If you don't think there's anything left to salvage or you don't want to try then we should part friends in the morning."

He went to speak, but I interrupted. "Don't make a hasty decision. Before you ask, if I didn't still feel something for you, I would not have made the offer. It's up to you whether you still have feelings for me. Take time to think about it. Come on, I'll show you your room."

We both put on underpants, suddenly a little coy around each other, as we padded down the hallway to the room I had always kept in case he dropped by and did not want to share my bed. He put his clothes away neatly in the wardrobe as I sat in an armchair and watched. It reminded me of the early days in Seaspray Bay and told him so. He smiled at the recollection.

He was obviously tired. He and his mum had risen very early that morning to get to the funeral on time. He got into bed and I kissed him good night, telling him I would let him sleep in the next day because, if Eric had planned this as thoroughly as was his wont, Mrs. Carter would be in the bedroom next door when we awoke tomorrow.

I went to the door but his voice stopped me. "Damien?"

"Yes, Josh?"

"Would you spend the night with me? Please."

I understood the offer. Even though it was my flat, it was his bedroom and he was making a reciprocal offer to the one I had given him. I went back to Josh's welcoming arms.

So began the long road back.

CHAPTER TWENTY

~

THE LONG ROAD BACK

*L*et there be no doubt about it, it was a long and difficult road. We had our moments of anger. We knew what barbs and accusation pushed the other into a frenzy. Eric, on more than one occasion, had to go referee to remind us there were patients in the surgery. We slept alone more than we did together, occasionally Josh would stay out all night and I would do the same, usually with Rodney. We never brought men home; it was an unwritten rule by which we both abided.

When we did share a night together, no other lover satiated me like Josh did. In a moment of candour, he admitted as much to me. From that flimsy bedrock, we planted the seeds which groped their way to flower.

Josh was as popular as the receptionist among the moneyed classes as he was amongst the workers, treating them all equally. There were a few titled ladies and gents, though I find it difficult to refer to them in those terms, who complained about a man in that position, usually using the excuse that it was demeaning to one of his sex. What they actually meant was it was a job for a woman and they could not countenance a man in such a subservient role. Queer was an accusation too far.

Of course, it didn't help, that Josh's democratic treatment of all mankind also extended to Sir Michael Cycledes. He saw no reason that he should tug his forelock or kowtow in any way. What was worse, in Cycledes' opinion, was that Josh was spreading this scandalous blasphemy to others of his ilk in the waiting room. My enemy became Josh's enemy and, sensing a soft spot in my armor, Cycledes turned his attention to my receptionist.

While the others in the building found the battle amusing, it was sapping morale and something had to be done. I took precautionary measures by involving Clem from the beginning. We devised contingency plans, always letting Josh in on the strategy. He found it vastly entertaining, failing to see the traps that were being set. As a result, he fell right into it.

The Board convened an extraordinary meeting when Cycledes screamed for justice. As they had acceded to his demand, I knew it was serious. I sat in stunned silence while he spewed out his venom, not against me, but against Josh. It was all very well that the others in the building would support me; after all, I was a well-respected medical practitioner and a gentleman, but Josh was an entirely different mammal altogether. They were not nearly as prepared to excuse his behaviour when a serious allegation was laid at his door.

It was a very serious charge that was levelled at Josh. A police matter, although Cycledes had said, "I do not wish to involve the police at this stage. I don't wish to see this august organisation become the subject of scandal. But, I warned you all from the very first day, that allowing Dr. Bouton into these chambers would be little short of disaster. Now his catamite has proved me correct."

"What is he supposed to have done exactly, Sir Michael?" Sir Godfrey was attempting to keep tempers at bay because I was purple in the face with anger and about to snap off Cycledes' head.

"Stolen my wife's Chinese necklace!" he exploded as if it was the most precious thing in the world. But then again, it was. We had all seen the famed necklace of jade and diamonds, that rumour had it was worth more than its weight in gold. It was a rare artefact from the Ming Dynasty that he, in his arrogance, used to flaunt his wealth and prestige. It was not good enough for the handful of patients that would see it on display in his surgery, he wanted to world to envy him and covet his property. He had taken a masterpiece of Chinese craftsmanship and had it converted into a bauble, for Lady Cycledes to wear around her neck, so displaying two of his prized possessions at once.

I was about to interrupt when Sir Godfrey hushed me by raising his hand.

"How exactly did Mr. Carter come to steal your wife's necklace? Surely, you keep it locked away. You are not suggesting that Mr. Carter is a safecracker?"

Cycledes attempted to look chastened but failed. "That part is my fault, gentlemen. My wife had given me the trinket to have the clasp tightened as she was afraid it was too loose and might snap. I should have been more vigilant but I left the necklace lying on my desk for weeks."

A murmur went around the room. I suspect we could all imagine Cycledes leaving the valuable object carelessly draped across his desk not because he'd forgotten it but rather to show off his conspicuous wealth. No one, however, dared voice that opinion.

"Irresponsible of me, I admit."

"How do you allege Mr. Carter managed to steal such a valuable item?"

"I don't allege, I know he took it. I have witnesses."

This had just gone from the vaguely ludicrous to the deeply troubling.

"Witnesses?" Sir Godfrey repeated. "They actually saw him take the necklace?"

"Not exactly," Cycledes admitted. "But as good as."

"Please explain."

"The day the necklace disappeared Mr. Carter was in my office."

"Now, hold on a second," I interjected. "Josh, Mr. Carter, is in and out of Sir Michael's surgery on a fairly regular basis."

"How is this so?" Sir Godfrey asked.

"Sometimes I refer my patients, only those with the requisite pedigree you understand, if his expertise in the matter is superior to mine. We swap patient files as a convenience and a courtesy, to save time and a lot of cross questioning. I can vouch for Sir Michael's bad memory because he often, perhaps I could say always but I'm not sure, forgets to return my files and I have frequently had occasion to send Mr. Carter up to retrieve them."

Cycledes obviously decided that, on this occasion at least, humility was a better defence than bluster.

"I do admit it, gentlemen, but then you know how many committees I chair, and how my hospital and charity work runs me ragged."

"Not to mention all that golf one has to squeeze in," I added maliciously.

"Go on, Sir Michael," Sir Godfrey suggested while glaring in my direction.

"Let me see, when Mr. Carter came in demanding a file on the spot—"

I interrupted. "I instructed him to demand the file as you had been promising to return it for more than a fortnight and I had, at that precise moment, Lady Treacher in my surgery." Fortunately for Lady Treacher, nee Molly Lorner, God's gift to the Tivoli, her sexual history was securely locked up in my office, away from Cycledes' prying eyes.

"Be that as it may," Cycledes continued, refusing to react to my needling. "My receptionist was then engaged with an important patient, telling Mr. Carter to enter my office and find the file on my credenza where I keep information for later collating. My receptionist will confirm, on oath, that Mr. Carter spent a longer time than usual in my surgery before he emerged."

"Did he have the file with him?" Sir Godfrey asked.

"He did."

"Go on."

"Later that afternoon, I noticed the necklace was missing, when a patient drew my attention to it by asking where the lovely bauble had gone. After that patient left, I immediately asked my receptionist who had been in my office. Apart from my patients, there was only Mr. Carter. I leave it to yourselves, gentlemen, to draw your own conclusions."

I wasn't about to leave it there. "So, assuming that the necklace has been stolen and is not just another example of your forgetfulness, the suspects must include any of the patients between the last time you remember seeing the necklace and the time it was brought to your attention that it was missing, your receptionist who had ample opportunity, and Mr. Carter."

Cycledes bellowed. At last, I had managed to get under his skin But he'd played his trump card and Josh was as good as accused, charged and found guilty.

Back in my apartment, I called a conference. We were in serious trouble. Josh was in danger of imprisonment. I outlined the case against him. He was sullen and withdrawn. "Josh, I don't for one minute believe you stole the necklace." Eric and John seconded my statement. "But we have to fight back. We can't deny you were in his surgery, that you were in there longer than would, on the surface, appear necessary."

"Have you seen his office?" Josh said in his own defence. "It's a pigsty. He has no method. Everything is just piled high until Wendy, his poor over-worked secretary, has a chance to get around to it." Josh looked aghast. "You don't think it was her, do you?"

"I don't think it's anyone yet. The most damning so-called evidence is from one of his patients, who also happens to be one of ours as well, someone not noted for their love of Cycledes. We'll try to contact him in the morning. But this is where we have a problem. Josh, you were seen coming out of the men's toilet near Cycledes' office with, and I quote here, 'a very disreputable male with whom Mr. Carter was swapping something which the stranger immediately put in his pocket'."

Josh blushed. He attempted to explain himself but just triggered an attack of stammering.

"Josh, just be quiet for a moment. Please. I know what you were doing in the toilet, you were having sex, and while I admire your adherence to that old maxim about not shitting in your own backyard I would that you had taken him to a floor other than that of our arch enemy."

"I'm sorry, Damien. I'll pack my bags."

"You'll do no such thing. I have no intention of allowing Cycledes to beat me. I don't mind that he has it in for me, but when he takes it out on my loved ones, then that means war."

They were fighting words, brave words, but I had no idea where to go from there. I had called the strategy meeting in the hope that someone, anyone, would come up with a suggestion.

Supper that night was a dismal affair. I called in reinforcements but Rodney was of little help either. He had sent out the call for dirt on Cycledes but had come up empty-handed. It looked as if I would be handing in my resignation from the chambers the following day. Under Cycledes' seemingly magnanimous gesture, the Board had given me twenty-four hours to retrieve the necklace from Josh, dismiss him from my employ, or else vacate the building.

If the necklace was beyond retrieval, and to avoid scandal, Cycledes agreed that he would contact his insurance company and say it had been stolen on their next holiday.

Of course, there was no way Josh could return something that he had not stolen in the first place, and I would not allow him to go to prison, so the looming alternative was to resign my spot in Macquarie Street.

We all went to bed early that night. I lay awake trying to see a way out of our dilemma, when there was a tap at the door.

"Come in," I called.

Josh entered in his Sunday best. I sprung out of bed. His bags were near the front door. I slammed my bedroom shut, leaning against the door to prevent his escape.

I had to play it cool. "All dressed up, Josh. Just for me?"

"I've never brought you anything but bad luck, Damien." He looked at the floor as he spoke, not daring to face me.

I kept it light. "On the contrary, Josh. I thank whoever or whatever is responsible for our meeting every single day of the week."

"It's not working out, is it?"

"Why do you say that?"

"I wouldn't need other men if I loved you enough. I wouldn't allow strangers to take me in the men's lavatory."

"Do you enjoy it?"

"Sometimes."

"I enjoy other men sometimes, too, Josh."

He looked at me and I saw a flicker of jealousy. "You have other men besides me?"

"Of course I do. It's not like we're committed to each other. You're a free agent. Until you move permanently to my bed, you are your own man."

"I thought you didn't want me," he said. "You never come to my room."

"Of course not. That would be taking advantage of you. You would feel that you had to give in because I'm your boss. I don't want another situation like you had with Enzo."

He understood immediately. His perceptions had been all wrong.

"You really do love me."

"I always will."

"I really buggered up, didn't I?"

"Maybe a little," I smiled.

"I'm sorry," he sobbed.

I grabbed him quickly because he looked ready to run from the room. As he cried, I removed his coat and his shoes. They were easy, his shirt and trousers proved more difficult. I rang for Eric. He was at the door in a matter of moments; I never insisted that he dress up if I called for him late at night. In fact, on a number of occasions I'd rung just so he and John could join me in my bed. They could refuse if they so wished but seemed to enjoy it as much as I did. Besides, it kept up staff morale. That had been before Josh moved in.

I whispered instructions to Eric, including the removal of Josh's luggage from the front door. He returned about fifteen minutes later with two steaming cups of cocoa. I propped Josh up in bed, handing him his drink after I had added a liberal amount of sleeping draft. It was dishonest of me but I was not about to let him go.

"Whatever happens, Josh, we'll face it together," I said forcing the soothing drink on him.

"I've ruined your life, Damien. Can you ever forgive me?"

"You haven't ruined anything. There's nothing to forgive."

"I'll go, Damien. That way you can keep your practice here in Macquarie Street."

"Josh, there's only one thing I want to keep. It's you. This residence means nothing without you to share it."

They were nice sentiments and calmed Josh but, in the pit of my stomach, I knew that if I left here in disgrace I was as good as ruined. It was a price I was prepared to pay.

I alleviated his concerns until his head dropped on the pillow. I took his mug, the dregs of the sleeping draft lukewarm in the bottom, tucking the blankets around him so he would feel protected. I hoped when he woke up, he would see sense and not run out on me. There was no way I could monitor him twenty-four hours a day, nor did I want to.

The jangle of the phone interrupted my care for poor exhausted Josh. Eric knocked at the door and entered, meaning it was an emergency. The fates were conspiring against me tonight.

"It's George," he said. "There's been some sort of accident, and they can't go to the hospital."

"Tell him to come here."

Eric disappeared and I could hear him giving instructions over the phone, telling him to catch a taxi and that we would pay at this end. George and his boyfriend had never been to Macquarie Street, preferring the relative anonymity of my Pyrmont surgery, so I knew that it had to be bad for him to ring me here. Eric dressed hurriedly to go downstairs to meet and pay for the cab and bring the injured upstairs. He had already woken John who was in the kitchen, preparing tea and sympathy, plus pots of hot water.

It certainly took my mind off my own dilemma.

I had no idea what to expect, what to prepare for, which was frustrating, particularly if it was life threatening. In the end, there was more blood than serious injury. George turned up with a very bloodied Jack whom he carried like a lifeless doll through the foyer to the lift, dropping blood at every step, Eric explained to me. John went down to scrub away the evidence; we didn't want to leave anything further for Cycledes to complain about.

"What happened, George?" I asked as I examined his boyfriend for serious injury. He was certainly cut and bruised, his face was pulped and seemed to have borne the brunt of the attack, although the abrasions on his arms and legs indicated he's been dragged some distance.

George was frantic with worry. I grabbed him by the shoulders, forcing him to sit, his pacing irritating me so that I could not concentrate.

"You know, Jack, doc."

"Not that way, I don't,' I said.

"You must be the only one then. I love him, no matter what, but everybody tells me to find a better man than Jack. Trouble is there is no better man. He's kind, he's gentle, and he does love me in his own way. It's just he's...he's everybody's. Tonight he picked on the wrong man to proposition. The bloke was disgusted but Jack wouldn't take no for an answer. The bloke threatened him so Jack had enough sense to back off. He was waiting when we left the pub. He beat the shit out of Jack. Cut him a bit. When I called out for the police, the attacker ran off. You can see why we couldn't go to the hospital. Questions would have been asked."

George put his head in his hands.

I kneeled in front of him and took his hands in mine. "He'll be all right, George. It looks much worse than it is. He's going to be sore for a week or more but there's no permanent damage. We'll check that out tomorrow. He may have to go to the hospital for tests but if I send him they won't ask questions. Now, you go to the kitchen and get John to make you up something. All right?"

He wiped his nose with the back of his sleeve. "Thanks, doc."

"Send Eric in if he's free."

Between the two of us, we cleaned up Jack as best we could. We removed his clothes to wipe the grit and blood from his wounds. He came round while we were washing him down with flannels. I had attempted to clean his face first, worried his nose was broken. Fortunately, it wasn't. He groaned so I knew he was in a lot of pain. I couldn't give him anything for it just yet until I'd ascertained the extent of his injuries and if there was any broken bones or internal complications.

It was a laborious process as Jack got frisky at the idea of two men examining his nude body. It seems superficial cuts to his face and chest did not prevent his cock from hardening. Once I'd given him a thorough going over I moved him to a spare room, with Eric's assistance. George nominated to sit in a chair by his bed, watching over him through the night.

Josh was sleeping soundly, so I went to the kitchen to join Eric and John who were having a nightcap, John rinsing out the cloths he'd used to wipe up

Jack's blood from the marbled foyer and from the floor of the lift. Eric poured me a tea and topped it with a slug of brandy.

I didn't know how to start.

"I've come to a decision about the problem with Cycledes," I said.

I had to tell them as it affected their lives as well.

"I hope you aren't going to throw Josh to the wolves," Eric said.

"No. I never considered that as an alternative. I find it highly suspicious that Cycledes doesn't want to call the police over a necklace that is supposedly worth more than the average working man earns in a year. He must know that Josh can't return the thing because he doesn't have it. So he gives us the only choice we can take, and he finally gets what he has wanted all along. Me out of Macquarie Street."

"You want me to break into his surgery and see if I can find it?"

"That wouldn't achieve anything. If you found it and there were signs of a break in Cycledes would only say we were putting it back to save Josh. No, I have no alternative but to resign from the chambers."

"We're behind you one hundred percent of the way," Eric added.

"Even though it means…"

"We have a little money saved," John added. "We'll be all right for a while."

"Now that you've given us a taste of what it's like to be together, we'll never go back to the way we were before."

"What will you do?" I asked.

"With my references I can get a job in a restaurant, or a café if I have to," John said.

"And I have enough experience I could work in an hotel," Eric added.

I knew it was all bravado. The economic situation meant they would be just figures on the ledger of the unemployed. But I did appreciate their support.

"If I can ever make it up to you…"

They hugged me and headed off to bed. It had been a long night.

I went to my surgery and set about writing my letter of resignation. It had to be done in such a way it could never be used against me in the future, and it had to cast no aspersions on Josh. It took time to compose to my satisfaction and I must have fallen asleep at my desk for that's where Eric found me the following morning.

First, I checked on Josh who was still groggy from the drug I had given him and promptly fell back asleep. Then I went to see Jack who, to my surprise was sitting up in bed, all chipper, slurping away at a warm broth Eric had prepared as his jaw was too sore for solids. George was feeding him and Jack was eating up the attention.

"Hey, doc," Jack said by way of greeting. "This won't affect my looks, will it? There won't be any permanent scarring?"

"None that I can tell but I want you to get checked at the hospital. I'll write a referral and take you over myself as soon as I've washed. You'll be sore for a couple of days. You were very lucky, Jack."

He took it all in his stride. "Story of my life."

George continued to feed him but would have to leave soon for work. When I got back after bathing he was gone.

"You treat him abysmally; you know that, don't you?" I scolded.

"I can't help it, doc. I love him, sure, but does that mean you have to be exclusive? I don't think so."

"But your promiscuity is so..." I was lost for words.

He smiled broadly, proud of his achievement. "Yeah, it is, isn't it?"

I had Eric help me sit him up in a wheelchair for the short push to Sydney Hospital where he'd receive expert treatment and examination. He was my private patient so they would not question him too closely about his injuries. I would deliver Jack, come back to front the Board at one o'clock, and offer my resignation. Josh was awake, seated in the kitchen having breakfast upon my return.

"It won't work, Damien," he said. "You'll always hold it over me. Or I'll feel guilt every day for the rest of my life."

"I will do no such thing. I swear it by all I hold dear," I said seriously. "You won't feel guilt either. I forbid it."

I had a quick bite to eat, censoring Josh from mentioning the subject again. He went to open the surgery while I dressed for the morning's roll call of illnesses, serious and psychosomatic. The morning flew by. I wasn't aware of it until Eric informed me there had been a phone call from the hospital that Jack was being discharged, asking that I please collect him as soon as possible as they needed the bed.

Glancing at the clock, I had a good hour so I dashed up Macquarie Street to retrieve my patient. He had been given a clean bill of health and it was now just a matter of rest and recuperation. He was in high spirits; to the extent he was even putting the hard word on a male orderly when I arrived to get him.

"Down, boy." I slapped him lightly although the orderly, a strapping man in his forties, was quite capable of delivering another beating if provoked. I was amused that he was either interested in Jack's proposition or had no idea what was on offer.

"Home, James," Jack commanded imperiously as we reached the street, some pedestrians recoiling at the sight of his face, although he still looked enough like the Jack of good health to be recognisable. He waved to attractive lads as they passed, demanding that I follow the more likely candidates, and insisted I take him around the block for the exercise. I refused on all counts.

Back at the chambers, I pushed him into the foyer, grateful there was no one with whom he could flirt. He whistled in appreciation of the gilt and marble now that he had an opportunity to really look at it. It was very different viewing now than when he arrived unconscious the previous night.

I pushed him quickly toward the lift in order to avoid running into anyone when he suddenly snapped on the brakes, almost toppling the two of us.

"Whoa. Hold on a minute," he said. "Wheel me over there."

I thought it best not to argue with him, thus prolonging our time in public. I wheeled him to the directory and he found my name.

"That's impressive, doc."

He ran his finger down the names stopping at Sir Michael Cycledes. "I thought so. I've been here before."

My heart beat fit to burst.

"When?'

"Last time was a few days ago. You may not believe it, but I mix in some pretty high circles. My looks and what I do with 'em gets me in some hoity-toity places, let me tell you."

"Like Sir Michael Cycledes?" I encouraged.

"Yeah. You wouldn't think to look at him he would be built like..." Jack held his two hands apart at a distance that would have looked in proportion on an elephant but would have been grotesque on a human. So, obviously Jack wasn't seeing him for a medical condition.

"What do you do with him, Jack?"

"That would be telling. I've got me reputation to uphold."

"Unless you start spilling the beans very shortly, you'll find yourself strapped into a runaway wheelchair, careening down Macquarie Street toward the tram sheds and almost certain death."

Shoving him in the lift, I had a mere twenty minutes to interrogate him. Back in the surgery, I called Eric explaining briefly about Jack and Cycledes, asking him to get the information I needed even it meant breaking a few fingers. Jack obviously believed me. "You can't do that!" he yelled.

"Explain to him, Eric, why I can and most certainly will if he doesn't co-operate. Offer him violence, offer him money, or even offer him sex. Anything. Explain the situation. Fast."

I went to change for the formal occasion that the Board meetings were while I hoped that Eric could get through to Jack the seriousness of the situation.

Twenty minutes later, I faced Josh's accuser across the large oak table. "So what's it to be. Bouton?" he sneered not even bothering to use my nomenclature.

"What were the choices again?" I asked coolly.

"That Mr. Carter produce the necklace in question."

"Impossible, as he didn't steal it."

"Despite all the witnesses."

"Correct me if I'm wrong, Sir Michael," I made sure I used his title. "But no one actually saw him with the necklace in his possession."

"A technicality," he huffed.

"Next choice."

"That he resign and move out of chambers."

"Again, impossible. He's a particular favourite among my patients and an absolutely top-rate receptionist."

Cycledes's face lit up as I had just one alternative remaining; the one he most hoped for. "Lastly, that you resign your residence here and leave within thirty days." He saw the envelope in my hand and went to grab it. I held it out of reach. "Is that your resignation?"

"No. I'm afraid that is not an option I can accept either."

There was a murmur from the Board.

"Instead," I continued. "I am going to suggest a few more alternatives. First, that Sir Michael go and check his surgery one more time to ensure he has not inadvertently misplaced the necklace. Second, that he ask his wife if, perhaps, she did not tire of waiting for Sir Michael to take it to have the clasp repaired and herself took it to a jewellers."

"Poppycock," Sir Michael steamed.

Now was the time for my bluff. "If neither of those prove satisfactory, I have instructed the Board secretary to call the police and have our rooms searched thoroughly, both yours and mine, while we wait here."

He reacted exactly as I thought he would.

"This is bloody outrageous,' he fumed.

I went for the jugular. "I can't see that you would have any objections, Sir Michael, unless you hid the necklace yourself."

I had as good as accused him of fabricating the charge against Josh, as I now knew he had. But I had given him an out if he wished to back down. He decided to bluff it out himself, striding purposefully toward the door. I blocked his way.

"Ah, fair's fair, Sir Michael. You have accused my receptionist on the flimsiest of evidence, without even calling the lad you saw with Mr. Carter in the men's toilet. He is a patient of mine whom I have just tracked down and he is willing to swear under oath that he became disoriented in the building and when entering the lift it went up instead of down. He got off on your floor as he felt ill. At that time, Mr. Carter was leaving your office and saw him, helping him to the men's room where he vomited. What you saw being put into the lad's pocket was my prescription for his illness."

I hoped it sounded plausible. I didn't know if anyone around the table was buying it.

"That's all bullshit," he screamed. "Let me out of here. Now."

He raised his hand to strike me but I did not flinch. He read triumph in my eyes. It rattled him.

"Perhaps, I have been a little hasty, gentlemen. With your permission, I will do as suggested, and search my surgery once again, although I know I won't find anything." He directed the last few words at me. "I will also speak to my wife. I will be back shortly and then you can call the police."

He waited for me to move aside. Instead, I said, "Sir Godfrey, would you mind accompanying Sir Michael while he searches. For his own sake, everything must be seen to be above board. I would hate suspicion to fall upon him because he'd been alone with enough time to dispose of the evidence."

"I would have thought a gentleman's word would have been sufficient," he said, scarcely suppressing his rage. Everything in Cycledes's behaviour pointed to his guilt.

"To the other gentlemen of the Board, perhaps, Sir Michael. But as you delight in telling me often enough, I'm no gentleman."

Pushing me aside, muttering that he would have 'my guts for garters' he flung open the door. He was prevented from leaving by a lad in a wheelchair. I saw the startled look of recognition on his face. He backed into the room.

"What is this?"

I was humble. "Please forgive me, gentlemen. This is one of my patients, the victim of a street attack last night. I have just brought him back from Sydney Hospital. I was running late and did not have time to take him back to my surgery so I brought him up with me. I was sure you gentlemen would not mind. I took the liberty of contacting one of my staff to come and collect poor Jack to convey him back to my surgery." As if on cue, Eric stepped out of the lift. "Here he is now." I took a chance when I instructed, "Eric, be so good as to pop upstairs and ask Lady Cycledes if she would join us. It won't take long."

Cycledes sputtered and prevaricated but I shut him down with, "I'm sure you'd want everything to be above board, Sir Michael. No interference with a witness." I'd already secretly gestured to Eric and he'd headed off with speed.

Most of the Board sat in bemused wonderment watching the drama unfold. They knew there could be only one winner and I hoped a few of them were rooting for me.

Sir Godfrey got up to speak. "I think Dr. Bouton's suggestions are admirably sensible. If you ensure us you have searched your surgery thoroughly I, for one, believe you, Sir Michael. So, let's have your good wife and see if she can throw further light on the subject. If not, then I'm afraid, it is incumbent upon us to ring for the police."

Sir Michael was perspiring now, mopping his brow with his handkerchief, wondering where all this would end.

"Did you search everywhere, Sir Michael? Could not the necklace have fallen on the floor when you pushed a file across the desk and then perhaps a patient or even yourself kicked it, inadvertently of course, say, and I'm only speculating here, under the credenza where you keep your files?" I asked maliciously.

The Board members listened intently. I was a little too specific in my speculations for them to spring from anything but inside knowledge.

Just as I'm sure he was about to curse me to hell, his wife turned up with Eric. Lady Cycledes was a sprightly old boiler of a woman, her chins hanging down like rows of chook jowls. She had mischief in her eyes.

"What have you done, Michael?" she chided. "This nice man," she indicated Eric, "told me you have gone off half-cocked about my necklace going missing. You are so forgetful lately, if I didn't know better, I'd suggest you consult a doctor. But, of course, you are a doctor, although you could scarcely consult yourself. Don't you remember, darling? I told you I had got so sick of waiting for you to have the clasp repaired I took it to the jeweller myself. And here it is." She produced the necklace with a flourish from the pocket in her day coat. "All fixed. He cleaned it as well so it sparkles brighter than ever."

Sir Michael could not leave the room quickly enough although Sir Godfrey informed him he should think over carefully the wording of the apology he would deliver to me at the next meeting.

Jack couldn't help but rub salt into the wound by calling after the retreating figure, "Hey, guv, next Tuesday as usual."

Sir Michael's far from elegant 'Fuck off!" reverberated down the corridor.

Sir Godfrey closed the meeting, shaking my hand effusively asking that I please tell him the whole story one day, which I solemnly promised although I had no intention of ever doing so. Eric, Jack and I went back to my surgery, closed for the lunch period, to celebrate. Eric broke out the good liquor. Jack was put out because he was not allowed alcohol with his pain tablets. I promised he was always welcome to come back for his share.

"Hell, we might even all fuck you for what you did for us today," I joked.

Jack looked at us expectantly. "Really?"

We laughed; his fantasy disintegrated.

"How did you convince the old chook?" I asked.

"That was the easy part. I told her that Sir Michael had got himself into a bit of a pickle for accusing someone of stealing her necklace and that the police were likely to be called in. It was likely he would be charged with slander, his career and social standing ruined. I'll give her this, she's a plucky one. She just said, 'What do I have to do?' We found the necklace where you said it was Jack. She put it in her pocket and I told her what to say, just as you instructed Damien. Sheer genius. And she carried it off. Of course, she will extract some expensive bauble or two from Sir Michael as recompense."

Everyone applauded and I took a mock bow.

"None of it would have been possible, however, without Jack. If he hadn't seen Cycledes name on the directory downstairs then we would not be celebrating."

Jack, it transpired, was a regular visitor to Sir Michael's surgery after hours, especially when the knight's good lady was out on her charitable rounds. Sir Michael's charitable activities consisted mainly of buggering young, rough working class lads over his desk while they shouted the bluest of profanities which, it seems, got Sir Michael rock hard, something his wife was either unable or unwilling to do any more. And in return, the lad would receive charitable largesse. What Sir Michael didn't realise was that Jack would have done it for the love of cock, because Sir Michael was blessed in that department. He took the cash anyway.

"To promiscuity." I raised my glass.

In his numerous times with Cycledes, Jack had noticed the necklace lying on the desk. He had never been tempted to steal it, although it would have been easy enough, so when, on his last visit, it was missing, he commented on it.

"He couldn't help himself," Jack said. "He was so proud of the ugly thing he had to bend down and get it from that bench thing in his surgery. It was underneath. I thought it was a stupid hiding place and told him so. He put his finger to his lips and told me there was a reason for it. I didn't care. I pretended to admire it because that's what he wanted but what I wanted was his cock. Later, as I was getting dressed I saw him down on his hands and knees pushing it back into its hiding place."

I was exhausted, totally worn down. I had no one booked for an appointment until the late afternoon. I told Eric to turn anyone away before four o'clock, unless it was an emergency, and went to my bedroom to nap. Josh followed me, standing in the doorway, almost afraid to enter.

I turned to him, my face beaming.

"Come here, Josh."

He sprang into my arms and we fell back on the bed.

During the morning, he had moved all his belongings into my bedroom.

CHAPTER TWENTY ONE

~

FUTURE TENSE

$\mathcal{J}$osh and I slowly inched our way back to a loving and committed relationship, which is not to say that either of us didn't stumble from time to time. It happened rarely, but when it did, we were honest with each other and tried not to allow jealousy to enter the equation. We had discussed infidelity, deciding on monogamy as our preference, but being mere flesh and blood we knew that sometimes, especially in the beginning, we might fail. We had no hard and fast rules, our one condition being that if either side had a problem we would sit down and discuss it.

I trained Josh in nursing skills and he became an invaluable asset to the surgery, something that helped his self-esteem which had suffered severely over the years. He bounced back, and within a short period was once again the companion that I had so loved in Seaspray Bay. He could never be exactly the same; his experiences had hardened him although, on the positive side, he was much more sexually adventurous. Of course, I had changed as well, but cynicism and pessimism are not attractive traits. I did banish them slowly, giving way to a happier disposition now that I had my lover back. There was, however, always that ache in my gut that one day I would wake up and find him gone.

As the weeks turned into months, that feeling gnawed less and less although I was concerned for the difference in our ages and set about, with

Clem's help, planning for Josh's future. He was my partner but I held the purse strings, something of which I was acutely aware. Mum Doreen left him a small bequest, as she did to Eric and John, Mrs. Carter, George and Jack, as well as myself. Surprisingly, she left her house to Rodney to help the destitute on the Pyrmont peninsula. With the help of his union mates, he upgraded the ancient terrace, giving it a new lease of life, inviting in those thrown onto the streets by the rapacious appetites of the foreclosing banks.

The renters by the hour who had taken advantage of Mum's hospitality had to look elsewhere but did not go uncatered to, albeit the new landlords and landladies were of more steely and greedy disposition than Mum's. She had stashed her rent money in the bank, leaving a sizeable amount to be dispersed among the locals, dispensed by Rodney through his union. I was pleased to see that diligent investment enabled him to perform good deeds without white-anting the original capital to any great extent.

Josh's mum would sometimes come to stay with us in Macquarie Street, but was always eager to return to her small village to look after the grandchildren; Eileen had a son, and a daughter. Gossip was that they had a half-sister when Carol fell pregnant and was quickly married off to the first man who would take her for a wife. There seemed little knowledge that Danny was the likely father although Mrs. Carter's letters never gave a hint that there was anything amiss in Eileen's marriage to the odious man.

We also became closer friends with Jack. It began as a guilty appreciation of all that Jack had inadvertently done for us but, as we got to know him, a genuine affection developed, to the extent that I hired Jack on a casual basis to help out at the surgery when Josh was otherwise occupied or needed assistance. My one proviso was that Jack leave his sexual habits at home. It became somewhat difficult when his partners began to turn up at my surgery. We neither encouraged, nor discouraged him in his sexual excesses, we just stood by with medical attention when it was required, as it often was. George had eventually grown tired of his lover's indiscretions, casting Jack adrift when he found more amenable distractions with a young man with similar moral tastes to his own. Jack and George parted on friendly terms, swearing to remain fast friends, but we saw a great deal less of George now.

It was on the occasion of another of Valerie's infrequent letters; that I realised just how much I missed her but rejoiced in her success. Now that she was the toast of the West End it left her little time for her friends Downunder. Josh and I toyed with the idea of taking a six-month sabbatical and sailing over to visit her and Cecil. Ty had settled in with a slightly older gent who ran a costume hire business near Covent Garden. Word was, it was a flawless match. He wrote less frequently than Valerie, understandably, since we'd never had much time to cement our friendship before he left. But I did like the lad.

It was my midday break. I always took ninety minutes minimum between the morning and afternoon appointments to recharge my energy. My work was exhausting even though I spent most of my day behind a desk listening to people's gripes.

I heard the bell ring. Not for the surgery but for the residence. Josh was out on some errand or other, or perhaps at Pfahlert's where he liked to meet up with friends during the lunch hour, though he was always back in time for the afternoon session. Sometimes we would lie down for a brief nap or, better yet, a bout of lovemaking, because I was often too exhausted in the evening.

Eric's announcement that Daniel Page was at the door stunned me. I wondered how many ways there were to kill him and dispose of the body because he could only be here for one reason: blackmail. I had often feared his turning up although I never let on to Josh, as it still pained him to hear me speak ill of his former friend, no matter how badly he had treated the two of us. Was it even wise to allow him into my home?

The point was moot as Eric announced his presence while I had my back resolutely to the lounge room door. I heard him shuffle awkwardly in the silence. I took my time to get my anger in check. He had a real cheek coming here now, just as everything seemed to be going so well.

I turned to confront him. He had his head bowed, his cap off his head.

"What do you want?" I said brusquely. "I'll give you no money, let's be clear on that."

"Good God, no!" he cried out. "I didn't come for money."

"What other mischief have you come to cause then?"

"I came to make amends," he mumbled. "Or try to. And see Josh one last time."

"Are you going somewhere?" I asked to make conversation rather than out of any genuine interest.

"Away," he said. "I won't be back. I am sorry for what happened in the past, Dr. Button. But it's gone. It's over. I can't take back what I did no matter how much I want to."

"How did you find us?"

"Josh's mum told me. She said I should come here and make my peace. She said I might find myself here."

"I wish she hadn't. Josh and I have a whole new life together and ..."

"I envy you, sir," he interrupted.

"Envy me?" I said. "You have a lovely wife and two fine children. Three, if the rumours are true. I thought you were a happily married man."

"Married!" he spat the word out. "Marriage is hell!"

"If it's to the wrong person, it can be," I said.

I signaled for him to take a seat. I buzzed John and asked that tea and refreshments be brought up. I may have detested the man seated opposite but I had been brought up to be civil.

He, however, was no slave to civility. "I hated you, you know. You came to the town and took what was rightfully mine. It came so easy to you. Fancy ways, money. All the things that can dazzle a young bloke."

"Josh is not some sort of chattel you can buy and sell. Anyway, he was yours for the asking. You were too scared to stake a claim. I wasn't. My money had nothing to do with it."

"I had no experience of asking. Not another bloke. I didn't know you could. That's why I went with Eileen. To keep Josh close by."

"What has happened that you are so down on marriage?" I asked.

"It was going all right for a while. I just pretended she was Josh whenever we...you know. I think I might have called out Josh's name once or twice. After baby Josh was born she turned cold. I accused her of seeing another bloke behind my back."

"You didn't think that was hypocritical considering you were seeing another woman?"

"You mean Carol?

"Yes, Carol."

"That was just another way to keep Josh around. It almost worked, too."
I heard a chuckle in his voice. "He got aroused when he saw us. Just like I
planned. But he wouldn't join in."

"Why don't you go home, Danny. You're not welcome here." Social
niceties be damned, I was tired of speaking to him.

"I'm not welcome there either."

I sighed. "Why not?"

"The accident."

"Accident?"

He'd kept his face lowered in what I had assumed was an attempt at
supplication but at that point he lifted his head. Even as inured to injury as I
am, I gasped.

"Explosion. Eileen didn't want me after that. She took the kids and moved
in with her new bloke. Carol didn't want me neither. Nobody did. Can't say
as I blame them."

The handsome young man from the Bay was now blind in one eye, a
terrible red scar of burned skin slashed down the left-hand of his face. It was
an evil disfigurement. Danny's demeanour crumpled, he began to sob.

"I miss him, sir. I miss him so much it hurts. All I want is to ask him to
forgive me."

"Come over here," I commanded.

He hesitated, but did eventually move toward me. I held his chin, moved
his face to the light to get a better look at the burn. It had been adequately
handled, but I had access to the latest treatments, something beyond the means
of a public hospital on the coast. I ran my fingers across his face. He didn't
flinch.

"It's no more than I deserve, sir," he said. "It's my punishment."

"It's not a punishment, it's a rotten accident," I would brook no discussion
of supernatural claptrap. "Yes, I think we may be able to do something for
you. Not your eye, unfortunately, but your face." The doctor in me overcame
my prejudices against the poor young man.

Josh bustled in with the tea and biscuits, obviously having returned home in the meantime and been press ganged by John for the task. He apologised for the interruption and turned to withdraw.

"Josh?" Danny said.

Josh stopped, hunching his back in anger. He turned to glare at his former friend. If he was shocked he showed no sign of it. He showed no emotion, waiting for me to cue him.

"I was about to ask Danny if he would like to join us for supper this evening. For old time's sake. He's had a long journey and came straight from the station."

Josh was puzzled by my seeming friendliness to our avowed enemy. I hoped he had enough residual affection for his old friend that he could overcome his hatred.

"You must be hungry, Danny," I said.

"I had a cheese sandwich at Gosford, sir," he said. He kept his head lowered most of the time to hide his face.

"Ah, I know them well. They taste like a thin layer of soap between two pieces of cardboard."

Danny snickered.

"See if John can put together something in the kitchen, Josh. Then ask him to come and see me."

Danny looked whipped and beaten, and must have suspected we were speaking in code, that he was walking into a trap. "I'm not a charity case," Danny said, mustering as much pride as he could.

"I'm not suggesting it for a moment," I replied lightheartedly in an attempt to assuage Danny's humiliation. "It's no more than I would do for any acquaintance who had travelled such a long distance to visit."

Josh raised an eyebrow but was good-hearted enough to lead Danny away. I heard the concern in his voice when he asked, "What the hell happened?"

While I waited, I retrieved one of my medical journals from the bookcase, thumbing through it, and jotting down notes, as I read. I gave the list of unguents and potions to Eric with an official written order. He knew where to go to collect them.

At the door, he hesitated for a moment. "The young man must be suffering greatly as he was so remarkably handsome before the accident."

"Indeed, he was," I said. "Would it inconvenience you to add another place for supper?"

"Danny?"

I nodded. "And please see that John is informed. I'm sure there will be more than enough prepared but just in case."

"Of course."

I enquired, "Has Jack returned? I sent him out earlier with a prescription for an invalid patient."

"Not as yet." Eric couldn't help but smirk. "Probably ran into someone he couldn't resist."

Sighing, as his behavior was one of the banes of my life albeit I was grateful for his intervention in the Cycledes debacle, I said, "I have hopes that one day, before it is too late and he finds himself in trouble with the authorities, Jack will settle down. It would make life easier."

"Perhaps he is merely bored and needs something more challenging that being a mere errand boy."

In any other circumstances, Eric would have found himself unemployed speaking to his employer in so blunt a fashion. Fortunately, I am not such an ogre and appreciate his forthrightness, especially when my concern for my patients prevents me seeing what should be obvious in those on whose good graces I rely.

Habits of a lifetime meant Eric's face was shrouded in concern that he had overstepped this time. I smiled. "I thank you for bringing it to my attention. I'll set my mind to remedy the situation."

Eric seemed much relieved when he left to purchase the creams I required. I needed to make some gesture to show his opinion was appreciated whether I ultimately agreed with him or not. To have he and John as my companions and servants, allowing me the freedom to live my life openly in my own home, was a luxury I could ill afford to abuse.

Unlike other members of the chambers whom I knew 'changed' for dinner, or 'tea' as Mum used to call it in the vernacular, I decided comfort was in order rather than social rigidity. However, I did change out of my constricting doctor's 'uniform' even though I was not as much a snob as Cycledes who greeted his patients in tailcoat.

Once attired in more comfortable clothes I adjourned to the kitchen where we usually ate, using the large imposing dining room only for dinner parties and to impress. The casual atmosphere in the kitchen meant we could talk to John as he prepared the meal and Eric would not have to run back and forth between the kitchen and the formal dining room with the various courses.

It had taken a while to convince them it was the best solution to a minor problem. For obvious reasons, none of us wanted to introduce another servant into the household so John did all the cooking on his own, employing extra staff on the occasion of banquets and official occasions, none of which Cycledes ever attended meaning the atmosphere was most convivial.

Eating in the kitchen meant Eric could join us at the table after serving the meal and John, once everything was baking or roasting or simmering to his satisfaction would join us to rest his tired feet and nibble at his meal.

Danny had made every excuse he could think of to avoid joining us so the atmosphere was gloomy rather than our usual happy bonhomie. Eric and John who'd heard tales of Danny's infamy were inclined to treat him with mute hostility, Josh was fidgety and uncomfortable as we spooned John's delicious soup. We all scrupulously avoided staring at Danny's scars.

I tried to enliven the meal with tales of some of my more outrageous experiences, particularly when I resided in Pyrmont but it failed to lift the oppressive mood.

Danny appeared tense and nervous as we ate the delicate soup John had prepared, gripping the spoon that Josh had shown him to use in such a tight grip it would have snapped if made of less sturdy material.

He slammed the poor metal instrument down on the table and we all started in surprise, turning out attention to the wretched Danny. "Look, I have something to say." He glared at John and Eric as if he wanted them gone. "This is private," he snapped.

"They're family," I said quietly, hoping to calm his mood.

He seemed conflicted for a moment then awareness crept in. "You mean…" As if to confirm his thoughts, Eric reached to clasp John's hand in his own. "You're all…" Danny was so surprised he wasn't capable of uttering a full question.

I put him out of his misery. "You're amongst friends here, Danny."

Josh, Eric and John looked at me with surprise that I'd used the word 'friends'. They were a long way from the usual definition of that word with our interloper.

Turning to Josh, Danny confessed, "I thought you went with him to spite me. I used to spy on you two. I would watch through the crack in the bottom of the bedroom window. When I realised you were doing it because you wanted to, and you were doing things I never could even have dreamed up, I got hard. And I got mad. Even when I was pulling myself while I watched."

I shook my head. "You wasted years, Danny. Just like Josh did. But it's hardly your fault. It's the way you're brought up. It took a lot of courage to admit what you just did and I admire you for it."

He looked up, surprised.

"Though it would be easier if you had come to blackmail us. That would be a straightforward problem that Josh and I could tackle head on. This way, you present us with a dilemma."

"What do you mean?" Josh asked.

It was obvious from how close he sat next to his former friend at the table that we had a number of issues to resolve. Danny was unfinished business.

There's wasn't time to patch up years of mistakes in one evening. But we could make a start.

Of course, fate has a way of intervening and just as we were managing to get on a surer footing with one another during dinner, Jack crashed through the door reeking of fumbled assignations and quick relief. He was dishevelled which was far from being unusual.

"Sorry I'm late. Had a bit of business to take care off." He plonked himself at the table and picked up his spoon. John rose to prepare his dish. And then Jack really saw Danny for the first time. "Holy fuck, mate, what happened to you?"

There are a lot of things for which to criticize young Jack but, on this occasion, he blew the stuffiness and the caution right out the window with his outrageous outburst."

"Jack, this is Danny—"

He looked about the table in surprise. "You mean the miserable sod that caused all the problems for youse two?"

Danny actually laughed. "Yeah, that would be me."

Jack was hoeing into his soup in an effort to catch up, the few manners I'd taught him nowhere to be seen. "Christ, mate, it looks like you got your just desserts."

Danny nodded. "Yeah, mate. Yeah, I did. But it was a wake-up call."

"How so?" Jack had no idea when to stop with the inquisition.

"It showed me who me friends were back home…well, not home any more. And I knew I had to make amends with Josh. And Dr. Button before…" He looked sheepish about not completing the sentence.

His comment reinforced my initial concerns.

"Where are you staying this evening, Danny?" I asked.

He hesitated before answering. "A hotel near the station, sir."

That was sufficiently vague to arouse suspicion.

"I think, perhaps, you might find it far more comfortable if you stayed here, don't you?"

Josh was as surprised as Danny at the invitation. I should have discussed it with him first but I believed time was of the essence in this case.

"I can send Eric for your bags if you like." I suggested.

"No," he answered quickly. "I'm not staying in the city long."

"I'm sure Josh would be happy for you to stay as long as you like. As would I."

Josh knew me well enough to nod his agreement although he had no idea what I was thinking.

Danny lost patience. "Why are you being so bloody understanding, after all I did to you?"

"Ask me that question again when you leave if you haven't worked out the answer for yourself by then."

The remainder of the meal went off without a hitch with Josh politely asking after people he knew in Seaspray Bay. He had never returned, not even to see his mother, since he fled in the wake of the discovery his fiancée's fickle nature. Danny winced as he spoke about the mine explosion that ripped apart his life, explaining that he'd instructed Josh's mum not to pass on the grisly story to her son. That's why we hadn't heard of it.

I knew there was unfinished business between the three of us – I was envious of the past Josh and Danny shared that I could never know – but it's resolution evaded me. Fortunately, there was more immediate business to attend to. "I think I have an idea for Danny's injury. Jack, would you show him where the bathroom is so he can have a soak and I'll be up in ten minutes or so. Oh, bring his clothes back to Eric so he can clean then up a bit."

Josh's face clouded as he watched Jack tug Danny along the corridor. Eric and John gave me sly smiles.

Turning to me, Josh asked, "What are you up to, Damien?"

I shrugged. "Jack needs a hobby to keep him out of trouble."

Josh didn't argue, merely retorting, "Then you should buy him a kit for stamp collecting rather than sic him on Danny."

Was he jealous? Did he still harbor feelings for his former mate?

I waited fifteen minutes before I knocked gently on the bathroom door. There was a muffled response and I entered to discover Jack naked in the bath with Danny. It was an outsize bath for just such occasions although usually reserved for Josh and myself. Jack went white with guilt because I had caught him passionately kissing our guest who attempted to push him away as soon as I entered. Jack was reluctant to let him go.

I pulled a stool over to the side of the bath. "I'm sorry to interrupt but I need to try something. If you'll be so good as to look up, Danny."

He did as I asked. Jack's eyes pleaded with me and I nodded my permission. He leaned forward to wrap his lips around Danny's remarkably beautiful cock. I have never heard a gasp as loud. "What's he doing?" Danny yelped.

"Why don't you take a look while I open these tubes," I said.

Danny gripped the sides of the bath as Jack sucked his cock with a skill that would leave him depleted. "Oh fuck, that is so good," Danny moaned.

I took his face in my hands, applying a little of the balm from one tube to his burned face. Danny's reaction was instantaneous. He forgot all the pleasure Josh was giving him, screaming, "Oh God, that stings so bad."

I quickly wiped it off. "I thought it might but I had to be sure." I went through the same experiment with another three unguents until we settled on one that Danny said was cool and pleasurable although I think the second part of his description had more to do with Jack's ministrations than mine. I rubbed it into the wrinkled skin of the scar, instructing Danny to come and see me in the surgery the next day when I would take a better look.

Danny's body was as firm and muscular as Josh's own, his cock somewhat thicker but not as long. Mouth-watering was the word that sprang to mind.

"Right you two. Twenty minutes and then I want to see you in bed. Danny can use the spare room. I've already had Eric make up the bed."

"Where am I going to sleep, the bed in the spare room's not big enough for two to sleep in?" Jack complained.

"Does Danny want you in his bed?" I asked as innocently as possible. Both men had erections which is all the answer I really needed. "Go on then," I conceded, "Use the room in the surgery but don't touch anything."

We have a special room off the surgery for patients who come down from the country and are forced to stay overnight

I handed Danny a dressing gown. "Try this on for size while your own clothes are washed and ironed."

I left Jack smiling approvingly and Danny more confused than ever.

Eric was in the kitchen with Danny's clothes, a threadbare suit, probably a hand-me-down that was of a fashion a generation ago.

"You were right, Damien. The young man had a few pence in his pockets and no tickets for left luggage or forward ticket. He obviously had nowhere to go; no future and he came to the city to make amends before… What a tragic waste it would have been."

"They'll be in the surgery bedroom tonight."

"They?" Eric asked smugly.

I ignored him. "I suspect, though, it will be more like a week before they surface. Serve them breakfast in bed if you would."

"I don't know where your ideas come from, Damien, if you will allow me to say so. In this case, I hope you know what you're doing."

"So do I," I sighed. "And it may be a good idea to see about getting a larger bed for the spare room."

It was three days before Jack resurfaced, Danny tagging along, looking guilty, still in the dressing gown I'd given him in the bathroom. Neither he nor Jack appeared for meals, or anything else for that matter although we did hear them late at night splashing about in the bathroom after we'd all gone to bed. Three days in which Josh was so irritable he was almost impossible to live with.

When I insisted I needed to examine his face again, Danny became defensive, spending the first ten minutes of my examination begging my forgiveness. That got tedious fast and I'm afraid I snapped, "It's Josh's forgiveness you need to beg, Danny. Do you think I'd be trying to help you with your scars if I hadn't?"

"I don't want pity either," he sulked.

I looked skyward in exasperation. I put down the cream I was applying to his face.

I had to restrain myself from shouting. I've never had much patience with self-indulgence.

"How's Josh?" He looked as if it might be a forbidden topic.

"Like a bull with a sore head."

Danny was crestfallen. "Oh, he doesn't want me here?"

I went to wash my hands in the surgery sink. "I don't think Josh honestly knows what he wants. What do you want of him?"

"I want to go back to the way things were before," he confessed.

"Before what?" I asked carefully.

"I'm not good with words. I meant, I want to be friends like we used to be."

"Like before I arrived?" I asked. His lack of an answer spoke volumes. "That was a really unhealthy relationship. I would hope that you'd want something better." He went to interrupt but I stopped him. "Either way, you and Josh need to talk it through, decide what the future holds."

He snapped. "Tell me, doc. What sort of life am I gonna have with a face like some monster out of motion pichers. Eh? Adults give me a wide berth when they see me in the streets and kids scream or throw rocks. So, tell me, what sort of life am I looking forward to?"

He raised his voice to such an extent that Eric burst in thinking there was something wrong. I shook my head so that he said quietly but with enough admonishment that it wouldn't go unnoticed, "They can hear you in the waiting room." He withdrew to get on with his duties.

A chastened Danny looked utterly defeated.

"Danny."

He turned to face me.

"There was no luggage, was there?"

He cast his eyes down.

"You're not still thinking that way, are you?"

He shook his head.

"Good, that's all I wanted to hear. When you and Jack have had your fun, and you and Josh work it out between yourselves, we'll see what we can do about your face. You can stay here for as long as you like. I must warn you that Jack is fickle although, all credit to you, I must say I've never seen him spend this long with the same man. Perhaps a leopard can change its spots."

"This is all very new to me. I guess I'm just learning the ropes." Danny looked sheepish.

"Looks as if you're an avid student."

Danny laughed.

"Meanwhile, I'll get Eric to take you shopping for new clothes. All right?"

"I have no money," Danny admitted. "I gave it all to mum to look after me kids."

He needed to keep some self-respect so I said, "You can owe me."

He left the surgery without saying another word. It was a long, hard road that lay ahead for Danny but with a little bit of support I had no doubt he was resilient enough he'd make it. But for now I had a surgery full of people who needed my full attention. I buzzed Josh, "Send in the next patient, please."

CHAPTER TWENTY TWO

~

PRESENT INDICATIVE

*I*t was a busy morning and Josh's bad temper did not help the situation. Eventually, it got the better of him and he went to lie down in our bedroom. "Headache," he muttered by way of an excuse. I had no receptionist and was forced to call upon Eric to help out.

Jack was unavailable as I'd had to send him out on an urgent errand, the only kind I ever seemed to have these days, leaving Danny at a loose end, but I didn't have time to worry about that when one of my patients collapsed in the waiting room. It had been touch and go before the ambulance arrived to take her to Sydney Hospital for emergency treatment.

I washed my hands and took off my coat to relax. Josh and I couldn't go on like this. I would have it out with him at the earliest opportunity.

He wasn't in the kitchen for lunch which we normally took together unless he had a pressing engagement elsewhere. It was an opportunity for both of us to unwind from the stresses of the surgery. The patients could be demanding or offhanded or any of a thousand other slight niggles that would escalate as the morning progressed. At lunch we could both let off steam.

Not today, it seemed.

Eric coughed. "Ah, young Josh asked me to inform you that he's rather unwell and will not be taking lunch with us today."

I waved Eric away in a rather irritated manner, not believing Josh's excuse for one moment.

"I could take him something to eat," a voice said from over by the stove. I hadn't noticed, my mind was so full of the complexity of the current situation, that Danny was at the sink washing dirty pots and pans.

I was about to snap a reply but thought better of it. Yes, he was the person who was unwittingly causing all the simmering tension in our home, but it wouldn't help to draw attention to the problems between Josh and I.

"That's a kind offer, Danny, but I will see to it. Or Eric."

"It won't be no trouble at all," he said, either blithely unaware of the problems he was causing or deliberately setting out to needle me. I saw John briefly touch his arm and shake his head. Danny muttered an apology.

I was left to my funk as John finished off his preparation and Eric served up the meal which was eaten in silence, the others at the table obviously afraid that anything they said might set off my mood.

When we'd finished, Danny hopped up to do our dishes. "You don't have to do that, Danny," I said.

"I like to pay me way as best I can helping out until I can get a job. I'm not a charity case."

I'd leave him his delusions. He was, indeed, a charity case. He didn't need me to chip away any further at his self-respect. He had enough problems ahead of him.

John slid a tray across the table to me. "I prepared a little something for Josh in case he feels hungry."

A peace offering. I could do that.

I carried the tray along the hallway to our bedroom and knocked but received no reply. I opened the door quietly, whispering, "Josh, I've brought you some lunch. You should eat."

He pretended to be asleep so he would not have to speak to me.Placing the tray on a bedside table, I quickly undressed and hopped into the bed, snuggling against his back.

"Josh, I know you're not asleep. Talk to me."

Silence.

I tried again. "Had I known you would get so roiled by Danny I never would have allowed him in the door. But that moment has passed and now we must make the most of it. I can ask him to leave. But if that's too cruel, I could give him a little money to set himself up somewhere else. What is it you would like? All you need do is ask it of me."

He snuffled and turned slowly to face me. His eyes were moist and his cheeks damp. "I'm such a mess, Damien. I don't know what I want. I thought I'd left all that behind me but now I'm so confused."

I kissed his eyelids. "None of us ever forgets our first great love, Josh. And given the history of your relationship with Danny it is perfectly understandable that you would be so conflicted on seeing him again."

"What should I do, Damien? I can't go on like this."

"I can't make your decisions for you, love. You must make that decision yourself." My heart almost broke when I went on, "You must speak to Danny in private. Speak honestly. Tell him everything you feel."

Sighing deeply, he added, "I suppose so. But there is no privacy here, Damien. And I don't fancy having such a discussion in public."

"I'll arrange for Jack to be absent this evening and you can go to visit Danny in his room. I'll make sure you're not disturbed."

"What if…" he hesitated.

I didn't want to think about what ifs. "Whatever decision you make will be the right one. I trust you, love."

"But will it be the right decision for us?" he asked.

"There is no 'us' until this matter is settled." I wasn't harsh, I was merely honest.

Josh must have agreed because there were no further questions although we lay in each other's arms for another twenty minutes or so until I was required back in the surgery.

As I dressed for duty, I placed the tray on Josh's lap. "Take your time and when you finish, if you feel up to it, join me in the surgery. I'm quite lost without your help."

A happier Josh joined me about an hour later but an unhappy Jack was told to leave Danny alone that evening.

"Aw, Danny and I wanted to try out the new bed in the spare room tonight. Christen it, so to speak," he complained.

"I'm sorry, Jack, but Josh and Danny need to clear the air."

"Yeah, it's been a bit tense around here since Danny arrived. Nobody seems to like him," Jack said.

"Except you." This was as good a time as any to play the strict Victorian guardian. "Just what are your intentions, Jack?"

"Can't a bloke just enjoy a good time without having intentions?"

"Of course, but Danny is vulnerable, more so than the usual sorts of men you have as partners."

Jack was indignant. "You don't think I know that? It's me who holds him in my arms while he sobs his heart out. It's me what tells him he's a looker even though his face is like…god knows what. Life hasn't done him any favours."

I apologized. "I didn't mean to imply you are stupid or insensitive, Jack. Please forgive me. I'm just concerned for his welfare."

"Well, right now, he thinks he's just another charity case, his self-respect is a beggar at the gate."

"It's just for tonight, Jack, if you'd be so good as to make your excuses and disappear. Danny and Josh need time together to sort things out, not only for their sake but for the sake of the whole establishment."

Jack made his excuses at dinner after he and Danny had a whispered conference in the hallway and left immediately after the meal. Danny insisted John sit and put his feet up while he washed the plates and the cutlery and the greasy pots and pans.

"There's really no need…" John began.

Danny gritted his teeth. "I feel pretty useless these days so let me do this. I can never pay you what it's worth that youse welcomed me even after all I done." He turned back to the sink and began to scrape the pans.

Josh stood up to join him, taking a tea towel to dry the plates already stacked up to be put away. It was time for the rest of us to make our excuses. "I've got a new single malt I've been dying to try and wonder if you gentlemen would care to sample it with me in the lounge room?" I asked Eric and John.

They took the hint and the three of us left Danny and Josh to it.

"I'm glad of your company this evening," I told them.

They both held me and I felt the better for their close friendship. I don't know what I would have done had I been forced to face the situation on my own. I thanked them for their friendship and poured us all a generous helping of my new whisky.

We clinked glasses.

Eric got to the point. "What if…"

"Josh's welfare is the most important thing to me. If he's unhappy with me and would be happier with Danny then I will be the first to congratulate them."

"I'm sorry that young man ever turned up at the door," Eric said bitterly.

John was a the peacemaker. "He didn't come to take Josh away, he came to make amends as best he could."

"Danny has always been the ghost in my relationship with Josh. Always in the background, unseen and unspoken. This is the opportunity for an exorcism," I said.

Eric had to have the last word. "Or heartbreak."

Our little party broke up soon after and John took the glasses to the kitchen to wash them. On his return he nodded. It was acknowledgment that Danny and Josh had finished up and retired to Danny's room.

My room, for tonight I was on my own, seemed cold and desolate without the man I loved. The man who was down the hallway with his unrequited first love. My imagination wove nightmares beyond anything the two of them could possibly get up to and although I sat in bed reading I turned the pages mechanically without taking in any of the words.

Finally, exhaustion overcame my much too vivid imaginings and I lay down to a troubled sleep hoping the morning would bring down the curtain on the past and allow us all to get on with our lives.

I wasn't sure how long I'd been thrashing about when I was awakened by a dip in the bed as if someone had joined me. A pair of strong arms enveloped my weary body and a voice whispered, "Kiss me, Damien."

I had no idea if this was Josh's way of saying goodbye or whether it was a new commitment to our relationship. Either way, I put my heart into caressing Josh with my lips and he responded in kind.

My impatience got the better of me but when it came time to ask the question, the finality made me mute.

Josh looked at me sadly. "It's over, Damien."

My heart sank and I gulped in a sickly amount of air to try to catch my breath.

"Did you…" I asked.

"I kissed him, Damien."

I watched while he attempted to formulate his response in his mind.

"There was nothing. I felt nothing. He admitted he'd always wanted to kiss me but he also felt nothing. We giggled like school children at how naughty we were. Then we held each other and talked about how young and stupid we were in Seaspray Bay and all the adventures we had. 'I'm very happy for you, Josh,' he said. 'You found yourself a good man. I hope one day I might too.' He fell asleep and I crept out of the room to come back to the man who is my whole life."

Josh and I consummated our relationship all over again that night until we were both utterly exhausted.

What a difference it made to the atmosphere in our home. Happiness begets hunger and it drove us to the kitchen well before the sun rose, John and Eric already up and about, gloomily getting themselves ready for another day as if it would be their last. It didn't take more than Josh and I arriving together, smiling brightly, for them get their hopes up, considerably lightening their mood.

John dared broach the subject that had preoccupied all our minds for too long. He needed official confirmation to feel secure. "Are we to assume that our futures are looking quite rosy at present?"

Josh laughed. "I know we've all been holding our breaths for longer than we should have, my fault and I apologise for the discomfort…" There were polite murmurs of disagreement before he continued, "The best thing that could have happened, although it didn't seem so at first, is Danny turning up as he did." He held his hands up to prevent interruption. "I don't mean his injuries, I wouldn't wish that on anyone. But Danny in the flesh has laid the ghosts to rest." Josh reached across the table for my hand to kiss it gently.

John looked teary eyed as he went about preparing breakfast ahead of a much brighter new working day.

Jack, unusually for him, turned up at sparrow-fart having spent the night with friends who, we were told later, were happy to see the back of him. He seemed relieved that Josh was happily at the table with me, confirmed when he asked all-too-casually, "Is Danny up yet?"

Now was my chance. "Why don't you go and wake him?" I suggested.

Jack was tearing down the hallway calling Danny's name before I'd even finished my suggestion.

"I swear that boy is developing feelings for young Danny," John said as he set another two places at the kitchen table.

Josh lay his head on my shoulder. "I think the feeling may become mutual given time," he said.

No one was at all surprised when neither Jack nor Danny turned up for breakfast.

Lydian Press

ABOUT THE AUTHOR

Naughty or nice? Sugar or Spice? Whatever way you like it, Barry Lowe writes M/M Romance and Erotica that's as addictive and satisfying as your morning cup of coffee. If you like it short and sweet with a happy ending then saucy romance is for you. But if you like a stronger brew with fetish, cuckold relationships, taboo, and all things steamy then try the Erotica – but watch out for the heat!

Go to https://www.facebook.com/barry.lowe.3591

ROMANCE BY BARRY LOWE

PLAYS

Available in eBook and Print

THE DEATH OF PETER PAN: Gay Historical Romance

NOVELS & ANTHOLOGIES

Available in eBook and Print

ROMANCING THE BONE: Gay Romance Erotica

COCK-EYED OPTIMISTS: Gay Romance Erotica

BACHELOR BOY: Gay Romance

EVERYTHING'S COMING UP ROSES: Gay Romance

THE BI-WORD: Bi Romance

SELECTED SHORT FICTION

Available as eBooks

GETTING TO BLOW YOU

NICE WORK IF YOU CAN GET IT

ELEVATOR SHAFT

GEORGE AND THE CHRISTMAS DRAGON

HOMO FOR THE HOLIDAYS

LOVE WITH A SIDE ORDER OF PELICANS

CHRISTMAS IN JULY

HOW MUCH IS THAT DOGGIE IN THE WINDOW?

THE DAY OF THE CLIFFORDS

HE WON'T SEND ROSES

HARD ON HIS HEELS

THE NEW DAD'S CLUB

For all Barry's titles please visit his page at: lydianpress.com

Lydian Press is dedicated to bringing you the finest GLBTQ erotic literature on the web.

Visit us on the web at:

http://lydianpress.com

www.ingramcontent.com/pod-product-compliance
Lightning Source LLC
Chambersburg PA
CBHW060408180626
46817CB00007B/2548